Telling Stories

Old & New

Books by Walter Cummins

Story Collections
Telling Stories: Old & New
Habitat: stories of BENT realism
The Lost Ones
The End of the Circle
Local Music
Where We Live
Witness

Novels
A Stranger to the Deed
Into Temptation

Nonfiction
The Literary Traveler, with Thomas E. Kennedy
Programming Our Lives: Television and American Identity,
with George Gordon
Managing Management Climate, with George Gordon
Florham: The Lives of an American Estate,
with Carol Bere and Samuel Convissor

Edited
Writers on the Job, with Thomas E. Kennedy
Shifting Borders: East European Poetry of the Eighties
The Other Side of Reality: Myths, Vision & Fantasies,
with Martin Green and Margaret Verhulst

www.waltercummins.com

Telling Stories

Old & New

Walter Cummins

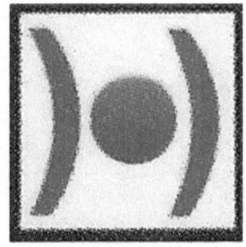

Del Sol Press
Washington, D.C.

Telling Stories:
Old & New
by Walter Cummins

Published by Del Sol Press
Washington, D.C.

First printing 2015

Cover photo: Source 123rf.com

Printed in the United States of America

ISBN 978-0692352403

For all the storytellers

Acknowledgments

"A Kind Hand," *Wisconsin Review*; "A Minor Dislocation," *Potpourri*; "Any Fancies," *Samisdat*; "Bird with Strings," *Perigee;* "Dance with Me," *Serving House Journal*; "Flower Killer," *Del Sol Review;* "Fred and Ginger," *A Quarter After Eight*; "Heart Failure," *Oasis*; "Hike & Seek," *Runnin' Around*; "Kaiser-Frazer," *West Branch*; "Linda and Eunice," *The Express*; "Mystery Woman," *Referential*; "*Ne Parle Pas*," *Contempora*; "No Rights in This Matter," *Twigs*; "Ruins," *The Fiction Review*; "Seeking K," *Mad Hatter's Review*; "Surprise," *Gingerbread House*; "Telling Stories," *South85*; "The Marriage Knot," *Aspect*; "The Other Price," *Skidrow Penthouse*; "Things," *Spafaswap*; "Treasure," *Stranger Kaddish*; "Tucker and Rob," *Valpariaso Fiction Review*.

Contents

Stories Old

A Minor Dislocation

L ater, after his unit moved on, Taylor happened on an old postcard of the village. He recognized the view immediately, though everything looked very different when he was stationed there. No whitewashed buildings along the river or steepled church high on a hillside, not even a single day of blue sky in all those weeks. The village he knew had been grey, a place of shattered windows and crushed walls. But, most of all, there had been no bridge, just twisted stanchions and jagged road ends on either side of the river, not the graceful arched span that spread across the front of the card.

The infantry occupied the village first, his convoy next, though at that stage of the fighting it hadn't taken much of an effort. The enemy had been defeated months before their leaders would formally surrender. He, a second lieutenant assigned to set up a supply depot, led the line of trucks in his jeep. Because no standing building in the village center was large enough, he commandeered a mill on the other side of the river. The bridge had been bombed out in the attack, but that wasn't important. The village itself didn't figure in anyone's planning. His army needed a way station on the way to somewhere more significant.

Taylor had to displace the mill owner's family. It was the part of his job he liked least, even though they were the enemy, even though all the wreckage and death he had witnessed made their suffering trivial.

An elderly man, two women, and several children had been sitting around a wooden table near an open fire when he pounded the metal knocker and pushed open the door. His men poured inside the stone-floored room, helmeted, boots muddy, eager for the warmth. Taylor knew enough of the family's language, had delivered this same message so many times that he found no trouble making himself understood. The people were nodding before he spoke, on their feet, the children huddling against women, the man's eye blinking as if in spasm.

"You must leave now," Taylor told them. "At once." The older children began to cry. "Is this all of you?" he asked the man. "Does anyone else live here?"

The man pointed to a stairway and called out a word, not a name, at least not one that Taylor knew. The old woman came down slowly, a step at a time, always leading with her right foot. She was a small plump woman in heavy, laced shoes, already wearing a dark coat, a wool shawl tied around her head, a bundle under her arm, as if she had been packed and waiting for someone like Taylor to arrive.

She stood in the doorway and glared at him with pale grey eyes. He wasn't sure whether it was an expression of hatred or defiance. He wanted to tell her, "Your side lost. You are defeated," but instead said, "Take what you need for tonight. You can come back for more tomorrow."

The old woman waited while the others rushed up the stairs and grabbed all they could. His men were already unloading their equipment in the sheds, hauling wooden crates, when the family returned to the kitchen. Taylor watched them move down the hillside toward the river, pausing at the edge while the man measured the depth with a branch, then waded through waist-high water, hoisting the satchels and suitcases, the small children on their shoulders. Once on the other side, they followed the road that curved uphill and disappeared into the cluster of buildings that was the village.

Someone would put them up, Taylor told himself. They probably had relatives. In a village like this everyone was everyone else's cousin. It was a minor dislocation.

He expected them back in the morning for more of their belongings. They had taken so little, no bedding or foodstuffs, just a change of clothes. But no one came, not that day nor the following nor the one after that.

The next week the old woman appeared on the path along the mill side of the river riding an old blue bicycle, nothing but bare tires and a frame. She sat erect on the seat, stretching her short legs to turn the pedals. Taylor wondered how she had crossed the water; there wasn't another bridge for as far as he could see in either direction.

He assumed she would want to get inside the mill for the belongings now stripped from the rooms and stuffed under the eaves. But she leaned the bicycle against a stone shed in the yard and dropped to her knees, pulling half-grown turnips from the earth and sticking them into her coat pockets.

They're starving, Taylor thought, desperate for a few scrawny roots. Cousins or not, the village didn't have enough food for everyone. War had destroyed the fields.

Taylor drove his jeep through the river, half expecting to be swamped. But the water had receded since the night the family left and came no higher than his axles.

Soldiers guarded the village, not from his unit, men he had never seen, patrolling the narrow streets with rifles slung over their shoulders. Some paused to salute Taylor; others pretended not to see him.

He went into a tiny bakery, aware of his boots resounding from the bare wooden floor. The baker and his wife pushed a curtain aside and came out of a back room, standing close together with heads bowed. Taylor asked about the family by the name he had seen on letters and papers around the mill.

"They are fine," the baker said.

"Do they have food? Do all of you have food?"

"Enough," the baker's wife said.

They would tell him nothing. Back on the street, he looked for the man, the younger women, or the children, wondering if he remembered any of them well enough to recognize if they were part of a group of cousins with similar features. Only the old woman would stand out. Taylor saw no one he knew, no one who would meet his eye. He drove back to his duties.

He and his unit had much to do—supplies to log in and inventory to distribute. He was responsible for an accounting. They all worked from early morning to late at night, exhausted from their part in the war, though the fighting was miles away. Taylor barely had time to think about his own family, much less the old woman and her people across the river.

Then she appeared again one afternoon, standing on the step with the old blue bicycle braced against her side, waiting until he opened the door, unwilling to knock at her own home.

He motioned her inside. "This is yours." He gestured toward the walls and spoke in her language. "It was yours before and will be yours again. We are only temporary." She echoed "temporary," the way he had pronounced it, as if it were a new word.

"How is your family?" he asked, and when she did not answer added, "your grandchildren, your daughters?"

"I have no daughters."

He smiled, as if she were being overly precise. "Daughters-in-law."

"I have no sons," she said, and he understood at once, knowing also that she would have scorned any gesture he offered. But he had no idea why she was here.

"Is there something you want?" he asked.

She glared at him, then down at the floor. "For the children."

"What for the children?"

"Food."

"Of course," he said, relieved that she finally asked. Taylor opened the doors to her cupboard, indicated the shelves packed with rations for his men. "Anything. Take whatever you want."

"For this," she said, twisting a ring from her finger, a pale green stone in an etched gold setting.

Taylor saw that it was an antique, beautiful, probably valuable. "I can't," he said. "It's not necessary."

"Take it!" she demanded, forcing the ring into his hand, bending his fingers around it with furious strength.

Although he was breaking rules, violating his own accounting, he packed a box for her, selecting items himself when she would not choose. The box was large, too unwieldy for her bicycle. Taylor offered to drive it to the village in his jeep. But the woman shook her head, saying only that someone would come.

When she climbed onto the bicycle and rode down the path to whatever place she crossed the river, he held the ring out at arm's length and watched her move away through the circle of gold.

The woman's two daughters-in-law arrived the next day, on foot, their dresses wet below the waist. They were plain women, one dark, one fair, both with stunned eyes, as if they had just witnessed something beyond belief. They made no objection when Taylor placed the box of food in the back of his jeep but would not get inside, walking behind him as he crept along in first gear, not even standing aside when the river water splashed their faces.

In the village, they pointed to a cottage. He stopped and left the box outside the door, driving away before the old woman came out, sparing her the sight of him.

But in the evening, when it was dark, he drove back across the river, parking just off the broken edge of road, and walked up among the houses. Soldiers were on patrol, fewer than he had noticed during the day. Taylor stood in the shadows of the cottage across from the one the family lived in. He could see them all in the front room, along with others, cousins, who were strangers to him. The adults stood against a wall saying nothing, but the children, a crowd of them, sat in the center of the room, an older girl passing out items from the food he had given the old woman for her ring. The children tore open chocolate bars, ate slowly and eagerly, savoring each bite. Then they looked at each other and burst out laughing. Two started to dance and soon they were all on their feet, dancing to a tune they sung themselves. They're having a party, Taylor realized, astonished that such a thing could be happening in this place. When he saw the old woman in a corner, weeping but making no gesture to wipe the tears from her face, he turned away, embarrassed to be watching.

15

Taylor and his unit stayed in the mill another few weeks, but he didn't see the old woman or any of the family. He never crossed the river again, and they never came to him.

When his men cleared out all the supplies and personal belongings and loaded the trucks, Taylor went back inside one last time, into the largest bedroom, and put the antique ring into the empty drawer of the table beside the bed.

As he drove away, he wasn't sure about what he had done. Perhaps the old woman would never find it. Perhaps it would lay in the corner of that drawer, a precious object misplaced from her life.

Linda and Eunice

E unice met Linda five minutes before their first class of their first day at the university. They literally bumped into one another in the doorway, where Linda had paused to estimate the situation just as Eunice was rushing in for fear of being late. Eunice apologized, and Linda returned a perfect smile, the one she had been trained to give at half-time shows during four years as a twirler. Of course, all the twirlers had practiced the same smile, but few picked it up as quickly as Linda or executed it as well. After a bumping like that many other girls would have taken seats together, using the accident as an excuse to build a friendship. In this case, the two parted as quickly as they had met and moved to opposite corners of the room, Linda up front where she could be seen, Eunice deep in the back where she could not. Though her smile had lasted two seconds, Linda's glance at Eunice took only a fraction of one, enough time to dismiss her and begin a search that instinctively led to a pretty dark-haired girl in expensive jeans. Eunice spent much longer looking at Linda, long enough for the familiar despair to catch at her stomach, before she moved backwards and banged her ankle against a chair rung.

The class began a course called "Communications Skills," which met four times each week for practice in writing, speaking, and reading comprehension. With only twenty-four students, it was the smallest class either girl would be in until her junior year. Usually they sat in lecture halls as one of several hundred listening to an amplified instructor. Linda and Eunice shared two other courses, occupying the same auditorium for "Western Civilization" and "Introduction" to Sociology. Throughout each lecture, except for the days Linda cut, Eunice sat far behind and could watch the sun that filtered through the skylight glitter from the girl's golden hair. Linda noticed Eunice once or twice as they filed out into the hallway, regarding her with a brief flicker of familiarity.

The "Communication Skills" course was taught by a very young graduate student named Gumner, who looked rather seedy with the beginnings of a full beard. He had graduated from an Ivy League school and cluttered each period with a feeble one-track wit, mocking the university for its athletic mania, for its farmers' sons, for its clumsy milling Friday night dances in a gargantuan quonset hut known as the Fieldhouse. In reality, he was a nervous wreck from the obligation to stand in front of a group of sullen faces and contrive fifty minutes of content four days each week. Constantly, his voice cracked or mumbled off into incoherence. He repeated some sentences three or four times and used the word "obviously" so often some students began to giggle whenever it came out of his mouth. The giggles made him blush and stammer. By the next fall he had dropped out of graduate school and taken a job as an apprentice in an advertising agency.

Eunice was terrified of him, of a sarcasm she couldn't even comprehend and of the red circles, slashes, and symbols that obliterated her returned compositions under grades that alternated between C- and D+ with comments like, "You don't have much to say about this subject—do you?"

As soon as Linda saw Mr. Gumner enter the classroom with briefcase and vest, she asked herself the question she always asked when confronted by young men of authority: what would I say if he asked me for a date? The instant she realized her response would be "No," Mr. Gumner retreated to the place of a petty annoyance in her life. Whatever she wrote or however she spoke, the grade always turned out B. She rarely made an effort because all young men teachers and most older ones inevitably gave her B's. Any real work she did was for the women and usually resulted in a B too. She wanted badly to be known as a B student; it made a nice frame to set off her other achievements.

Near mid-semester Mr. Gumner assigned, from the departmental syllabus, a demonstration speech. Students had to bring some object into class and describe its use or operation. Eunice lay awake for hours that night trying to devise a plan to avoid the assignment. Even if she feigned illness, she would have to make it up; she couldn't imagine herself refusing to give the speech. For previous speeches, standing before the class in itself was a torment, but she had solved the problem by remaining fixed behind the lectern and reading quickly from notecards, afterwards enduring Gumner's attacks on her lack of animation and eye contact.

But the thought of this demonstration speech caused her new anguish because it would force her to make gestures and look out at the faces in the room. But worst of all was the certainty that others would be watching her. For several days she did nothing but brood over the topic, eventually spending hours browsing through the downtown stores in hopes of discovering an object. Finally, she chose an embriodery kit, a skill she knew nothing about, and memorized points from the instruction sheet to recite during her sixty-second performance. Mr. Gumner gave her a D+.

Linda, who did not pick her topic until she rummaged through her closet fifteen minutes before class, brought water skis. She placed them on the instructor's desk and climbed on top from a chair, having removed her leather boots while Eunice was speaking; she wore shorts that came down to mid-thigh. Some of the boys whistled. Mr. Gumner tilted his chair back and bit down to stifle a grin. On the comment sheet, he noted, "Your content may have been a bit thin, but your form left little to be desired."

That was an overstatement, though not unusual for a male response to Linda. Men and boys treated her as if she were a beauty, when objectively she was barely pretty. A few good features overwhelmed her weak ones; attention focused on the fine golden hair, the blue eyes, the full lips, while ignoring the knobby chin, the pug nose, the slouch to the shoulders, and the thin bowed calves. It was almost as if males wanted her to be much better looking than reality permitted. Even as a child she had been considered the pretty one and, because of it, fell into a life of popularity. People, even girls, liked her because she wasn't conceited, acting with the

19

confidence of someone special but tempered by her realization of the luck involved.

No one had ever considered Eunice beautiful; no one had ever blinded himself to the flaws of her thick squat body or her bad skin or her puffy face, distorted as if she were continually holding her breath. The second of three daughters of a Caucasian father, a Navy chief petty officer, and a Chinese-Hawaiian mother, the combination in her belied the Eurasian attractiveness that graced her two sisters. Where they were exotic, Eunice seemed the victim of a genetic blunder, a plump Caucasian who suffered jaundice. Even her sisters, who were quite close, regarded her as an outsider.

By coincidence several weeks later when the speech subject was sororities and fraternities, the schedule placed Linda right after Eunice. Although she had meant to read notes on a brief history of Greek letter societies taken from an encyclopedia, Eunice found herself backed against the blackboard ranting as if secret thoughts had erupted after a long festering. Her eyelashes sticky with tears, her vision clouded, she couldn't see to read and sputtered the word "Unfair!" Sororities are snob societies. They choose only the prettiest, the best dressed. Clubs in a university should help people become better. But sororities exclude. They look down at the rejects as inferiors. They can hurt deeply. They can scar for life. Sensing that she was incoherent, Eunice stopped abruptly in mid-sentence and plunged down the aisle to her chair, not lifting her eyes from the names and initials scratched into the writing arm until the class had ended.

Eunice's outburst had upset some people in the room, not because of what she said but because she had broken an unstated code by involving her emotions in the ritual of education. But Linda, stepping before a room of friends, spoke as if she had not heard a word of Eunice's protest, thumb and forefinger plucking her sweater to emphasize the Kappa pledge pin that rode the incline of her taut left breast. "I'm at home in the sorority. There are seventy girls in the house and they're all my sisters. I know I belong. The sorority will be one of the most important things I'll ever experience. I belong in a national organization, and all over the country in almost every city there will be sisters I can turn to. And I know for the rest of my life that I'll never be alone because they're my kind of people."

Next year as a sophomore Linda was able to move into the Kappa house. She loved every minute of it, the swapping of clothes, the confidences after dates, the singing at dinner. By November, Eunice's roommate requested a change. Eunice heard the girl complaining to the senior counselor. "She never talks and she doesn't wash her underwear." At first the peace of being alone pleased Eunice, but soon the empty bed, its bare mattress rolled on the boxspring, became haunting. At the semester break she moved into a rooming house on the same street as Linda's sorority.

The girls passed occasionally, Linda so involved with her companions that she never saw her former classmate scuffing at the sidewalk. Once when she saw Linda alone too, Eunice stopped her on a bold impulse. "What happened to Mr. Gumner?" she asked abruptly. "I don't see him around."

"Gumno? I never think about him. He's a very forgettable person."

By the spring Linda was going steady, having chosen a boy from about the dozens she dated. "I think I like him," she told her sorority sisters, and they squeezed her hands in theirs and squealed.

The boyfriend, named Jon, a first-year medical student was nice looking in a rather formal way; his well-molded face didn't bend easily. Everyone who saw him knew he would become successful and wealthy. Most Kappas found him a bit dull, but never said a word to Linda. Usually an unthinking young man who did what was expected of him with a precise efficiency, he sometimes wondered if he would have fallen in love with whatever girl he had dated at that moment in his life. But he didn't pursue the thought. He found no flaws in Linda and sought no quarrel with whatever chance had brought them together. The only thing that upset Jon about Linda was her strict code of sexual conduct. For example, she let him slip his hand inside her blouse to fondle her breast, but never inside her brassiere. She always insisted upon a layer of cloth between their flesh.

Linda's code became a constant subject of discussion for them. Writing an assigned paper about *The Sun Also Rises* for Mr. Gumner, she had said, "Lady Brett Ashley did all sorts of things I wouldn't do." "What's that?" Gumner had asked in red, following the inquiry with a large round question mark. Jon argued from his knowledge of human physiology, but Linda never faltered in her defenses; he couldn't help respecting her for them.

While Linda drank beer from Jon's mug and screamed laughter to games of thumper at Saturday night fraternity parties, Eunice sat in her room and listened to music on the radio until one Saturday the pattern on the wallpaper began to make her sick to her stomach. She walked into town and stared at the articles in the windows of the closed stores, wanting none of them. When she heard singing from a bar, she summoned up all her courage to step inside. It was crowded with couples who sang to the accompaniment of an upright piano enameled bright red. School pennants and poster pictures of football heroes decorated the walls. Eunice found a small table in a corner by a radiator and enjoyed listening to their fun. The waiters didn't even notice her.

After that night she went out more often, usually to movies, but now and then back to that same bar to hear the singing.

In the summer when Linda taught Jon to water ski at her family's vacation lake, Eunice stayed at the university to work in the cafeteria collecting dirty dishes on a metal cart. With no classes to occupy her, she started going to the bar on weeknights, by now having learned to nurse a bottle of beer for an hour even though she hated the taste. But weeknights, there was no singing and few couples. Called "The Clinic," it was a hangout for medical students.

By mid-June the young men began to notice her. At first they just shrugged and turned away. But her continued presence annoyed them, as if they could not be as free in their pleasure with her watching. They began to insult her, deliberately bumping her table and spilling her beer, flicking ashes into her glass. A powerful student named Frank, once an undergraduate weightlifter, gave her a nickname. Useless Eunice. They would shout harsh greetings to her all through the evening, made crueler by their puzzlement when she came back again the next night.

Finally, a boy sat down at the table with her. He said his name was Bobby and seemed even more nervous than she was. She smiled and tried to make conversation although she had heard Frank and some of the others taunting him to join her. She thought they had bet money that he wouldn't do it but wasn't sure.

Eunice told Bobby about her work in the cafeteria, knowing that her talk was boring and that he didn't listen. One of his legs shook frenetically under the table and he interrupted her with an abrupt question that was almost a command. "Do you want to get away from here? Take a ride?"

She nodded and he was out the door before she had gathered up her purse. Frank led the whoops of ridicule as she hurried to follow.

Bobby told her he had three roommates in his apartment. She said that must be nice. "Can we go to your place?" he blurted.

She shrugged agreement. "It's not a big room."

"I don't care," he said.

He followed her up the stairs carrying a bottle of whiskey in a paper bag. When she said it burned her throat, he gave her two black and orange capsules and told her they would make her feel good without any discomfort. At first her head felt funny, then she seemed to float as if weightless until she lost consciousness.

She recovered to find herself flat on her bed with Bobby naked on top of her, thrusting up and down and moaning with excitement. She felt the pressure inside her, surprised it was without pain, but received no pleasure.

After that she let one of the medical students take her home from the bar every night. As it passed along the gossip chain, Bobbie's tale became distorted. The others assumed they had to give Eunice pills before she would go with them, and Eunice took the pills because the young men expected it.

By the fall when classes started she was already a local legend, a standing joke, sitting for hours at the same table with a fixed stare, automatically following any male out the door as a touch on her shoulders.

Occasionally, Jon took her home; quick in his passion, afterwards driven to explain his circumstances, fully dressed, sitting erectly on a wooden chair across the room from the bed where Eunice lay with a sheet up to her chin. He told her about the lovely girl he was pinned to, about the pressure that built up inside him and how his nights with Eunice enabled him to treat his girl with more respect. Each time he went with her he repeated the same story and thanked her when he left.

By the time Jon and Linda became engaged, Eunice was a heavy user of barbiturates, drawn to the release of oblivion with the first passion she had felt in her life.

She never studied and rarely attended classes. Failing all five subjects, she dropped out of the university at mid-year and reapplied for her job in the cafeteria, ignoring the catcalls that followed her among the tables.

Her father, now retired from the Navy and working in the post office, reacted angrily to the news of her withdrawal. He stopped sending checks. Her mother wrote letters now and then; her only contact with her sisters was an exchange of birthday cards. At Easter she tried a visit home but was sick from missing her drugs and suspected that everyone gave her strange looks.

Linda and Jon came back to the campus on the same train after an exchange of family visits, but they rode in a different car from Eunice and they never saw each other.

Not long after, in the spring, Frank took Eunice home for the first time. She accepted the capsules from him, but when he pushed her toward the bed, she knotted herself in a rigid ball and shook him off. "I don't like you," she told him. "You're the only one I don't like. You've always been mean to me."

Frank turned furious and slapped her face. "Pig! Slut! Filthy, rotten, stinking whore! You're trash! You're the garbage of the universe!"

He slammed the door so hard pieces of plaster dropped loose through the hollows of the house. Eunice went berserk, hurling her body from wall to wall of the tiny room, screaming that she hated her flesh.

For the next three days she rarely moved off her bed, except to get glasses of water to help her swallow the capsules she had hoarded. She didn't eat. In the empty hours she tried to picture the faces of all the young men who had been with her, but couldn't. She realized that she knew only a few of their names, and became so bewildered the faces blurred in her memory. Near the end of the third day she lost her sense of time and began taking more barbiturates every hour.

No one could say whether she took the overdose deliberately. If Eunice herself had been able to speak about it, she would not have known what to answer. Her flesh was so pained that night, her mind whirling with so much confusion. But when she closed her eyes for the last time, she experienced a strange sense of finality.

The body was not found for a week. The people in the cafeteria and the students in the bar had missed her, but did not take the trouble to look. It was the odor that led neighbors to investigate.

Eunice's corpse was brought to the hospital on one of Jon's duty nights. He had to help the resident perform the autopsy and assisted with his usual efficiency.

That Saturday he seduced Linda, so forceful in his passion that she submitted out of surprise. His action might have been considered rape if the girl had not been his fiancée and if her unwillingness had not been an act made convincing by years of practice.

For all her militant chastity, Linda turned out not to be frigid. In fact, she discovered that she enjoyed the act of sex so much it soon became one of her greatest pleasures. Linda was very fortunate in her life.

A Kind Hand

As Marsh turned the corner toward the river, a fish smell slapped him in the face. Huge trucks were backed across the sidewalk to the open warehouses, the rough idles of their engines rumbling against his skull. Men in bloody aprons, shouting to make themselves heard, hauled baskets of fish netted from the sea that morning. Marsh glanced down at the piles of dark bodies that writhed in death throes. They gazed back at him with unblinking one-eyed stares.

He stepped out into the gutter to pass them by and crossed the street to a pier where clusters of grey-suited businessmen and office women relaxed on their lunch breaks. Beneath the cloudless sky the river gleamed brightly, but it was not clean; debris floated past on clusters of scum and it gave off a vaguely fetid odor. Out in the distance the harbor widened into an open sea that met the horizon.

He turned to face the city. The clusters of skyscrapers seemed jammed to the river's edge, aspiring to the clouds, yet landlocked and going nowhere. He strained to find the window of his office thirty-five floors above the street. But his vision became fuzzy and for an instant he saw only a giant wall of stone looming above him.

A strong hand clasped his shoulder through the padded suit jacket. Devlin had approached from behind.

"Good to see you, Frank," Devlin boomed. "Glad you were able to find the place."

Marsh winced as he looked down at the tanned hand calloused with a workman's strength. Devlin spent his spare hours caring for his sailboat, scraping, caulking, painting in preparation for the month's vacation cruise he took each summer. Marsh had passed a Saturday on the boat several years before, left breathless by the sensation of free flight when a sudden wind billowed the white sails.

It was Devlin's idea to meet at the pier even though Marsh had called to invite him to lunch, forcing heartiness over the phone, embarrassed because he knew Devlin understood a favor would be asked, oddly resentful because Devlin would not mind. Before Marsh could make a suggestion, Devlin named the restaurant and the meal, sea food. Marsh felt cheated. Devlin, he was sure, meant no harm; seizing the upper hand was second nature with him.

"We don't do this often enough." Devlin grinned at him with affection. Both men were past fifty, but Devlin's hair was still dark and close cut. "You know, I haven't seen Hilda in three years."

"Has it been that long? Hilda doesn't get out much any more." Each night Marsh and his wife sat staring at television programs he couldn't remember the next morning. "She hasn't been feeling well lately."

"Laziness plain and simple. You're stuck to one spot."

"She has ... ah, female troubles."

A twinge of distaste crossed Devlin's face, as if he had just chewed into egg shell. He had married late; his wife was still youthful and elegant. "Most likely she'll need an operation," Marsh continued.

"Christ, I'm sorry, Frank."

"I guess we have to face the fact that we're getting older."

Devlin laughed. "Not if you put up a fight."

An ache of fatigue stretched from Marsh's shoulders to the small of his back. He had sought out Devlin for help, but could not bring himself to make the plea.

A fishing barge maneuvered alongside the pier, cutting engines and drifting while two deck hands leaped onto the prow to wrap ropes around the pilings. A name had been painted on its side, but most of each letter was worn away. Marsh made out something like the "Mary Care." He thought it was an absurd name; this misshapen stump of a boat deserved no more identification than a number. The only grace it possessed lay in the slim radar antenna bolted to the side of the cabin, projecting twenty feet upward and tapering to a fine point. That sleek rod reminded Marsh of Devlin's craft.

"I forget what your boat's called," he said.

"It's named after Claudine."

"And you're the captain."

"Captain and crew." Devlin smiled up at the sun. "Let's play hooky, Frank. We'll go down to my boat. His eyes took on a glint Marsh remembered from their youth.

"I can't. Things are pretty busy at the office." But at the moment Marsh could not recall his afternoon duties.

"How long has it been now?" Devlin asked.

"What?"

"Since you began working for the bank?"

"Fifteen years last January." His own words struck Marsh as a confession.

"That's a long time."

As the barge began to unload, all the gulls along the river seemed to swarm over the pier. Moments before they had drifted lazily; now they spun in excited circles, wild to get at the cargo of fish. Hundreds of them flapped and wheeled, swooping down to seize the pieces of gut that fell into the water or onto the planks of the pier.

The office workers backed away and the deck hands chased the gulls with angry swipes of poles, muttering curses of longstanding hostility. Marsh had always admired the graceful flight of birds, but the brute hunger of these gulls, the squawking snaps of their sharp bills, filled him with anger at their existence. He feared their intrusion would ruin his request for a favor.

Marsh turned his back on the birds and tried to make Devlin look away too.

"You're right," he said, "I've given the bank a lot of service." A rush of emotion clutched in his throat. "You know what I can't stand? What makes me sick?"

"No."

"The damned subway. I only have a five minute ride, but I get on on the right hand side and have to get off on the left. It's always so crowded I have to spend the whole trip working my way across the car, and every day I'm afraid that I won't make it. I lie in bed mornings and hate to get up just thinking about it. But what if I didn't get across? What difference would it make?"

Devlin put his hand on Marsh's sleeve. There was a gentleness in his touch that warmed Marsh's hopes. This friend would do anything for him. But now he didn't know what to ask for, what he really wanted.

A woman cried out. "It's stuck! The poor thing. Look!"

Marsh followed her pointing. A gull had dropped too close to the boat's antenna and pierced a wing on the sharp tip. For a moment the bird hovered as if stunned. Marsh was sure it would gather its instincts to lift free. But as the loose wing spread wide and beat with frantic effort, the gull merely twisted in a circle and pinned itself more deeply; the point of the antenna glittered in the sun a full six inches above the useless wing.

"Somebody help!" another woman cried.

Marsh looked uncomfortably at Devlin, sensing a futility in the neat collar and tailored business suit.

The other gulls swirled around the captive. Their motions were abrupt, their cries harsh. The two deck hands, dark seaworn men as grimy as their boat, climbed atop the cabin and beat off the other gulls until the impaled one screeched alone. They tried to push it loose, but the gull was beyond their reach.

Marsh imagined all the workers in the great office buildings crowded at thousands of windows watching this scene of solitary crisis, the concern of the city focused on one helpless bird.

The gull was ugly, its belly fat, the feathers yellowed with river filth, the sharp little beak cutting at the air with frantic squawks.

"Get loose!" Devlin yelled. He sounded like a man cheering at a football game. Marsh closed his teeth on his lower lip.

The women closest to the boat began calling out to the deck hands, urging that they do something. A few men joined the appeal. The two hands looked back at the crowd, their mouths sullen. With weary eyes they nodded to each other; one went inside for a toolbox. He began to loosen the bolts that clamped the antenna to the cabin. A sound of relief passed through the crowd. Marsh was surprised at his own great joy. Devlin shouted encouragement.

The second hand held the antenna steady as the bolts were

removed. Then together they slid it out from its brackets and slowly lowered it to the deck. The gull became more frightened; its good wing beat madly trying to tear loose, and blood spread on its feathers. You little fool, Marsh thought, they're trying to help you.

When the antenna reached the deck, one of the hands took hold of the bird with a stroking motion that brought its wings back against the body and kept the head still so that it could not peck. The group on the pier watched in complete silence. The other hand drew the tip of the antenna from the gull's wing. Marsh felt a sword had been pulled from his middle. People were laughing now.

The hand seized the gull by its legs and with a sudden striking smashed its head against the side of the cabin.

Marsh's knees buckled. He tottered forward blinded by dizziness, but Devlin held him back. He stood among the speechless crowd for a full minute after the deck hand turned his back and threw the gull into the river. Then Marsh broke away from the others and hurried into the street, sickened by the fish smells. Devlin trotted after him.

"The filthy rotten bastard," Marsh swore.

"It had to be done, Frank. The wing was broken."

"But why did he have to be so kind?"

Ruins

He lifted the lid to the garbage can and found the flowers, tulips and daffodils ripped by their roots from his garden, houseplants still packed in dark dirt, the clay pots cracked against the metal. In the yard behind the house the shrubs exposed hacked stumps. Limbs of the fruit trees dangled by their bark. A hatchet and garden shears lay rusting in the dew. When he knelt beside them, she twisted away from the window and snapped the curtains closed.

Blocks of the city's central district had been pulled down, leveled and bulldozed into flat lots of rough stones and fragmented brick. The sidewalks formed a perfect grid; rotting cars lined along the curbs as if people still lived in the memories of the row houses. At the edge of these empty blocks, other buildings, whole streets, were marked for demolition, wide white X's taped across the blank front windows. He and she had a home there once, when they were someone else. Now he wondered where the other people had fled with their lives.

The old Buick tilted against the garage front, engine running, driver's door swung open, a wooden beam crushed into the right fender. He walked slowly to turn off the key as if it were too late. The temperature needle quivered in the red warning zone. The metal of the fender was ripped in a deep gash, the headlight broken, the tire flat, sidewall torn open. She must have been driving desperately, approaching at an absurd angle.

The factories stood on a hill near the railroad tracks,

buildings a hundred yards long with great windows segmented into thousands of separate panes, most missing, jagged edges in the frames. These buildings had been mills, built a hundred and fifty years before, now, when he peered inside, totally empty. He had expected to see huge still looms with rotting cloth frozen in their shuttles. But the machines must have been ripped out for scrap. He pressed his face through a space of missing glass and looked along the splintering plank floor and up at the dark light fixtures swaying from the twenty foot ceilings. He shuddered at the hollowness. Her father had once worked in a factory like this, but her father had been dead for years.

His shoe came down on something sharp when he entered the dark kitchen. He fumbled fingers across the wall for the light switch, then blinked in the sudden brightness and saw the clock. 3 a.m. The linoleum was littered with broken glass, the cupboard doors wide. Every tumbler in the house was shattered—amber, green, clear, wine glasses and crystal. Whole shelves were bare. Jagged slivers glittered under the ceiling light. Exhausted, he began sweeping the debris, the clatter screeching against the still night. He wondered if the noise would wake her. He wondered if she were sleeping, if she ever slept.

Flames leaped ten feet high against the midnight sky, so hot they seared his eyebrows as he stood barefoot on the sidewalk, listening to the crackling from within, small explosions of metal, the crash of collapsing beams. Black smoke, thick as tar, billowed from the upholstery. A chemical smell burned tears from his eyes and ate into his lungs. I'm being poisoned, he thought, but stood gasping through an open mouth.

Her face terrified him. It was a face he knew as well as his own.

But never so ravaged, the eyes dark and fixed, locked with a fervid stare, the hair wild, twisted into jagged coils, the mouth knotted, teeth grinding so fiercely he didn't hear the sirens.

Ne Parle Pas

It was the spring of 1973, a glorious day. Yet Jerry decided he'd had it with Paris but with no idea where to go next. Then he saw Lisa in the Louvre, of all places. It was in the *Salle de Etats* where the greatest paintings hung, though Jerry didn't know where he was, just having wandered up and down corridors past a blur of art, wondering what the hell he was doing in a museum. Just as he realized his feet were aching, he saw the Mona Lisa and, a second later, the living Lisa. Of the two, he preferred flesh and blood.

At first glance he thought she was French because of her gleaming dark hair, narrow jeaned hips, and high, full Parisian breasts. But the TWA flight bag looped from her shoulder told him she was American. Wherever she came from, she was the best thing he had seen during his two weeks in Paris. While she stood at the outer edge of the people clustered around the Mona Lisa, he examined her with more real desire than he had felt in several years. If the museum guard at the door watching the crowd with suspicious French eyes had suddenly come forward to offer him, as a gift of M. Pompidou's government (say, because he was the millionth tourist to enter the Louvre that year), the priceless painting or the girl, even though he could have sold the painting and lived in ease for the rest of his life, he would have picked this girl he didn't know without a moment's hesitation. Christ! She might have been married or syphilitic. He didn't care; he wanted her so much his stomach twisted in python knots.

How to make an approach? Usually he calculated a full conversational gamut before maneuvering after a new girl. But this time he just plunged forward, stopping dead in panic when he realized she was with two friends, attractive enough girls if they hadn't been so close to her, one in a college tee shirt carrying a copy of *Europe on $5 a Day*.

Only three feet away, Jerry overheard one friend. "It says the DaVinci's by the door are better."

"I don't know," the spectacular girl said. "I think this is the greatest painting in the world."

"Well, we're tired of looking at it."

"I want to stay."

"We want to go ahead."

"Then go."

"All right. We'll look for you by the entrance in an hour."

"If I'm not there, I'll meet you at the hotel."

Unbelievably, the two friends left her and Jerry stepped closer until he was right next to her. Following the path of her lovely dark eyes, he looked at the painting too and recalled an hour in an art appreciation class, the Mona Lisa projected on a screen while he half dozed with his feet on the chair in front of him. It was a dumb course and he usually cut, but this one recollection turned out to be a godsend.

"It's the mouth," he told the girl.

"What?" She seemed surprised to hear a human voice.

"The mouth is the center of the painting. It's what attracts you. The force is compelling. If you look long enough, you can't keep your own mouth from moving. It transmits tremendous power. Even after all these centuries, you have a human contact with that woman."

The girl stared harder at the painting until her own mouth started to twist, forming a momentary pucker that nearly drove Jerry to kiss her right there. He couldn't remember such an overwhelming attraction to any girl. But he fought to control himself and keep the words flowing.

"See. It's happening to you," he said.

"My gosh! You're right." She rewarded him with her own smile. "You certainly know a lot about art."

"I studied it in school."

"You were an art major."

"Just an interest. A minor, you might say."

To his own amazement, he heard himself offering to take her on a tour of the room and improvised a series of capsule lectures on color, light and shadow, design patterns, and emotional messages that bewildered him, as if he were suddenly speaking in tongues, The girl (he knew her name was Lisa by then), instead of laughing in his face as he expected, nodded with awe.

"Why does Uccello always use so many poles and shafts?"

"Phallic symbols." The term spilled right out of him.

"And that must be why he has so many horses. Masculine potency."

"Of course," Jerry said, as if her association were child's play.

Lisa never did meet her girl friends that day. After the Louvre she and Jerry crossed the Pont Neuf and walked for an hour around the Île de la Cité, then passed over to the Left Bank and ended up at a sidewalk cafe on the Boulevard Saint Germain, the whole time with Jerry telling her about Paris, passing on incidents that had happened to other people and impressions given him by strangers as if they were his own. When she told him she had only been in Paris three days, he said he had been there four months although there wasn't any good reason not to say two weeks.

To his eyes they made an odd pair in cafe mirrors, she so tall and lovely, her skin tan and clear, he an inch shorter, soft in the middle, shaggy, his face barely visible under and behind all his hair, with a beard that grew high on his cheek bones, up to an inch below his eyes.

But they spent the next five days together, Jerry picking her up after breakfast and not returning her to her hotel until long past midnight. The most fun was shopping for food , bread and pastries in the boulangeries, meat and cheese in the charcuteries, for park bench lunches. Neither of them knew French, so they struggled through with her French phrase book, giggling helplessly in the faces of hostile proprietors who seemed to take their mangling of the language as a personal insult. "*Ne parle pas*," they kept saying to explain their own incomprehension.

It wasn't until Sunday afternoon, after days of walking that covered fourteen of the twenty-three tours specified in her Michelin

Guide, that he made love to her. The girlfriends were sunning themselves in the Luxembourg Gardens and they finally had privacy in her hotel room. Jerry was sleeping dormitory style in a hostel, so his place was useless.

The sex was joyous. My God! This is great, he kept thinking the whole time. Afterwards, his hands brushing up and down her warm smoothness, he said, "You're incredible."

"*Je t'aime*," she answered back.

He was so thrilled at her response that he buried his face in her hair to hide his tears. When he calmed, he pretended cool amusement. "I thought you couldn't *parle pas*," he said.

She giggled. "I practiced those words all last night."

At five o'clock she said they'd better get dressed and fix her bed. Peggy and Michelle would be back any minute.

"I don't want to leave you," Jerry argued.

"We'll go out somewhere together."

"I mean I don't want to move an inch apart."

"Silly." She kissed the tip of his nose. "Why don't we go away? Just the two of us?"

"How do you mean?" Her offer stunned him.

"Out of Paris. Into the country. Someplace we can really be all by ourselves and talk for hours."

"Is that all? Talk?"

She blushed and he loved her all the more for it. "You know what I mean."

"Where in the country?"

"Anywhere. A tiny, tiny village with dirt roads and cows mooing all over."

"Great. We'll hitchhike."

"I've never hitchhiked."

"It's the only way to travel."

Later, both eating *bifstek frites* at a brasserie, she said to him, "Jerry, you haven't told me anything about you."

"Are you kidding? I've been on a nonstop talking spree since the moment we met."

"That's all been about people and places, things that happened and how you reacted. 1 mean, you know that I'm twenty years old, where my home is, where I go to college, my major, that Michelle is my roommate."

To his surprise, although he had known all along the situation would arise but had no plan, he found himself making up an autobiography. Because she was only twenty, he couldn't tell her he was well into his thirtieth year. Because she would be a college junior, he couldn't tell her he had flunked out after one semester of a freshman year long ago. Because she was anti-war, he couldn't tell her he had killed four years in the Navy. Because her home town and school implied family money, he couldn't tell her he had never worked at more than odd jobs long enough to pick up a stake of cash to bum around the States and now, for the first time, Europe.

"I'm a Martian computer," he told her.

"Stop teasing." She covered his hand with hers. "If *je t'aime*, I really want to know."

By the time he finished talking, he was twenty-three, had graduated from a university a year ago, and had been traveling around the world ever since. Eventually, he might go to law school, or more likely become an archeologist to see even more of human civilization. Two days later when they hit the road, he had hidden his passport deep in his rucksack. Later, one night when she playfully insisted on seeing his passport photo, reluctant as he had been to give in, she didn't even bother to notice his birthdate. His relationship with her had been one stroke of good luck after another.

After they started hitchhiking, Lisa had a change of heart. The first ride took them to the outskirts of the city, but then they stood at a junction for an hour, thumbs out, while cars whizzed by.

"I don't want to do this any more," she told him.

"You mean we'll go back to Paris?"

"No silly. The country."

"How?"

"Take a train. Rent a car."

Jerry sat down on the roadside and laughed. "With what? Do you know how much money I have? You told me you've got even less."

"But I've got these." She drew two plastic credit cards from her wallet. American Express and Diner's Club.

"Jesus Christ!"

"Daddy insisted I take these in case I ever got stuck."

The cards in her hand scared him. He took them as certain signs that he would lose her. "Another ten minutes," he pleaded.

Luck again. A man in a Peugeot stopped after nine. He began spouting in French as soon as they tossed their gear into the luggage area and climbed into the back seat. Jerry took it to be a long question and didn't understand a word. He and Lisa hugged tightly and spoke in unison: "*Ne parle pas.*" All the way to Tours, the man sneaked looks at Lisa in the rear view mirror. Le bad tough luck, you frog, Jerry kept thinking, still dazzled by his fortune.

They camped for a night outside Poitiers, snug in his sleeping bag near the bank of the River Clain just fifty yards away from three caravans in a clearing, but private in a thick growth of trees.

The next day they covered much less distance. Rides came infrequently and only carried them a short way, usually between two neighboring towns. Finally, they got into trouble in a Renault Dauphine and found themselves dumped in the middle of nowhere. A farmer and an old woman in black, probably his mother, had picked them up at a Total garage. Jammed in the back seat with their gear, heads brushing the roof with each bounce, Jerry found himself singing, "*Ne parle pas, ne parle pas*, I can't *parle* a damn," to the tune of "Chicago." Lisa joined in. The car stopped so abruptly they pitched forward into the faces of the farmer and the old woman, who were shouting bursts of nasal outrage. Shouting, gesticulating, probably cursing, the farmer kicked them out of his car.

Wherever they looked, they saw nothing but vineyards. Still, the sun was shining and they embraced in hilarity. A sign pointed to a village called St. Pierre two kilometers away. Things weren't so bad.

During the walk into the village, Lisa told Jerry about her

language education. "I took three years of Latin in high school, more than enough for college entrance. I got A's every marking period, but forgot everything the year I stopped. Daddy wanted me to take French in college, but I picked Spanish because it was easier. I should have listened to Daddy. Whenever I go my own way, I get into trouble."

"Honey, a girl who looks like you could be mute and nobody would care."

Jerry expected the praise to please her. But instead she turned away and pouted in silence until she asked him, "Why is it that you never learned French? You do so well at everything else?"

"I never had the time for languages. Too much rote memorization for my tastes. I had better things to do with my education."

St. Pierre could have been a ghost village for all the life they saw when they first entered. Only animals moved—a few cats, chickens, and the cows Lisa had dreamed of. Unlike the neat villages of freshly painted white houses they had passed through all day, St. Pierre looked depressed, the stucco crumbling, the stone walls like arbitrary heaps, the roof tiles buckled, tattered handbills smeared on the sides of sheds. Every now and then bursts of flowers sprang up from the weeds behind the rusting iron fences. A few cars, mainly old Deux Chevaux-like constructions that seemed assembled from the back of a cereal package, sat dormant in the yards. All the windows of the village were shuttered tight.

"Oh, Jerry!" Lisa said. "Isn't this picturesque?"

"Great. It's the place we've been looking for."

She found St. Pierre in her Michelin Guide for the Cote de l'Antique, a guide all in French because no English translation existed. They were only twenty kilometers from Royan. "Oh, Jerry, we're near the ocean!"

Miraculously, a few hundred meters west of the village they found a converted windmill for rent. Lisa translated the notice with her phrase book. Using a combination of sign language, a display of money, and pigeon French—*"Voulez vous rentir la moulin a nous"*—in the doorway.of the nearest farmhouse, they were able to arrange a month's rental—*"pour quatre semaines"*—for four hundred francs, which left them seven hundred of pooled resources for food.

The windmill, only about ten feet wide, had three rooms, one on top of the other, a weathervane, but no blades. The top room was empty, the middle furnished with a double bed and straw-filled mattress, a chest, a plywood wardrobe. and a crucifixion painted in 1899 by a man named E. Nowatowski, a surprisingly good painting for such tatty surroundings. The ground level contained a gas stove, a sink, a table, and two loose-jointed chairs. The toilet and shower were outside, not at a distance, but in a cinder block cubicle attached to the mill. Moss grew from the stone walls and everything smelled of dampness. Because the farmer, as best they could understand, refused to supply linen, they spread the sleeping bag on the mattress for sleeping and lovemaking.

The first week there was the most idyllic of Jerry's life. Warm sun, peace and quiet except for the natural hawking of chickens and mooing of cows, cheap wine, great sex, hitching to beaches of pure, fine sand. Jerry burned a bit and his nose peeled, but Lisa got tanner and tanner, more beautiful each day. He spent hours just looking at her.

Spiders turned out to be their first crisis. After a hard rain, when the dampness in the windmill was so thick they could almost squeeze it in their hands, the spiders appeared in corners of the ceiling and constructed elaborate webs between the edges of the furniture and the walls. They terrified Lisa. She screamed like a child at the sight of them. At first Jerry was amused by her display of weakness, pleased when she clung to him for protection. But the fear became a nuisance. She wouldn't move from one room to the next without him going in front of her to squash the insects. He ended up doing most of the cooking and cleaning while she huddled on the middle of the bed trying to understand the Michelin Guide with her phrase book. She insisted on reading aloud to him, one word at a time, little of it making any sense. For revenge, he sneaked fingertips up her back, pretending they were a spider, and roared laughter at her shrieks.

The next trouble came in the village shop, a combination boulangerie, charcuterie, and hardware store, with chickens and one suckling pig in a pen outside the back door. For two weeks they had been eating nothing but canned goods and packaged cheese because Lisa couldn't overcome her distaste of the exotic looking fresh food. They usually stopped in daily, and despite their protestations of "*Ne parle pas*," the woman shopkeeper insisted on carrying on an interminable one-sided conversation. One day the woman referred to Jerry as Lisa's "*mari.*" Lisa gave her a puzzled look while the woman kept pointing and repeating the word. Then Lisa got her meaning and giggled. She shook her head. "Oh, he's not my *mari.*"

From then on the village, which had never done more than ignore them, turned hostile. Mothers pulled their children to the other side of the street; the nun-like old women on motorbikes forced them off the road; the men who tended scruffy vegetable gardens beat their hoes at the earth like guillotines when they came into view. The farmer who owned the windmill, a rotund man in suspenders with a white mustache and a screwed eye, stopped his gruff morning nod. To Jerry the shuttered windows now looked like the mean, tight-lipped mouths of a condemning jury.

The rain that had brought the spiders was only an isolated day of showers. The bright sun returned. But in the middle of the next week came a period of unending drizzle, the skies grey, the wind chill, a film of wetness over everything like a sheet of gloom. There was nothing to do, nowhere to go. Jerry came to look forward to the day's shopping. Lisa slept till midday, then napped through most of the afternoon, when she did get up shivering and wrapping the sleeping bag around her.

"I was a fool not to pack a transistor radio," she told him. "At least we could have so me music."

"Do you want me to sing to you?"

"Jerry, let's get away from this place. I'm sick of stone walls."

"Where? It's the same all over France."

"Majorca. Crete. I'll charge plane tickets."

"We paid for a month. It would be like cheating to leave now. Christ! We're together. You said that's all that matters."

"But I'm so cold."

On a Thursday with rain still falling the temperature warmed a bit and Lisa decided to take a shower. Above the patter of the drizzle, Jerry could hear the steady splashing from the bathroom outside. Though he tried not to admit it to himself, he felt relief at being alone.

Then she screamed. His first thought was that the farmer was raping her. He took the stairway in two jumps and crashed open the bathroom door with the shoulder. Lisa crouched against a corner under the streaming water hopping from one leg to the other as if trying to draw both up under her at the same time. In the opposite corner a six-inch green lizard clung to the wall and darted its tongue.

Here was the most spectacular girl he had ever known, ever seen for that matter, better looking than a movie starlet or a playmate of the month, and here she stood naked before him, claiming to "*je t'aime*" him; yet she seemed ridiculous in her fright, grotesque in her contortions.

He picked up the lizard by its tail and flipped it into the weeds. When she moved to embrace him in gratitude, he closed the door and went back into the windmill.

"It's like living in a prison," she told him the next day. "Round stone walls ... A dungeon!"

"You haven't stepped outside in a week." He made her go with him on his shopping trip.

Being in the open, wet as it was, revived her spirits. She wanted to pick all the food. But once in the village shop she couldn't communicate, no matter how much she repeated pronunciations or pointed right at words in her phrase book. She wanted strawberries, "*fraise*," a "*demi kilo*" of sliced ham. The shopkeeper just threw up her hands. Jerry, after all his buying there, was sure the woman understood, but he merely watched, not involving himself, unable to feel anger.

"Jerry, make her understand!" Lisa was crying, beating her fists on the wooden countertop, turning hysterical in desperation. "I want her to understand me!"

Jerry grabbed a loaf of bread, dropped a franc on the counter, and led her out of the store. The bread was the only thing they had to eat all day.

"I can't figure why you got so upset," Jerry told her. "What's that woman to you?"

"Nothing. But I hate her. It scares me not to communicate. Being here with all these people makes the world so strange. Nothing makes sense."

"Do you have something you really want to say?"

"I want to talk about myself."

"All we do is talk."

"That's just surface. I want to tell you what's inside me, to try to make you see who I really am, about all the things that frighten me."

"What the hell do you have to be frightened of? You're beautiful, you're smart, and you're rich enough to have two credit cards."

"None of that is me." And for the next days, so many Jerry lost count, morning, noon, and evening, as long as the rain fell, he had to listen to the monologue of self-analysis that poured out of her, interrupted by outbursts of frantic tears or wild laughter. When she was exhausted from talking, she clutched at him in desperate lovemaking.

Jerry had trouble keeping it all straight. But as far as he could gather, she was sick with doubts about herself, worried that her surface was smothering her inner self, that her brains and beauty were no more at the heart of her being than an elegant wardrobe. People didn't treat her as real; they stood back as if she were a character performing on a stage. Daddy was partly at fault. He expected perfection, not in a bullying way, but quietly, as if perfection were the least she could do to acknowledge his love. So she got straight A's, won charm contests, and did everything well. But nothing she did seemed natural.

"What would Daddy say about me?" Jerry asked her.

"He wants me to be happy. But he'd probably object to you. You're not tall enough or handsome enough or polished enough."

"So you picked me for revenge."

She pondered a while, sucking her lip. "Picking you was the only honest choice I've ever made in my life."

"And what do you think the real you is?"

"I don't know," she told him and burst into tears.

"Maybe," he suggested, "the inner you is no different from the outer you. What's so wrong with being bright and beautiful?"

"It's not enough."

My God! she talked. His brain reeled from listening to her. No girl had ever been so honest with him before. Her verbal revelations were more intimate than a striptease. Yet Jerry found it all tedious. He didn't want to know. For a few weeks it had been ecstasy to have the surface of her. Now she was smashing that loveliness with every word. He felt sick of listening.

It struck him that in her desperation for depth she was exposing shallowness. Beneath her beauty she was nothing. Fearing a life of boredom, she was boring. He began to wish his first impression had been right, that she was a French girl speaking a strange language he could dismiss as a babble of sound.

To amuse himself, to give himself something to say, he convinced her to burn her credit cards as a gesture of liberation from her existence of secure ease. "Face a life of lizards, girl." And weeping she held the two cards in the flame of the gas stove. When Jerry saw the cards curl and blacken, when he gagged on their plastic fumes, he panicked. In leading her to destroy her options, he had made her his responsibility for real. The new burden oppressed him like a load of rocks in his rucksack.

The first morning the clouds parted, while she slept exhausted from another sexual-confessional orgy, he went out to do the shopping. Standing in the roadway with 60 francs in his pocket and two loaves of bread, a bottle of wine, and a hunk of cheese under his arm, he realized that all he had to do was make an aboutface and keep on walking in the opposite direction. He could be free of her that easily.

He turned very slowly, took ten steps, and then stopped. Without a real reason to return to her, he decided to go back anyway. He would shake her shoulder, wake her up, and tell her the truth about himself—that he was thirty years old and a flunk out and a bum. And he would tell her how boring and empty he found her, how he was even bored with the freedom of her lovely body. Then he would see what happened next. It couldn't be any worse than the stage they were in now.

Heart Failure

Teddy Keane breathed slowly and deeply trying to force control of the pain that tore against his rib cage like slashes of a jagged blade. He moved his hand toward his chest, halting an inch away as if on the verge of a reckless act. He lay on his side on the examination table, cheek pressed on his forearm.

The December wind rattled the window across the long room, fingering his bare back. Below mid-thigh where the hospital gown ended his legs shivered with goose pimples. He couldn't understand how they had neglected to give him a blanket. Reaching behind, he tried to pull the gown closed, but it was too small. The pillow case was wrinkled and discolored with rust, or worse. Teddy averted his eyes from its repulsion and swallowed back the pulp in his throat. He wanted to shift his head, but was afraid to move.

A spasm ripped through his armpit. Furiously blinking back tears, he yearned to be free from the weight of his body. I'm ok, I'm ok, I'm ok: the cry of fright caught in his lungs, pounded at his temples. He clutched the edge of the table and squeezed until his fingers were numb.

Someone pried his hand free. Teddy howled at the touch. Two young doctors in baggy white jackets stood at the table; they couldn't have been more than interns.

Embarrassed by the ridiculous gown and by his helplessness, Teddy forced a manly grin through the pain. Neither intern smiled back. He introduced himself and tried to make small talk. "Sorry to bother you on a Sunday."

"That's why we're on duty," one said. "There's a room full of emergencies."

"I saw them. Looks like you're going to have some rough customers. What do you do when they can't speak English?"

"What seems to be wrong?" the other said.

"I woke up about seven with terrible pains in my chest. My cat, Panther, was scratching and hissing. My left arm felt like a lead weight. I couldn't breathe. It was like being twisted into knots. I managed to get dressed and find a taxi. I've never had so much pain."

"Is it still severe?"

"It hits every now and then. I'm freezing in here."

"We'll see about a blanket. How old are you?"

Teddy looked down at the trim muscles of his blond-haired legs and warmed with new hope. "Thirty-nine. I've hardly been sick a day in my life. Christ, I play handball every week."

The intern nodded. He snapped the gown away from Teddy's chest, exposing a smear of lipstick. Teddy coughed a laugh. "No more of that stuff for a while, I guess."

"We'll see." The intern touched an icy stethoscope to his flesh and Teddy flinched.

The intern listened intently, adjusting the stethoscope several times and frowning. "Take his blood pressure, Fred," he said. The other fixed the strap around Teddy's biceps and pumped the rubber ball. He shook his head at the reading, tried again, and asked his partner to check. "It's irregular as hell," the other nodded.

Teddy recoiled, his mind stunned into clarity by their professional confirmation: the morning had become deadly real. A wave of blackness was smothering him. Clutching the intern's wrist for defense, he choked out, "How bad is it?"

The intern shrugged. "Can't say yet. We'll have to make more tests and place you under observation for a few days. Guess we'll put him in Ward 12. Right, Fred?"

"A ward?" Teddy said. "There's some mistake. I came to the emergency entrance because I was in pain. I've got Blue Cross."

"Sorry. The hospital is jammed. Semi-private rooms go to the critical patients."

"But this is critical. It's my life."

The interns ignored his plea and walked out to the corridor. The wind seemed fiercer; snow whirled outside the window. His teeth were chattering.

Teddy closed his eyes and imagined Mother and Ruthie entering the room together, even though the two women were strangers in life, Mother rouged and high-heeled at seventy-two, embracing him loosely with one of her pecking kisses and telling him it would be all right, an edge of impatience to her voice. And Ruthie, his forty-year-old girl friend, bearing a blanket to protect him from the cold. But Mother was stopping somewhere in Las Vegas on a trip to California, and last night with Ruthie had been ugly. A new pain struck, making him long for the stroke of their hands. They must come to him; he needed loved ones.

Furtively, his eyes searched the stark room for objects of comfort and fell on the end of his tie, silk foulard, dangling onto the muddied floor, beyond his reach. His clothes were piled on a chipped enameled chair beside the table. The crumpled suit frustrated him, taunted his immobility. Mother had chosen it at Armani, and paid for it, five hundred dollars, during her last quick visit to the city, for his birthday.

Ruthie said he was compulsive; she had laughed at him last night for hanging up his clothes before getting into bed with her. "My jungle beast," she had called him and growled. Annoyed, he lost interest. Panther had watched their sullen lovemaking from the dresser, his tomcat eyes flashing green in the moonlight, the only fire of passion in that room.

Ruthie was a tall broad-boned woman with feathered hair, very attractive in tailored suits; in bed her skin seemed thick and dry. He felt much younger, a boy beside her. She was a career woman, an executive for a cosmetics firm, earning more money than he did, he was sure, although he'd never had the nerve to ask.

At two a.m. he had put Ruthie into a cab, un-kissed, and five hours later awoke with the pain, Panther turning frantic circles on the blanket.

His watch vibrated in his ear with a precise ticking, an Omega that never lost a second. He caught the time at the corner of his glance; ten minutes since the interns had left. Teddy heard nurses talking in the hall, occasional laughter. Why won't anyone help me? he cried silently.

When he had told the woman at the emergency desk what was wrong, he was rushed in ahead of a waiting room full of people. One man clutched a bleeding hand, a baby was screaming. Filthy with poverty, Blacks, Hispanics, they all had stared at him with grim accusation. He was glad he had struggled into his suit, despite the pain, and remembered to bring his Blue Cross card. Teddy wished the people had heard what he whispered to the receptionist; then they would have understood and sympathized. Lying alone in the grim room, Teddy felt strangely unlike these people. They existed with disease and danger; his life had always been safe.

Finally, a tight-lipped orderly, adolescent, pimpled on the neck, came in and wheeled his table into an elevator. In an examination room a technician set him up for an electrocardiogram, smearing a salve on his wrists and ankles, strapping down probes. The mechanism of wires and dials and gauges terrified him with its mechanical inhumanity. The technician counted Teddy's ribs with his fingertips and applied the chest probe. While the machine charted the beat of his life, he averted his eyes from the graph and realized that to the hospital he was nothing but a physical malfunction. He wanted desperately for someone to promise he would be alive and free.

Bound by the straps, Teddy tried to pray, but could find no words to plea his despair, muttering the strange sound "God, God, God" again and again.

The orderly moved him to Ward 12, at the end of a corridor lined with wheel chairs, and roughly shifted him from the table into the bed. The nurse, a blank-eyed, dumpy blonde, lifted the back of his skull and slipped under a thin pillow. Without looking at his face, she probed for a vein in his arm and drew a plastic vial of blood; then she made him swallow a pill. Exhausted, fighting the need, he fell asleep.

In late afternoon he awoke, uttering a short whimper of panic when he opened his eyes to the strange room. He shut them tight. Someone touched his arm. He looked up into a parched old face grimacing at him with a toothless smile.

"Max Lokey," the old man said. "They slipped you a mickey." He sat on the edge of his bed, leaning over toward Teddy, his bald scalp scaly with red scabs. Shocks of grey hair stuck out straight at his temples. Beneath the hospital gown pushed up to his waist, his legs were swollen, purple with veins.

Teddy turned away from him and looked down to the far end of the ward, at the rows of beds, humps of sick men under white sheets. He heard moans and the constant hack of a fluid cough. In the corner against the back wall a cloth screen closed off one bed. He sensed a grotesque sickness behind it.

"Funny thing," the old man said. "This place is like an assembly line. About seven this morning the guy in your bed kicked off, and as soon as they change the sheets, they bring you in. What's wrong with you?"

Teddy pointed to his chest.

"Nothing. You're lucky. It's a favor to die from a heart attack. Me, I ain't got much of my kidneys left. They tell me I'm going to die in a few weeks. Shit. The pain I got alone would kill most men. That guy in your bed yelled from the minute they brought him in."

"But you're sitting up." Teddy said. "Are you sure? Have the doctors told you?"

"Goddamn right I'm sick. I'm going to die." The man was offended at Teddy's doubts. "How about that? Max Lokey dead. You want to know something? Nobody cares. There's nobody left. I bet you've got a wife and kids."

Teddy shook his head. "Just a girl friend."

"Ah ha. No wonder you're here. Too much of that stuff." Lokey pounded fist into palm.

"Will you shut the hell up, you old bastard."

Teddy turned to the strained voice behind him and saw a face deep with creases and dark with whiskers buried in a pillow. The hlanket was pulled up to the man's chin.

"That's my friend, Michael Vetucci," the old man said. "Don't let Michael bother you. He's rotting away inside. Shits black lumps of himself into the bed pan."

"Why don't you hurry up and die." Vetucci closed his eyes.

"Michael is unhappy. He has so much to live for. Wait till you see his wife. You'll love her too. She looks like a crowbar. I don't see how he can stick it inside her. I'd be afraid she'd snap it off."

"I hope you burn in hell." Vetucci spat the words.

Teddy peered out the window behind his bed. Grey snow coated the roofs of the factory buildings across from the hospital. The street was bleak. A thick night fog was settling in from the river over the city. He felt no pain now; he wondered why he was here. He wasn't like all these other men. Mother would make a fuss and they would release him. Then he realized she would be ashamed of him for being there.

He had no place to look. Vetucci frightened him; the old man swung his legs, exposing shriveled genitals. A cry of pain cut through the ward. For a moment there was a stunned quiet. Teddy shut his eyes. The old man laughed until he coughed up phlegm. "They're all afraid of dying."

For an hour Teddy was tortured by the sounds of the ward. He would not open his eyes. Dizzy circles of light swarmed on the backs of the lids. He longed to get up and run, but his legs had no strength.

While the others were served dinner, Teddy received a glass of special liquid. He felt hollow with hunger, forcing his hands down on his stomach.

The doctor came after six when it was night outside and the ceiling lights cast dim shadows around the edges of the room. Teddy threw quick glances at Vetucci and the old man and whispered that he would pay anything to get out of the ward The doctor answered, too loudly, that it was not a matter of money; the rooms were filled. Lokey whooped with laughter.

"But I'm all right now," Teddy said. "I'd like to be released. This whole thing has been a mistake. You can't hold me here against my will."

The doctor shook his head. "The hospital is responsible for you now, Mr. Keane."

"I must make a phone call. No one knows I'm here."

"I can't allow you out of bed. If you give me the number of your next of kin, I'll ask one of the nurses to call."

Teddy wanted to envision the shocked expression Ruthie would have on her face, but could picture only last night's scorn. "Never mind. I don't want anyone to know."

While an orderly drew another vial of Teddy's blood, Vetucci's wife entered the ward, hesitant, almost ashamed, to visit at her husband's bedside, a stick of a woman with a lantern jaw who looked as if she belonged in a hospital herself. Their faces were close together and they spoke softly.

The old man gestured and grimaced at Teddy. "Ain't you got visitors? What happened to your girl friend. She two-timing you?"

"I haven't told her I'm here."

"So when you do, your whore will come wiggling her ass in a mink coat. It grabs me right here that a rich man like you should have to sleep in a ward."

Teddy began to protest, but stopped. "You're goddamned right," he said. "I'm not like you. I'm ok."

"I'll help them dig your grave," the old man said. Teddy tried to make out what Vetucci and his wife were discussing, what a wife says to a dying man; but he caught only occasional words that meant nothing to him.

He would find someone to get a rush message to his mother. She would fly east and help him recuperate. When he tried to imagine her visit, he could recall only the illnesses of his childhood; Mother fixing a smile from his doorway, dressed to go out; the doctor gripping his hand, urging him to be a big man. When the lights were turned off, he hadn't written on the paper in his bedstand. Teddy could find no words that would make her believe what was happening to her thirty-nine-year-old son. The night nurse was annoyed at his buzzing her. She would not give him a sleeping pill. "Your doctor didn't order one," she scolded.

The darkened ward was filled with snoring and coughing and gasping. Vetaucci seemed to be weeping. Teddy covered his head with the pillow, trembling at his aloneness in the hospital.

In the middle of the night a wild scream shocked a knife of pain through his chest; he clung to the rungs of the bed and pulled himself up to the sounds of a struggle. The lights snapped on. Two women cried frantically beside an empty stretcher table. A nurse and two orderlies chased their patient to the door, locking his arms and half-dragging him back to the bed. He was a young Hispanic with snakes of black twisted hair and frenetic eyes that flashed terror: like Panther's eyes when Teddy had awakened in pain. The man shouted in Spanish while one of the women, an old lady, muttered and crossed herself again and again. The orderlies wrestled him into bed and strapped him down. He twisted furiously, shrieking animal cries.

The old lady must have been his mother. Her brow with wrinkles; she wore several layers of black garments that hung like tatters down to her ankles. A large crucifix glitter her chest. The other woman, no more than a girl, was wife or sister. She watched his struggles helplessly, large brown eyes wide on an olive face. Her body was angularly adolescent, yet large liquid breasts moved under her blouse. Teddy felt sure she wore no brassiere.

He shifted in his bed and she glanced toward the sound. Teddy gave her a soft smile. She turned away and wiped her eyes; the hand showed a wide silver wedding band.

The old man, Lokey, yelled to an orderly. "What's the Spic?"

The orderly tapped his temple. "Brain tumor, his chart says. Don't worry. We'll knock him out with a shot."

Lokey whispered to Teddy. "I bet you'd like to have that one in your bed tonight. With those tits, she'd kill you."

Teddy watched the nurse inject a needle into the Hispanic's buttock while the orderlies forced him still. In seconds he became quiet. The nurse turned out the light, and she and the orderlies left the ward. The women remained at the bedside. Teddy felt indignation at the looseness of the hospital's rules, at a disorder that denied him his insured privilege and placed him across from swarthy strangers.

Old Lokey was mumbling to himself and Vetucci's eyes were wide open on the pillow. With the mouth and eye sockets deep in shadow, the head of the Hispanic looked like a skull. Last night Teddy had been in bed with a living woman; tonight he was alone with the breath of the dying, one of them.

He tried to imagine oblivion, cold wastes of total silent blackness. Death would be a falling, the plunging of an elevator. But each time he closed his eyes he pictured only the city in the grey dawning to come: his bed unslept in, his cat unfed, his desk unoccupied. The final fleeting traces of Teddy Keane.

Teddy grieved that he had not clung to Ruthie's warm flesh, tormented by the irrational intuition that his inability to love her was the reason he was here now.

Across from him the old woman stood before a window, outlined into a black spectre. The girl waited on the other side of the bed, lost in darkness except for the shaft of moonlight that fell on her gay blouse. Its colors were vibrantly alive, like the plumage of exotic birds.

Teddy had a vision. Mother and Ruthie were leaning over him, each clasping, kissing one of his hands, their tears falling onto his cheeks, the pain of dying overcome by their love. And he, loving, watched their faces dissolve into light, merging, expanding, until it became the light of eternity.

He clung to his dream, savored it, but slowly lost his hold on it and returned to the reality of the ward, to the abrupt shadows of the night. The presence of the girl comforted him; a warmth for her loving grew within him, hopeful and soothing.

Struck with a notion that his own life had no future, Teddy felt a great need to tell her that her husband would go to heaven. "Miss," he whispered, "Senorita," so softly that even the men beside him could not have heard. The ward was so still. Awed by the strength of his message, he was unable to bring himself to speech.

The Hispanic turned his face into the moonlight. Freed from the shadows, his skin glowed. He seemed to be sleeping peacefully, the only one in the ward who was at rest. Teddy envied him his dying until he realized that this man was the one among them who most deserved life. Choking back sobs, he prayed that God would spare this man; he fixed his gaze on the girl's blouse and prayed.

Vetucci and the old man were finally asleep. Teddy, the last one awake, listened to the quiet breathing of the ward and realized that he must pray for them all.

Toward morning, he shot bolt upright from his dozing, shivering with chill.

In the bed across from him the Hispanic was also sitting up, staring straight back at him with horrified unseeing eyes, shrilling an endless siren wail. He had ripped free from his straps. The mother crossed herself furiously; the wife clung to his shoulders. Teddy squeezed the buzzer for the nurse until the plastic cracked in his grip.

He climbed out of his bed, suffocating at the knot of agony in his chest, took two steps toward the man and toppled forward as his legs gave way.

The nurse ran into the ward just as the Hispanic died, crushing his hands down against his skull, as if trying to stop a bomb from exploding.

The girl collapsed with weeping. The mother moaned her anguish. Nurses and orderlies led them from the ward, gentle with their bewildered struggles. Teddy yearned for the girl's tears, the chance that she would run to him in need of an embrace.

He lay helpless beside his bed until the nurse returned and dragged him up, hissing in his ear that he could kill himself if he got up again.

The body was examined by a doctor, who dropped the lifeless pulse and covered the face. When it was taken away, Teddy mourned his loss. For the next hour he watched the orderlies scrub the bed and the cabinet and the walls sterile. Outside the first glow of sunrise was smothered by fog.

Only the orderlies spoke. When one laughed abruptly, Teddy glared his outrage, joining the mute protest that animated the ward, feeling a painful joy to be bound within the comraderie of dying.

"Bastards," the old man said. "Someday it'll be their turn." For a second Teddy wanted to reach out and touch him.

He ate a breakfast of soggy oatmeal. Afterwards, the doctor approached his bed, expressionless. "False alarm, Mr. Keane."

"What?"

"You didn't have a heart attack."

Teddy froze in disbelief. The whole ward was staring at him, the one among them reprieved. He felt them cursing his life. "But I had terrible pains. In my chest."

The doctor shook his head. "What you have is a form of bronchial pneumonia that has symptoms similar to a coronary. It showed up in both blood tests. Just something that's going around these days. You can go home as soon as the nurse checks you out. Some antibiotics and a week or two in bed should be a sufficient cure."

Teddy grasped at the doctor's hand. "I live alone. I want to stay here."

The doctor patted Teddy on the shoulder.

"Your pneumonia isn't severe, Mr. Keane. Certainly nothing to be alarmed about. If you'd like, I'll call your family physician to make arrangements."

"I'm very ill and I have no one to help me."

"I'm sorry. The hospital is overcrowded with critical cases."

The doctor, professionally detached, left him. Teddy stretched out flat on the bed and clutched the sides of the mattress. A new pain struck like the blow of a fist, fingers piercing inside him and twisting greedily, all through his body, into his stomach, into his brain, into his chest. In the crowded ward he was alone with the frantic gasps of his own breathing.

Old Lokey's voice exploded in his ear. "You heard the doctor. You don't belong here. "

Teddy felt tears gathering. When his pain passed into a dull, steady aching, he lay still and looked out at the grim morning that stirred the city, prolonging the moments before he must dress to confront his life again.

Any Fancies

The clown, a little man in an orange fright wig and bright red long johns, stomped oversized shoes across the stage to the beat of a bass drum in flatfooted pursuit of the young honey blonde who wiggled her backside just a step ahead of him. Voluptuous in a silver sequined gown and spiked heels, she stopped short and he tripped into her, clutching her hips for support, then bounced like a spring while a guitar twanged the same note over and over through the loudspeakers of the amusement park. The girl shouted outrage, the clown murmured apologies with an expression of sexual anguish, and the crowd screamed laughter. Philip stood at the edge of the spectators with a bewildered smile. The exchange was all in Swedish, and he didn't understand a word of the language.

His wife disappeared behind a white partition near the funhouse, following the arrow that pointed to WC–Damer. For a moment Philip studied the roll of her thighs and the flapping bottoms of her wide-cuffed pantsuit, then gave his attention to the blonde on the stage, the net stocking curve of her leg up the slit skirt, the smooth flesh of her back.

He didn't realize the foreign voice was talking to him until the girl touched his wrist, pressed with her fingertips and did not remove them even when he turned to face her.

She spoke again, in Swedish. Philip shook his head. "I'm afraid I don't understand.''

"I know English," she said, quite easily, without any accent. " I asked if you would give me a crown. A kroner.''

He reached into his change pocket, moving his hand from her touch, and took a second to acknowledge that she was very pretty, another Scandinavian beauty.

She made him recall the sidewalk poster displayed all over Stockholm, hundreds of copies, sometimes four on a single street

corner , advertising a suntan lotion called Plus. "Snyggt burn. Plus."
It had been one of the first sights to greet Philip when he and Beverly
emerged from the Central Station.

In the poster two young women, both blonde, stood in the sun
against a background of glittering sea. The young woman in front
dominated; the second stood several feet behind, a few degrees out
of focus, smiling more than the other. Both were very tan, with
beads of water so vivid they seemed three-dimensional on their
golden skin, and both were topless. Lines of shadow, the angle of
the arms, focused attention on the right nipple of the woman in the
foreground . The whole poster revolved around the circle of pink.

"A crown," the girl repeated. She stepped so close Philip could
feel the warmth of her body, a tingling that vibrated across the inch
of their separation.

He moved back and tried to take her in with a single glance. Her
hair was a fine-sheen pale blonde, cut shoulder-length and carefully
brushed. Even though the night was chilly, she wore only jeans cut
off at mid-thigh, clean white sneakers, and a ribbed sleeveless shirt
scooped at the neck, with deep-cut semicircles in back that exposed
her shoulderblades. Her breasts moved freely under the cotton, small
and firm, the nipples pushing taut points against the thin cloth.

The blonde chased the clown now, running with hobbled high-
heeled steps, waving a parasol over her shoulder. She struck the top
of his head again and again. His knees buckled each time.

Philip jingled the coins in his pocket confused by the girl's
request. "Do you need change?"

"Only one crown," she said.

"I know. A kroner. But for what?"

"For me," she said, not smiling, her blue eyes very serious.

He looked again to make sure she wasn't selling something—a
ticket, a souvenir. His fingertips felt the shape of a kroner and
pinched it tight. "I'm sorry. We're not communicating. Are you
broke? Do you need carfare? Is that it?"

"One crown," she repeated, stepping close again, touching his
hand with her fingertips, "to buy me."

The clown stood at one side of the stage, made a shushing gesture to the audience, and began to tiptoe across to the blonde, who primped before an imaginary mirror, twisting first on one foot, then the other. He paused mid-stage to paw the air libidinously. As if suddenly maddened with desire, he bolted for her. She screamed, his legs went out from under him, and he crashed down on his face. The crowd roared.

Philip was sure the girl had confused an idiom in her translation. "Buy you?" He grinned and to hear better led her a few steps away from the others, into the shadow of a game booth.

She nodded. "Yes, buy me."

"How do you mean?"

"I go with you."

"For a kroner? You'd sell yourself for a kroner?"

She shrugged. "I like to belong to someone."

"For God's sake, why?"

"It's the way I am."

"Let me get this straight. If I gave you a kroner, you'd belong to me?"

"Yes. That's right."

He forced a laugh. "Forever?"

"As long as you want to keep me."

He studied her for signs of drugs or madness, but her eyes were bright and clear, intelligent. She appeared quite relaxed. He was the nervous one, sure that he was being a fool not to turn his back on her, but too intrigued to leave.

For a moment Philip thought she might have been the second young woman in the Plus poster, the one behind and slightly out of focus. He had stared at the poster whenever he saw it, embarrassed because no one else seemed to be looking so closely, as if he alone were corrupt enough to be fascinated by the naked flesh.

"Is it for money?" he asked.

She shook her head. "Money isn't important."

Perhaps it was a joke, hidden cameras recording his reaction. But a more reasonable answer struck him and he smiled at her.

"You're doing this on a bet, aren't you? Some sort of dare?"

"No. No one is making me."

"Suppose I buy you?" Philip asked, feeling ridiculous because his legs trembled at the possibility.

"Yes?"

"I mean, what would happen?"

"That would be up to you."

In the hotel when Philip registered, the desk clerk, a scented, balding man of shaky English, had presented him with a slick paper pocket guide to the city: lists of sightseeing tours and special events, ads for crystal, leather, restaurants. At the back, four full pages were devoted to notices for sex shows. One in particular obsessed him: "If there are any fancies of sex in your mind which you want realized— the Nana's staff wish you welcome to Cabare Nana in expectation of being to any help in this matter."

"Would you be like a slave?" Philip's voice quavered.

"Exactly like a slave."

"But there must be limits. Forbidden areas."

"None, if you own me. It would be up to you to command. To create possibilities."

"All my fancies?"

"All your fancies."

Desire charged his blood. He wanted to rub his hands under her thin shirt, fondle her breasts, rub his palms over the hard nipples. He wanted to plunge fingers beneath the snap of her jeans, over her flat belly, into the liquid center of her. He wanted to force her into a dark corner of the funhouse where whole rooms vibrated. He wanted to drag her onto the floor of a bumper car, curled on the floor beside the foot pedal, face in his lap, while other cars jarred them from all directions. He wanted to ravish her in the hall of mirrors, doing everything, seeing everything.

"I'm married," he told her, face burning. "My wife is in the toilet. She'll be back in a minute."

"I don't mind."

"I can't tell her I've just bought a girl as if you were some souvenir, a wooden horse for the mantle piece."

"She would own me too."

"You'd sell yourself to a couple?"

"Men, women, couples. People of all kinds. From all over."

"Have you done this before?"

"Many times. Whenever someone will buy me."

"And the wives. How do they react?"

"Most like me."

Philip went dizzy with possibilities.

The clown dropped to his knees before the blonde, softly imploring, wringing his hands, sinking lower and lower to the floor of the stage as he pleaded. When his cheek touched the wood, he slipped onto his back and tried to look up her gown; she ground a heel into his stomach. The crowd squealed with delight.

"What have the others done with you?" Philip asked, wiping the sweat from his forehead .

"I can't tell you."

"But if I bought you, I could order you to."

"I always forget. As soon as it's over, I don't remember anything."

"Because you're so ashamed?"

"Because I only care for what I'm doing when I'm doing it. Then I don't think of past or future. I give all my concentration to the present. I have nothing left to make pictures for memory."

"Do you enjoy yourself so much?"

"It's not a matter of enjoyment. Not of thrills and sensations. I give myself over to being owned. I lose myself in possession."

"But you're so beautiful," he protested. "You could make others your slave just by being beautiful. Your hair, your eyes, your skin. It's wonderful to look at you."

"Beauty is only for others to notice. Just an accident that does nothing to make me feel good inside."

"May I touch you?"

"Only if you buy me."

Quickly, before he had time to reconsider, Philip gave her the kroner and watched her slip it into a pocket in the front of her jeans.

He reached out to embrace her and put his hand on her bare shoulder, stroke it down her arm to her elbow and then let go. The touch of her smooth, cool flesh evaporated his fancies, left his imagination dry.

"Now," the girl said, "I will do anything you ask."

"But there's nothing I can think to want."

"I'm content to wait. Wait or do, it's your choice."

"What about all the others who bought you? Where are they now?"

"I have no ideas. Once they stop owning me it doesn't matter."

"Why did they stop? Why hasn't at least one of them wanted to own you forever?"

"I think it's because they are like you. They really don't know what to do with me. They have something in mind when they buy me. But then, whatever they try, whatever I do, it's not what they really wanted."

"How does someone stop owning you?"

"They just tell me to go."

"Please go now," Philip said, more sorry than ever before that he was not another man.

She turned and left him without a word of parting. He watched her move away with smooth graceful strides, long curved legs. The shape of her couldn't have been more perfect.

Beverly reappeared from behind the partition, pants cuffs still flapping. The clown wrapped his arms around himself, writhed in his long johns, and howled lust until his orange hair stood on end.

Things

On damp mornings my car won't start. I cover the hood with a blanket, spray the wiring, pour Heet into the gas tank. I snap off the distributor cap, wipe the points with a rag, and try again. The starter spins, the engine grunts; it hangs on the least fraction of resistance as if it is struggling to turn over, but falls back with a useless groan.

The TV picture doesn't hold still. A black line slowly works up from the bottom of the tube so that the top half of the picture shows at the bottom and the lower half at the top. Sometimes it flips so rapidly we get dizzy watching. I try to adjust it, delicately easing the horizontal hold. As long as my hand touches the knob, the picture will stand still; but the moment I let go it begins to flop again. I curse, slap the side of the cabinet, beat my fist on the top; the picture still rolls.

The dishwasher floods when we forget and load pots that block the drain hole. When it overflows, two inches of suds cover the floor, seeping under the cabinets, etching a dark stain into the edge of the hall carpeting. It takes us two hours to soak it up with towels. Five floor tiles buckled when water seeped under; we've never been able to make them lie flat again.

Our gas furnace dies on the coldest nights. By morning the house is down to fifty, and we sense the chill in our sleep, pulling blankets up around our ears and shuddering at the thought of touching our feet to the floorboards. No one knows what makes the furnace go out. The repairmen tinker and send bills in the mail, but they don't really understand. Perhaps a wind blows out the pilot light. Nothing can be done.

The roof leaks, not the big roof on the house, but a side roof over the downstairs toilet that juts out from the kitchen wall beside the pantry. It only happens during a downpour. A square of wallpaper on the stairway landing gets saturated each time; a jagged brown stain is eating across the paper, growing with every rainfall. Water drips through the toilet ceiling. Once it ran into the light fixture, and my son got a shock when he flipped the switch. I try to fix the roof, climbing a ladder, smearing a layer of tar with a serrated trowel, staining my pants, sticking my fingers together. But no matter what I do, the leak is always there.

The house has mice. I've caught glimpses of them, both the brown ones with large bulging eyes and quivering ears and the small grey ones that hug the baseboards as if on wheels. They nibbled neat scoopings through the plastic wrapping into bread loaves. We bought a bread box. But they survive by eatinq crumbs of the dog's food and leave their droppings on the countertops. We talk about buying traps, but haven't gotten around to it.

The dog is going blind. She's an old dog and we had to expect it. Our house is old too, and our car; rust is eating into the fenders, bubbling the paint above the headliqhts. corroding jagged hollows into the rocker panels. Most of what we own is old. Our chair rungs snap, the arms wobble. The dog bumps into things. We have to open doors slowly. Sometimes she wets on the carpet.

I live with a continuous backache, a pain that eats down through my left leg and numbs my toes. It hurts just to sit. The doctors took a MRI, but it revealed nothing, no problems with the discs. Sometimes I wear a brace to walk.

My stomach is sour. I chew antacid tablets by the hundreds. I belch, double up at the pressure of qas, gag after the slightest taste of grease. The doctor says it's nerves, but I sense something much worse, something beyond repair.

Fred and Ginger

He saw her—walking down the street, crossing a hotel lobby, boarding an ocean liner, passing in a taxi, queuing for customs, waiting for a plane, lifting a glass of champagne. And he had to meet her.

Though he loved her from the first, he was never lovesick, never whimpered with self-pity even when scorned, rebuked, ignored, insulted. At times he gave in and frowned a "Darn!" of disappointment. Yet he never lost hope, not even when she flaunted the opulent ring of a rich-but-wrong rival or stamped her foot and swore to hate him forever. He fought back with spunk, spirit, a snap to his step, a crackle to his wit.

When he wooed her—despite his love, despite the intuition that they were meant to be flawless together—he wooed with wit. If rich, feigned poverty. If poor, wealth. Assumed ridiculous accents. Approached haughtily. Approached shyly. Made a fool of himself but was never foolish. Bribed stewards and maitre d's. Delivered letters, flowers, room service. Offered strolls through parks, rides in roadsters.

Let her stamp her foot, turn on a heel, shake her head, pout her lip, hide behind a veil. His wince was only a double take, displaced by a smile, a cock of his head, because he knew even before she did that she was liking him more and more.

You couldn't call him handsome. Without his elegant jauntiness he would have been typed scrawny, cadaverous. But his rivals were all toads, weak-chinned, slimy, pompous playboys with slick little mustaches, dullards—all clumsy and cloddish. And his smile, just the arch of an eyebrow, had true grace.

It was his charm, of course. Who could resist his charm? As much as she denied him, told herself, told the world, that he was a heel, a rat, a louse, she was being secretly charmed.

Somehow, he knew he was charming because only a man with supreme confidence could have been so winning. Other men would have fallen on their faces. Yet you couldn't call it conceit. He was too playful for arrogance, too bright in his sense of irony. As much as he loved her, he never lost perspective, never made that love bloated or sodden.

Inevitably, he would sing to her, his voice high and thin, but his timing flawless, his phrasing remarkable. Once again he displayed hidden resources. Control was his secret. A man with such immaculate control had no reason to worry. How could she resist him after he sang to her?

But the meeting and the smiling and the wooing and the singing were only preparation for the moment he would dance before her, at times beginning slowly and deceptively with a single tap of his toe, at others bursting forth with a flourish that suddenly revealed him as a special being. When he danced, he was a creature of perfect motion, absolutely free, shaping gravity with the snap of a finger. Then she would dance, they would dance together, she following his pace, attuned to his lead. And there would be no doubt that she was his, that for all her foot-stamping and head-tossing and slow-burning, they would always be less apart and greater together.

Now and then they kissed. But kissing was not at their essence, not a prelude to a physical need. Their kiss was a choreographed step, a phase in their dance. Her gown would never be wrinkled, nor his starched front rumpled in the crude passion of ordinary humans. Their fulfillment came in dancing, the click of taps, leaps, twists, the flash of her calf. He would swirl her and swirl her and swirl her and they would be perfect forever.

The Marriage Knot

If Karen stood on the fourth step to the bedrooms, gripped the railing, and leaned forward until her eyes passed the edge of the kitchen doorframe, she could look down into the family room and see Karl's legs beneath the blankets on the studio couch. His chest and face were blocked off by the wall. She didn't know why she bothered to stand like that; it was her house and she could have walked right past him to get to the washing machine. According to Lenny, Karl slept in his shorts. She didn't care how he slept. All she knew was that she didn't like having him there, in her life.

That had been Lenny's idea, of course, letting the strays follow him home, offering them a bowl of milk and an old scrap of rug in the corner.

"It'll just be for a day or two," Lenny had told her, "until he gets his head together. Jesus, he can't go home the way things are with Gail and Margaret."

"Whose fault is that?" she had said, standing by the dryer, folding baby clothes, while the machine tumbled, clanking buckles.

"It's nobody's fault. What's fault got to do with it? He's my buddy, and he needs a place to sleep."

"Rent him a tent."

"Don't you like him?"

"I barely know him."

"Are you automatically taking the wife's side? Is that it?"

"I'm taking my side. I don't need your screwed-up friend on my studio couch. I've got you in the bedroom. That's bad enough."

He grinned, turned her around, and pressed her against the dryer with his body. "I never heard that complaint before. So I'm a problem in the bedroom."

She responded to him and wrapped her arms around his neck,

still holding a bib in her fingertips. "That's not what I meant and you know it."

The day or two became two weeks, as Karen knew they would. Why not two months? Two years? A great lump on her studio couch until ten in the morning for the rest of her life, messing up her schedule, ruining her day.

Karl worked as some sort of salesman, and no one seemed to care what his hours were. But she couldn't stand his sleeping past ten, and turned the kids loose to rush him with squeals, leaping onto the couch, bouncing the springs. "Uncle Karl! Uncle Karl!" Within a minute she would hear his bare feet slap across the floor to the downstairs toilet. Then he would appear in the kitchen in trousers and tee shirt to pour himself a cup of coffee.

She rarely spoke to him and told Lenny, "I feel like the goddamn maid. Seen but not heard. There to serve. He just sits bleary-eyed and barely even looking at me."

"So that's it. Injured vanity."

"I just want him to be civil."

Only once, after his first night on the studio couch, she had made his bed almost automatically; then furious that he had left it for her, vowed never again. From then on, when she ignored his mess, he folded sheets and blankets, emptied his ash trays, left the room neat; he even put his cup and saucer in the sink. He never ate breakfast, had lunch on the road, and did not come back to the house early enough for dinner. Half the time she was already asleep when he rolled in. Lenny stayed up to wait for him like an anxious parent.

Karen lay awake until Lenny came up to bed. "Did he have a warm nose?" she said.

Her remark startled him; he dropped the shoes he held in his hand. The clumps seemed to resound from the foundation. "What?"

"You're nursing him, aren't you?"

"The poor guy is miserable."

She sat up, snapped on the overhead light, and pointed a finger at him. "I just figured you out. I know why you're doing this. It's like being back at the fraternity house. The guys wait up half the night to console their brother with the fouled-up love life. He weeps on your shoulder. You give manly advice."

"Jesus, you don't know what he has to put up with from those two women. Gail is a featherbrain. And Margaret is a first class ballbuster."

"Is that a nice way to talk about your best friend's wife and mistress?"

She lay awake trying to imagine Karl's life, the instability, the uncertainty, living out of a suitcase beside somebody's studio couch. The more she thought about Karl, the closer she snuggled to Lenny's sleeping warmth.

She tried to comprehend how two so very different women could love such a man, if love was the word for lives like theirs. She supposed Karl was good-looking, at least to a Gail and a Margaret. His eyes were deep and clear; his jaw was strong. Once or twice she had seen him moving around the family room in his shorts. He had a swimmer's body, lean muscled legs and thick sinew at the shoulders, the body of a lifeguard adored by every fifteen-year-old on the beach. But once a girl turned sixteen, she could see right through him, nothing but strut and posture. Even with his soft middle and quarter-sized bald spot, Lenny was much more the man of the two. Steady, mature, capable of tenderness and passion, far beyond neurotic night prowlings. Who could love a Karl? Only a fool.

Two fools, Gail and Margaret. She reversed the question: who could love them? Only a Karl. All made for each other in a reject factory.

Gail, the wife, was brassy—attractive if you didn't look too closely, but shrill and dumb. One of the fifteen-year-olds from the beach. Her conversation was limited to quick meals, the best buys in boys' jeans, and television. Everyone Karen knew watched television, but—for God's sake—they had enough sense not to talk about it. Even with the spike heels, long purple fingernails, deep red lips, and black-dyed hair, Gail seemed more child than woman.

Margaret, the girl friend, was the exact opposite, a drab woman, pale and freckled, limp-haired, slope-shouldered. But she had the reputation of being bright, halfway to a PhD in French before she married her dullard husband. Everyone called her soft-spoken, but Karen, who had seen her only a few times at parties, considered her sullen, perhaps bitter over lost achievement. What little she did say was sarcastic, though her soft voice disguised that. Despite her drabness, there was something angrily sexual about her, as if she had hung on the edge of orgasm all her life and was desperate for a final shove.

Annoyed and aggressive, she started a conversation while Karl sat hunched over a steaming cup of morning coffee. He rubbed his eyes. "What?"

"I said, where do you go nights? To which of your ladies?"

"Do you really want to know?"

"Why not? It reminds me of a psych lab I had once. We put a white rat in the middle of a maze with food at either end to see which path it would take "

"That poor damn rat. You confused its instincts."

"But you're a thinking creature. Which direction would you drag your tail?"

"You can't make an experiment out of me. There's no logic to what I do."

"Don't tell me you just flip coins."

"Some nights Gail gets a sitter and we meet in a diner for the same endless heart-to-heart discussion. Now and then, I take her home and give her a good screwing. It calms her down. But I never sleep over. That would complicate matters. You know how marriages are."

"Just my own."

"Other nights I drop Gail at her door and rush over to Margaret's

72

apartment."

"To calm her down. You're the soul of charity, Karl."

In bed, in Lenny's arms, hearing Karl rattle around in the room below, she asked Lenny how he could have such a man for his friend. "He's not good enough for you."

"Am I that great?"

"Yes, you are."

He laughed. "What about all my faults? I'm going bald, I don't exercise."

"Your only fault is that your let bums like Karl take advantage of you."

"Come on. You can't label someone a bum because his life is messed up."

"Aren't people responsible for their lives?"

"Karl is trying to be. He's trying to make a responsible decision. Meanwhile, I'm being responsible to a friend."

"What do you call a person who uses two women and manages to feel self-pity at the same time?"

Lenny didn't answer. He sighed and turned toward sleep.

Karen worried all night. She had always known Lenny was good-natured. Now she realized the quality went much deeper in him. Her husband was a true innocent; he believed in people. And that knowledge frightened her. Lenny was someone very special, very vulnerable.

Karen sat at the table with Karl and asked him as she would one of her children. "And who do you love?"

"Maybe Margaret. Maybe Gail. Maybe both. Maybe neither."

"You're such a marvelous fellow, Karl."

"I never claimed to be better than I am."

"And your women, are they so wonderful?"

"No more than any other women."

"So you keep two to make up for their defects."

Karl started to stand, then gave up in frustration. "Cut it out,

Karen. I'm not hurting you."

"You're in my house."

"Lenny invited me."

"And I suppose you can't make up your mind whether you like him or not."

"Wrong. Lenny's a great guy. He's straight. If it wasn't for Lenny holding me together, I don't know where I'd be now. I owe a lot to him."

"Enough to get out of his house?"

Karl shook his head. "I can't. I'm not ready yet."

"Do you dislike me?" Karen asked Karl.

"Every time I walk past you, it's like opening a freezer door."

"Why do you stay here if you don't like me?"

He grinned even though he had tried not to.

"To punish you for being unlikeable."

"What's your reason for not liking me?"

"Christ! Do I have to have reasons?"

"If you're more than a rat in a maze."

He drained his cup, pushed the saucer away, and shrugged. "You've got bad breath."

She was so shocked she slapped his face with the back of her hand. Then after a silent minute he rubbed his cheek and she massaged her knuckles. His stubble had scratched her skin.

"You asked me," he finally said.

She blushed. "With sending Lenny off to work and dressing the kids, cleaning up, I never get around to brushing my teeth until lunch!'

"It's just something I've noticed."

She went up to the bedroom and stayed there until she heard the front door close. From the window, curtain pulled back on her forearm, she saw him load an oversized sample case into the passenger's seat of his car and then come around to the driver's side. What kind of a salesman, she wondered, doesn't even wear a tie? When his car was out of sight, she stepped into the bathroom and brushed her teeth for a good five minutes, battering blood from her gums with the stiff bristles.

Lenny passed on a new revelation. "You won't believe this, but Karl has taken to spending hours with Margaret's husband, analyzing her life and character and getting drunk together."

"Why doesn't Margaret's husband punch him in the mouth?"

"Because he knows that wouldn't solve anything."

"What is his solution?"

"He loves Margaret, but thinks she might be happier with Karl."

"What a noble soul!"

"For some people, being in love is tough, Karen."

"And you, Lenny? Would you find love simple enough to punch a man like Karl?"

"If I ever punched a man, it wouldn't be simple."

Gail phoned at noon. "When is he coming home?" she demanded without bothering to identify herself.

"I don't know," Karen told her. "I hardly ever speak to your husband. I thought he visits you. Why don't you ask him?"

"Why won't you people make him come home?"

"I'd be overjoyed to get rid of him."

"You want him in your house, don't you?"

"I want your husband like I want termites."

"He'd be home if it wasn't for you."

"Gail, I don't like your husband. He's a third-rate human being. Nothing, absolutely nothing, could make me happier than to know that I would never see his face again."

"He's screwing you, isn't he?"

Karen slammed the phone down and stayed furious all afternoon, exploding rage the moment Lenny came through the door.

"Gail is going off the deep end," he said. "She spends her days making phone calls. She's even been bothering Karl's customers."

"I won't have this!" Karen cried. "1 won't have my life touched by people like that. They make me feel dirty just to know them."

She burst into tears, and Lenny comforted her. "It's Gail," he said when she was calm. "She blames everybody for Karl leaving her."

"I don't like people spreading lies about me."

"Nobody believes Gail. Not when she starts ranting about Karl."

"What if he did try to seduce me?" she said in desperation. "Would you hate him then?"

"I don't believe in hatred."

"What in God's name would you feel?"

"Disappointment. I've tried to be his good friend. If he betrayed me, I'd be very hurt."

"Hurt enough to kick him out?"

"I suppose so."

"Lenny, he *is* a bum. Get rid of him right away. Before he hurts you."

He stroked her face. "Soon. When his life is straightened out."

"That man's life will never be straight."

After Lenny left for work, Karen took a shower and stepped out into the hallway in bathrobe and bare feet. She started to move into their bedroom to dress, but on an impulse that made her shudder hurried down to the family room, clutching her robe at her throat.

Karl slept with his mouth open, the blankets twisted down around his waist, bare-chested, one leg sticking out all the way up to the thigh.

Trembling, she fumbled at the buttons of her robe and let it fall open as she stood over him. I'm doing this for Lenny, she told herself, afraid she would scream when Karl opened his eyes. She gasped when his body thrashed over toward her, but he only covered his face with a forearm and began snoring.

It repelled her to look at his open mouth, his white morning tongue. Quickly she closed the robe, knotted the waist sash, and kicked angrily at the mattress with a bare foot. He sprang up into a sitting position, rubbed knuckles at his eyes, scratched fingertips through his rumpled hair. When he cleared the phlegm from his throat to speak, she felt a wave of nausea.

"What's the matter?" he said.

"I want you out of here tonight," she insisted.

He looked her up and down from throat to toes as if she were naked and smiled. "Can't be done."

"Why not?"

"Margaret and I are coming to dinner Saturday. Lenny's invitation."

"I won't have it!" she shouted, furious, unwilling to believe him.

"Take that up with Lenny," he said and bounded out of bed for the downstairs toilet.

Karen demanded that Lenny tell her Karl and Margaret had not been invited for Saturday.

He shrugged and tried to look sheepish. "It thought it might be good for them."

"Don't I get consulted about tramps at my dinner table?"

"It's not like that and you know it. Karl might be ready to make his decision."

"And you're playing father of the bride."

"People's lives are at stake."

"Don't my feelings count?"

"He needs me to get over this last hurdle."

"Lenny, please. I don't want you involved with Karl any more. Let him ruin his own life. Don't be responsible for any of it."

"Let's see what happens Saturday."

Gail called five times before lunch, pleading, abusive, hysterical, breaking down into genuine tears of misery. Karen hung up on her each time and finally removed the phone from the hook. But when Lenny came home and replaced it, it rang immediately. He nodded his end of the conversation, mouth grim, and finally said, "Promise you won't do anything until you talk to me."

"Karl?" Karen asked, frowning her annoyance.

"I have to see Gail now. Right away. She threatened to take an overdose."

"And you believed her?"

"Of course I did. She's frantic."

"Lenny, I forbid you to leave this house."

"Jesus, don't you have any sympathy?"

"I wish they were all dead. Karl is a corrupt man. Everything he touches turns rotten. Don't you see what he's doing to you?"

"I have to go. I'm in too deep now."

For an instant she thought she would slap him, for another instant that she would burst into tears. But she spoke with a lucidity that shocked her. "You're jealous, aren't you, Lenny? You're seeking your own misery."

"That's crazy." He edged toward the door, jingling car keys.

"What if Gail needs a good screwing to calm her down?"

"What the hell are you talking about?"

She stood at the window to watch him drive off. Then she ate dinner alone and gave the children their baths. After they were in bed, she stared at the television screen, comprehending nothing, lightly weeping.

When the late news came on and Lenny still was not home, she took Karl's plastic alligator suitcase from the laundry room and dumped all this clothing from the chest beside the studio couch, resisting the impulse to tear each garment, instead carefully folding it in neatly, even the bright red boxer shorts. Last, she squeezed in his shaving kit from the toilet shelf and had to sit on the suitcase to snap it closed.

She dragged the suitcase out to the front steps and left it under the bright yellow porch light. Then she bolted all the doors and turned off all the interior lamps. She waited in darkness on the sofa, swallowing continually, as if trying to force down a great hard lump that had lodged in her chest, wondering what she would do if Lenny returned first. And she knew that Karl's leaving would not be the simple ending she had once believed in.

No Rights in This Matter

At first glance Professor Blair wasn't sure it was Sally. The young woman stood in an elegant knit dress across the historian-glutted lobby of the convention hotel talking with a bearded man, her cigarette perfectly balanced between two fingers, her head tossed back in laughter as if her companion had just dropped a bon mot. This the lanky eighteen-year-old uprooted from a wheat farm straight into his Western Civilization classroom, a bewildered seeker awed by his studied knowledge. Then she wore bobby socks and saddle shoes; now she was sophisticated in suede.

She reached out to flick her cigarette into a tray, but rammed the lapel of a passing academic, scattering ashes over both them. She laughed again this time with embarrassment. Blair warmed with his rediscovery of Sally Baines. Her grey eyes scanned the lobby, paused at his face for an instant, but then swept past. Before Professor Blair could make up his mind whether or not to approach her, Sally disappeared with the bearded man, and he remembered an appointment to interview an applicant to his department. He pushed onto a crowded elevator and reached his room thirty seconds before a knock sounded at the door.

He shook hands with a young man named Frederick Cochran, lean and well-groomed in a dark suit.

"I'm terribly sorry," Blair said. "I got held up in the lobby and didn't have time to review your application."

"Maybe I should look, too," Cochran said. "I've done so much running around today I've forgotten who I am, and I'm not sure I want to remember."

Blair smiled with sympathy. "Do you have your doctorate yet?"

"Someday. When I get the dissertation done. If I do. I started the damn thing the day I was weaned, or maybe it just seems that way."

Blair flipped through the folders in his briefcase, but couldn't locate Cochran. "What is your graduate school?"

"Western."

"Of course. Now I remember you. I taught there for a bit years ago."

They discussed people, buildings, the parking problem. Then Blair took a wild stab. "This is probably silly. I'm sure I just saw an old student of mine from Western in the lobby. I'd like to get in touch to say hello. Perhaps you know her. Her name was Sally Baines."

Cochran laughed aloud, his face flushed with amusement. "Sally?" He laughed again. "Sally is my wife. Eight years worth."

Blair grinned too and pumped Cochran's hand in belated congratulations. In answer to a rush of questions, Cochran rattled off a quick resume of their life. He met her when she was a senior and he a master's candidate just out of the Navy. When they married, he left school to work as a salesman in Chicago. Their two sons were born then. But apathetic over his work, he quit to return to graduate school six years ago. At first Sally took a job in a bookstore, then received a teaching assistantship and became a graduate student herself, in history too.

"Wonderful," Blair said, proud of her. "I knew she would be a success. Your wife is a very bright gal."

"Too bright for her own good sometimes. Mine too."

Blair did not understand. He looked at Cochran closely. His brown hair was parted flawlessly, with flecks of grey at the sides, and Blair realized that despite the boyish smile, this man was not as young as he first seemed, probably only five or six years younger than Blair himself.

After Cochran promised he would have Sally get in touch, Blair began to reminisce. "I'll never forget the first day Sally came to my class. It was her first in college, and she entered with classic ineptness. Five minutes late, tripped in the doorway and scattered books and papers across the floor up to the base of my lectern. I kneeled to help her gather them, and she was shattered, great big tears in her eyes."

"I know all about it," Cochran said. "She almost quit school that night. Had her bags half-packed."

"She was so shy. She never said a word in class and barely the nerve to nod to me in the corridors. But I was struck by the naïve brightness of her papers. They seemed to pour out a secret thrill at discovering that such elaborate systems as Greek and Roman civilization had ever existed. She misspelled the names of men and cities, outraged chronology, but truly saw."

"She can see all right. X-ray Vision."

"It was my first year of full-time teaching, and she was my opportunity to help mold a fine, raw mind. I invited her to my office once. She wouldn't stop talking. I couldn't get rid of her after that. I suspected she slept in the hallway outside. But I didn't have the heart to rebuke her. She sought me out to discover what she could be. During graduate school I had assumed my only job would be to convey facts and concepts. Sally became an awesome responsibility. She taught me the moral obligation of being a teacher."

"She still is."

"Is what?"

"An awesome responsibility."

"She used to babysit for us."

"So you were the guy."

"I became her confessor, soothing tears after a fight with her roommate or a D on a physics quiz. Sort of a second father."

"Don't underestimate Sally. She knows how to get the most out of her teachers."

"When I moved to Cornell, she cried hysterically and swore her life would be ruined if I left. At first she wrote every day, but eventually, inevitably, I stopped hearing from her."

"Beware a woman scorned."

"But the story has a happy ending. She married you."

"Let joy reign unconfined." Cochran stood up and looked long at his watch. "Say, I'm taking too much of your time. You probably have a busy schedule."

Before Blair could explain that he really wanted to interview him, Cochran was out the door, and Blair realized that even from his initial responses the man had not behaved like a job seeker.

Between interviews, browsing through the publishers' book exhibits, Professor Blair literally bumped into Sally. He wanted to hug her, but merely pressed her arm.

"I saw you in the lobby before," she said, "but thought you'd forgotten me."

"Don't be silly. How could I forget my favorite student and my least expensive babysitter? Thirty-five cents an hour."

"But you don't need sitters any more. They must be in their teens by now."

"And you have your own sons, Mrs. Cochran."

She reddened. "How did you know?"

"I met your husband. Sheerest coincidence. He came for an interview, but doesn't seem interested in us."

"You're not alone in that."

"He's an impressive fellow. Rather nice looking."

"Oh, he's beautiful. Primps in front of the mirror half the morning."

"And you've changed yourself. When I first knew you, you were too bashful to wear lipstick. You're a big girl now."

She blushed again, this time as if ashamed of having matured.

"Your eyes are different too," he said. "They used to be like a tourist's. Now you seem to know what you see, what you're doing. The dazzled quality is gone."

"Is that good?"

"Not for a schoolgirl, but for a woman."

"You're still trying to teach me, Professor Blair."

He noticed the wall clock. "Damn. I have to run. More interviews. Does your department still have its annual convention party?"

"It's a sacred tradition by now."

"Will you be there?"

"For a while."

"I'm counting on it. We'll have a long talk."

From the elevator car, squeezed in at the back, he saw Sally with a tall man of his age who was leaning down and speaking close to her ear. She nodded very seriously at his words, as if memorizing instructions. As the doors slid closed, he watched the man touch her shoulder and stride off quickly.

When Professor Blair arrived at the ninth floor suite for the Western party, the first person he recognized was Fred Cochran. Blair asked him where Sally was, and the man merely shrugged. He seemed to have been drinking for quite a while, his tie crooked, his hair messed at the part line. He recognized Blair, but didn't care. Blair recalled the fatigue and depression of being interviewed, and he understood.

"How's job hunting?"

Cochran shrugged again. "One place is as good as another. I'll go somewhere."

"Where does Sally want to go?"

"Why don't you ask her? She doesn't tell me anything."

"Did she ask you to apply to us?"

He shook his head. "I don't tell her anything either."

Blair patted him on the arm and turned away. "You'll feel better once you have a few definite offers in hand."

He worked his way across the room, exchanging enthusiastic, but brief, greetings with people he had not seen in years, until he spotted Sally alone in a corner, looking dejected, a bit sullen.

He kneeled beside her. "What's wrong?"

She shook her head. "We have a long, hard trip."

"And, if I guess right, an argument with Fred."

"Fred, Fred, Fred," she sighed.

"Edith and I had the worst fight of our marriage the week I had to decide on my first school. There are so many unnerving questions."

"You've been very successful, haven't you?"

"I suppose I have."

"Books, grants, prizes. You've done it all. Not to mention wife and family. You must be a happy man, Professor Blair."

Sally drew a cigarette from her handbag and waited for him to light it. She turned her profile and exhaled a cloud of smoke. He recognized an odd loveliness about her. She wasn't pretty; but he saw an attractive quality in the breadth of her forehead, the clear outline of her cheekbones, mainly in the penetrating grey eyes. He found himself wishing she were a stranger he had just met.

"Did you like me when I was eighteen?" she asked suddenly.

"I gave you more time than all my other students together."

"There are people who spend a lifetime with someone they can't stand."

Blair smiled uncertainly, "It was my choice. You were my pupil. I suppose I let you seek me out because I was curious to find out what you were, what you could become. I wanted to have a part in your development. Half the time I wanted to hug you, the other half to spank you. I saw a great potential. But I was annoyed by your pettiness and your little deceits. For all your shyness, you used to mock everyone else in the class—the athletes, the lovers, the sorority girls—without realizing how jealous you were."

"I didn't like myself then. I was a terrible person. I didn't cheat academically, but in everything else."

"I tried to tell you that—subtly—every time we talked."

"I knew. Still I came back to your office again and again."

He lit another cigarette for her and smiled. "You were a bit of a pest."

"I was in love with you." She said it without embarrassment, clinically, and met his eyes. Years before whenever she had a difficult confession to make, she would put her head on his desk and sob.

"I suspected you had a crush on me. That's why I made you our babysitter. So that you would know Edith and the kids. There's nothing like dirty diapers to drive the romance from a man's image."

She tossed her head back in laughter, just as she had done with the bearded man. "I'll never forget the night I found you sitting in the kitchen with a towel around your shoulders while your wife cut your hair."

"You learned that I had feet of clay."

"I felt so sorry for your poverty. It was the one time in my life that I felt superior to you."

"There's a healthy shock in discovering your teachers are human."

"And a great loss. If it hadn't been for that night I would have seduced you."

Stunned, Blair tried to smile, "But that would have ruined a fine friendship."

"There are better things than friendship."

"But now you have Fred Cochran and two sons."

"I keep tripping over his feet of clay."

She crushed out the cigarette and lit another, almost a nervous reflex.

"He's had too much to drink tonight," Blair said. "Does he drink often?"

"Whenever there's a bottle nearby. Nothing else will lure him out of his easy chair."

"But he's so impressive at first meeting."

"To know him is to watch him fade away."

He braced his hands on her shoulders and felt them tremble beneath his fingers. "This isn't good. Have you told him how you feel? Have you had a sincere talk?"

Sally stood up quickly and brushed her cigarette against his wrist. He flinched back at the sting.

"Excuse me," she said. "I have to go to the ladies' room."

He followed her past the open door to the bathroom out into the corridor and held her arm. "Where are you running off to? You're still a bewildered kid."

She pulled free of his grip. "I have to get more cigarettes."

"Let me go for you."

"You can't spank me now," she told him, "not in front of all these people."

Inside the party suite, Blair exchanged professional gossip with the few people who remembered him. The bearded man who had been chatting with Sally in the lobby came over and introduced himself as George something. He flattered Blair, made references to his books, obviously feeling around for a job. Meeting him made Blair realize that Sally should have been back with her cigarettes by now. He asked this George if he had seen her.

"How do you know Sally?" George said.

Blair explained. "We were in the middle of a conversation," he said. "I'd better find her. She's probably wondering what happened to me."

George gave him a strange knowing look, the hint of a leer. My God, Blair thought, he suspects I want to seduce her.

Fred was in the front room, teasing a homely, mannish girl who wore a square-cut suit, making her stand on tiptoe to reach a drink he held over his head, bumping her chest with his shoulder each time she lunged. He was quite drunk now and insolent at Blair's question. "How the hell should I know? What Sally does and when she goes is her own damn business." He splashed the drink into the girl's face and laughed, "Am I my wife's keeper?"

Blair took an elevator to the lobby, but the leather sofas were nearly deserted. The man at the cigar counter gave him a tight-lipped grunt when he described Sally and asked if she had bought cigarettes from him.

He stepped out to the street, but a chill rain drove him back inside. He rode up and down the elevators, wandering through corridors for more than an hour, assuming she was lost; it would have been just like Sally to lose her way in the huge hotel.

When he turned a corner on the seventh floor, he saw her standing in an open doorway and called her name. As he trotted toward her, she walked away and the door swung closed, but Blair got a glimpse of the tall man who had whispered to her by the book displays.

"Sally!" he called again. She ignored him. When he caught her, she turned to confront him, cheeks burning. He finally understood the true change of her eyes: they were hard now, knowing and bitter.

"I'm still deceitful," she said, "but no longer petty."

"Who is he?"

"My teacher too. A graduate course."

She broke away from him and he let her go.

Early in the morning, missing breakfast, Professor Blair abandoned his colleagues—scholars, educators, civilizers of the young. He did not even call to cancel his other interviews, but sat three hours at the airport awaiting the first plane that would take him home, as fatigued as he had been on the troopship that brought him back from a war, his closest real contact with history.

Treasure

When Kurt pushed back the grey metal door and stepped out from the bank onto Paradeplatz, he stood dazzled by the golden glow of the midday sun high above the spire of the Fraumünster. The piercing rays made his eyes ache. He reached thumb and forefinger under his rimless glasses to pinch the bridge of his nose and for a second saw nothing but a fiery blur.

Starting at dawn, he had spent the morning in a small basement room, dark but for the lamp on his worktable. For seven hours he had stared at handwritten papers half a century old, breathing in decay as he scanned for significant words, then dropped each sheet into a shredder while a guard stood silently at the door, saying nothing, looking straight at the wall ahead.

"I have to get outside," he had told the guard and looked at his watch. "I have an appointment." The guard, stiff in a tan uniform belted with black leather, gave no sign of acknowledgement, but turned the key in the lock and held the door open so that Kurt could pass. Before he took two steps from the room, he heard a slam, a metallic echo following him down the corridor.

All that time in the room Kurt had been eager for daylight, a deep breath of clean air, a breeze from the Zürichsee. And now, finally in the open, he was blinded by the radiance.

Kurt stood against a bank wall and blinked until his vision cleared. He set his briefcase on the sidewalk, propped against a sharply creased trouser leg, and reached up to adjust the knot of his tie, a slim man with close-cropped greying hair in an impeccable dark pinstriped suit. There was no breeze to ease the heat of the day. Still, he buttoned his jacket and smoothed a lapel.

Other men similarly dressed passed with their own briefcases, nodding to each other as they nodded to him, entering and exiting the thick portals of bank buildings. Before him green tram cars assembled from several directions at the Paradeplatz interchange, gliding almost silently, then halting with a slight creak of brakes; lines of people stepped down and boarded quickly, as if rushing to be somewhere else.

Then all the cars departed at once and, for just an instant, the square was empty of vehicles. There across the way, waiting outside the window of the Sprüngli café, Erika smiled at him and gave the merest of waves, so subtle most people wouldn't have recognized the gesture. But as he crossed to her, stepping over the shining tracks, he wanted people to notice, to be aware that he was a man about to meet a startlingly attractive young woman, blonde hair drawn back to accentuate the bones of her face, rich dress fabric clinging to the curve of her hips.

As they touched fingertips and he bent to touch his lips to her cheeks, first the right and then the left, he knew that anyone watching them would know immediately that she was his mistress. Who in Zürich would not know? A man from a bank greeting such an elegant woman in the middle of the city.

"So," he said. "Have you been waiting?"

Erika lifted her wrist to glance at a thin watch, the hours marked by diamond chips on a black face. "Not so long. Didn't you say earlier?"

"The manager gave me unusual work today. A special assignment"

"Was it important?"

Kurt made a dismissive gesture. "Old papers. They had to be looked at."

"And then what?"

"I destroyed them." He waited an instant for her to laugh in uncertainty, then laughed with her, unsure what he would have said next if Erika had believed him.

She fanned a white-gloved hand in front of her face, just twice, and sighed. "What a warm day. Why don't we go inside?"

He held open the Sprüngli door for her and immediately, once they stepped in from the street, breathed a rich scent of chocolate and coffee. Throughout the large room, people sat on metal chairs around small marble-topped tables, lifting morsels of pastries with their forks. The clatter of silverware, the hum of conversation, expressions of delight at the taste of delicacies.

Even at this hour the room was crowded, but Kurt spotted an empty table far down by the window. He put a hand on Erika's shoulder and guided her across the floor. Once with Erika several weeks before, he had passed directly in front of his wife's friend, here with her children, adolescents in school uniforms, perhaps a year or two younger than his own sons. The woman had nodded and he nodded back, neither of them speaking, aware that she would tell nothing to his wife. She too had a husband with a position in a bank, a different one. He knew the man slightly from training weeks in the Swiss army. They both were officers of the same rank.

"Now, what should I order?" Erika said when they took seats, reading the menu, gazing out to study the cakes and tarts arranged in a glass case. She asked as a child would, eagerly, delighted by the possibilities of so many choices. Kurt took more pleasure in her manner than he did in the treats—a stunning woman pretending naïveté.

"Can't you make up your mind?" he asked.

"There's so much that I like."

"Then why don't you choose for me too? That will give you the opportunity for two different tastes."

"To double my pleasure?

"Exactly."

The waitress stood over them, a pen poised over a small pad. "My friend will order." Kurt gestured toward Erika. "She always knows what delights me best." Erika pointed at the case and spoke softly to the woman, as if sharing a secret.

Kurt lifted her hand and leaned forward to touch his lips to her palm. Close to her, he saw that she had perspired in the sun, and was amused by the tiny beads glowing on her forehead. He shook open the handkerchief from his jacket pocket, took a corner between two fingertips, and pushed back her fine blonde hair to dry her brow.

Then he folded it carefully and patted his own face, sharing the sensation of intimacy.

A shadow fell across their table, and Kurt sensed a presence blocking the window. He glanced up to see a heavyset woman standing over them, very close to Erika, her broad hips almost touching the edge of the marble top. He expected her to move on at once, but she just hovered there, looking over their heads toward the back of the cafe. Kurt followed her gaze, expecting to see something unusual. But there was nothing but the diners clustered about their plates, the waitresses in crisp dresses serving coffee and pastry. From Erika's expression, he knew that she expected him to do something.

"Is something wrong?" he asked.

Instead of responding, the woman pulled back an empty chair and sat down with them.

"Excuse me," Kurt said, "you've come to the wrong table." He tried to catch her eye. But, expression frozen, the woman folded her hands on the marble top and stared straight ahead as if he did not exist.

She was in her late fifties, dark, with a loose fleshy face and brittle, black-dyed hair coiled atop her head. She wore wide-framed glasses and dangling enamel earrings. Tiers of thick bracelets fit tight around her heavy arms, and large gaudy rings glittered from the fingers of each hand, none of them a wedding band, all of it cheap, costume. Her multicolored dress seemed much too heavy for the warmth of the day, the cloth bulky, as if padded. Kurt had the sensation that she was wearing several layers of clothing, that she had emptied a jewel box and adorned her person with every item.

Erika gave him a perplexed glance. Maybe she is ill, he mouthed, touching a finger to his temple.

"*Güten tag,*" he said, forcing a smile, trying to engage the woman directly. "*Bon jour. Buona sera.*" Nothing. Not the slightest reaction. He shrugged: What was wrong with her?

The waitress delivered their pastries, Erika's rich dark layers of chocolate filled to overflowing with a thick cream, his bright red berries glazed in a pale crust. Kurt expected the waitress to address the woman, ask if she wanted to order, at least greet her. All she did was serve the plates. *"Einen Güten appetit."*

Is this allowed? He was about to ask and point at the woman, but the waitress turned and walked away before he could speak, giving no sign that she had even noticed the strangeness at their table.

Kurt stabbed a berry with the tip of his fork and lifted it to his mouth. He felt discomfort at eating in front of another person who had nothing. Despite the size of the woman, he had the odd suspicion that she was famished, that she had been days without food. He wondered what would happen if he held out his plate to her and gestured that she should help herself. But he knew that would upset Erika. He dug at the crust, felt it crack under his pressure. "Good," he told Erika as he chewed. "This is very good."

But she bit down hesitantly, barely moving her mouth. And the woman was watching her closely now, the muscles of her face tightening and relaxing in time with Erika's.

Erika pushed her plate away. "I'm not hungry."

Kurt decided to start a conversation as if they were alone, to just ignore the woman sitting so close, so conspicuous in her silence, as if she were growing larger each minute in their presence. He thought to ask Erika of her shopping. "Let me hear what you bought today," he said. She visited the same stores almost every day, often buying nothing, at times a surprise for him, a special scent that he would wear after his evening shave the nights he stayed in the city. "I have duties," was what he told his wife, the same words he had used to be with the woman before Erika.

Erika shrugged. "I found nothing I liked." Her eyes shot at the woman, then quickly retreated.

"But we have so much." He indicated the city outside the window.

"Tell me about your day at the bank. All those old papers," Erika asked.

Kurt flushed and shot a glance at the woman, then brought a

finger to his lips. It wasn't a subject to be discussed in public. Kurt turned to see if the woman was listening. Her face still fixed, she seemed to be looking ahead at nothing, her hands sprawled on the tabletop like dead animals. Then he noticed that on the thin chain of a necklace, almost hidden in the folds of flesh at her throat, she wore a tiny Star of David, small and plain amidst the oversized garishness of all her other jewelry.

He signaled to Erika as his lips formed the word Juden, silently, and darted his eye toward the star. She followed his glance and twisted her mouth when she saw.

Although their waitress stood at a table on the far side of the room, Kurt beckoned her with a sweep of his arm, aware that the gesture was excessive. He had been coming to this place for years and had never done anything so extreme. He paid immediately and did not wait for change, aware the note he pulled from his wallet was twice what was necessary. Before the waitress could react, he was on his feet, Erika immediately beside him. He turned back to the woman with an abrupt snap of his jaw, as if to say, the table is all yours now. To his surprise, she looked directly at him with hard, dark eyes.

Kurt and Erika moved quickly through the tables, out onto the street. A haze now coated the sun, and the afternoon thickened with gray, turning sultry with a sudden heat quite inappropriate for this city. Crossing onto the Bahnhofstrasse, he was already sweating heavily, his face drenched. He paused in front of a shop window to rub the salt from his eyes, Erika beside him with her mouth open as if gasping.

"I've never been so uncomfortable," she said. "What's wrong with that woman?"

"Probably a local character. She must be well known in there. Did you see how the waitress just ignored her?"

"She must be mad."

"The mad Jewess," Kurt said, unsure whether to smile, whether or not he had made a joke.

"She doesn't belong here."

93

"Let's just forget about her," Kurt said. "I want to buy you something."

"You don't have to. It's more than enough to have this time. To be with you."

"Yes, it's unusual to have an afternoon free."

"Your reward for whatever you did with those old papers." She smiled, and Kurt made himself smile back.

She took his hand and led him to join the throng moving past shops that displayed expensive clothes, glassware, elegant jewelry. She paused before the fashions of Hermes and Chanel, admiring scarves.

"Shall we go inside?" he asked expectantly. She was a woman who had a gift for wearing scarves. He took great pleasure in wrapping her with silk.

When they stepped toward the entrance, Erika dug fingernails into the flesh of his wrist. "Goddamn her! Goddamn!"

"What? What's wrong?"

"Can't you see?"

There, centered in the doorway, blocking their access, was the woman, rigid as a statue, hands at her sides. Despite the dozens of people passing on the street, she fixed her gaze on them.

"Let's go!" Kurt pressed his hand into Erika's back to turn her around, the two of them stepping quickly, Erika stumbling in high heels, as they rushed down into the narrow streets of the old city. Although Kurt had known this part of Zürich for many years, it all seemed unfamiliar now, as if they had wandered into some strange place. He followed Erika as she slipped into a shadowed alleyway between two gray buildings. It smelled of dank mold as if impenetrable to sunlight.

Kurt began to sneeze, first sniffles and then violently. He felt a constriction in his lungs, a band tightening around his chest. "I've got to get out of here."

In the light again, he opened his mouth wide and gulped air. Erika's blouse was drenched, her hair hanging limp, pasted to her cheeks.

"Why don't we just get away?" she pleaded.

"This is insane. How can we let some crazy Jewess chase us from our own city?"

"Why us? What did we do to her?" Erika looked about to break into tears.

"All right," Kurt told her. "We'll go to our place."

They would avoid the Bahnhofstrasse, he decided. Rather, they would take side streets until they could cross the Limmat to reach the flat he had arranged for her. That meant going in the opposite direction from his car, walking several miles on one of the worst days of the year, one of the worst in all his memory.

Kurt's feet were beginning to hurt, the insteps swollen against the tight laces of his narrow black shoes. His trousers clung to his legs. Everything about Erika seemed to droop. He thought of reaching out to take her hand but feared she would shake him off.

At Münz-Platz, his heart jumped. The woman stood in front of the fountain with her arms folded across her bosom. Erika didn't notice and he said nothing, just kept moving, winding in and out of the strolling tourists, the two of them walking so fast that people paused to stare.

When they reached the Rudbrun Brücke to cross the river, the woman was waiting in the middle of the bridge. Erika saw her this time, let out a gasp and buried her face against Kurt's shoulder. He pressed her tight against the railing and edged slowly to pass as if the woman threatened violence.

The closer he got to her, the more he sensed that no one else on the bridge was paying attention, even though she stood as a barrier in their paths, a gross figure wrapped in a dress that hung like a tapestry. No one swerved to avoid her or even glanced in her direction despite the oddity of her presence. He wanted to call out, don't you see! But, of course, he said nothing.

As they mounted the hill toward the Predigerkirche, Kurt made himself look behind. The woman had not moved; she was far back, still in that one spot, and he let himself relax, slowed down. All they had to do now was climb the rise and take several more streets to reach the flat.

"It's fine now," he told Erika, rubbing his hands across his wet face, tugging at his shirt collar. Each time they had to pause at an intersection to let a car or a loud scooter pass amid the odor of exhaust and rubber, he stole a glance to be sure the woman was nowhere in sight. People emerged from doors in the buildings that faced the street. A few acknowledged him, and Kurt nodded back, relieved to be in a part of the city that lay at the heart of his private life.

In minutes they would be inside the flat, with its cool white walls and soft, padded furnishings. They would shower, refresh themselves, open a chilled wine, and then make love. He touched her face. Her eyes started with surprise, and for an instant she shuddered. "It's just me," he said.

Along the steep sidewalk to her street, Kurt paused to look back over the city, a spectacular view, a sweep of roofs and building towers, the river and the sea, and beyond at the horizon, snow-capped mountaintops. He gazed out in the direction of his bank, aware that more papers awaited him in the morning, precisely logged accountings of gold bars, listings on yellowed paper that made him think of death. By the end of the next day, they would all be gone, the narrow strips turned to ashes. But now he would not think of that.

Inside the building of her flat, Kurt tightened with a surge of desire as the door closed behind them. He seized Erika on the stairway, closing his hands on the wetness of her back, the sweat that saturated her fine dress. With his hips he forced her against the stairwell and moved to kiss her, but she pulled away, quickly.

"Not yet," she said. "Not when I'm like this."

"Like what?"

"Unclean."

In the unlit hallway, his eyes had to adjust to the grey haze, the stale heat that hung before them like a curtain. Kurt had to peer close to the flat door to find the slot for the lock. "I'm exhausted." He sprawled against the enameled wood, his clothing saturated, suddenly drained with fatigue as he slipped the key from his pocket and slid it into the lock.

Inside the flat, as Kurt opened the door, there, her presence a stain on the pure white sofa, sat the woman, the Jewess, glaring at their entrance, hands sprawled in her lap. When Erika screamed, the woman opened her mouth, wide, gaping, exposing large gold fillings sunk deep into her molars like secret treasure.

Kaiser-Frazer

The day the war ended I put on my sister Carla's feathered hat, her twin, Laura's, varsity twirler's jacket, a lace shawl of my mother's, my father's old gardening boots, then stood in the middle of our front lawn and blew a tin bugle at the honking cars.

By the next summer my ten-year-old life reeled with change. A self-service supermarket had opened beneath red, white, and blue banners on Broad Street. Prefabricated houses covered the vacant lot that had been our ball field. Figures on a tiny grey screen glowed from the window of Pete's Radio. Carla and Laura, two years out of high school, quit their jobs in our town to catch the 7:38 each morning to the city. My mother was in the city too, in a hospital for months of recuperation from intricate vein stripping surgery meant to control her high blood pressure. My dad had died suddenly the previous November, a week before he was supposed to decorate my bike for the Armistice Day parade. To fill the hours, I slept till mid-morning and wandered to the edges of the town in the afternoons, unable to make myself join the other kids in their games.

One afternoon on my way to shop for the groceries Carla and Laura had listed on their flowered notepaper, I discovered Tom Maxville. When I stopped to ponder the white coating that blanked the windows of a long abandoned store on Main Street, a young man, really an adolescent, staggered down the alley beside the building trying to balance a ladder under one arm and carry a bucket of paint and wide brush in his free hand.

Untended brown curls spilled over his ears and forehead, down the back of his neck. The clothing flapped about his scrawny frame, a tee shirt and dungarees smeared with grease, splotched with yellow paint. With his large head puffed out even more top-heavy by all the hair, he looked like he might snap in two.

As he swayed back and forth, his face scrunched into such an exaggerated grimace I would have laughed if he fell. But when he set down paint and ladder, he met my eyes and grinned so hard I forgot my usual shyness with teenagers and returned his "Hi!" I peered to see through the streaks of whitewash on the inside of the windows. For all the years I could remember the store had contained nothing but a dusty counter and broken boxes.

"What's going on here?" I asked him.

"The future!" he proclaimed.

"Huh?"

He laughed so wide-mouthed his eyes disappeared in a squint above his grease-dabbed cheeks.

"The newest and the best!" He was almost singing.

"Best what?"

"Automobiles! We're making history here."

"Cars?" I noticed the rips in his tee shirt and gave him a doubting look.

"Kaisers and Frazers!" His voice rang.

"What are those?"

"Thirty years from now you remember you asked me that. It'll be a good joke to play on yourself."

"You're making those names up." I suspected he was teasing me.

"We'd never have won the war if it hadn't been for Henry J. Kaiser. He built more ships than anybody. And now he's making cars."

"Who's Frazer?"

"A friend of his."

That impressed me, two friends building cars together. But I still wasn't convinced. "How do you know your cars are going to be any good?"

"Because they're using all the new know-how. They don't have any of the old stuff to forget."

"What do yours look like?"

"That's a secret."

"Do you know?"

"Sure." Tom put a finger to his lips and whispered, "But I've got to watch out for spies."

"The war's over."

"From the other car companies. They're eating their hearts out."

I asked Tom if he was going to be the salesman.

"Me?" That tickled him. "I'm only seventeen."

He explained he was working as all-around helper and handyman, pretty much on his own until his boss returned from a training program at headquarters ready to sit back and start filling out order blanks. Right now, Tom had to paint the building. Grey chips were flicking away from the wooden frames around the windows and from the cinder block foundation.

I blurted an offer to help:

"Sure. You can scrape with me. But don't make a mess of yourself."

He handed me a tool and introduced himself, amazing me by reaching out to shake my hand. We worked side by side for an hour, Tom chattering on about how in a few years the world would be filled with Kaisers and Frazers. Then I remembered my sisters' grocery list and had to run off before the store closed.

The next morning I dressed in old clothes dug from my mother's rag bag and dashed out of the house a few minutes after Laura and Carla left to catch their train, the two of them carrying white purses and striding identically in their high heels. I had to wait until 9 for Tom, drawing in the dirt with a stick and wondering how I would explain my being there. But he just passed me the scraper as if I were expected.

Even I could see that Tom was a sloppy painter. Blobs of yellow spattered the sidewalk, spotted the window glass. He dug after loose bristles with his fingernails but whistled happily, oblivious of any mistakes.

After working for an hour or so, he reached into the pocket of his dungarees for a Clark's Bar, twisted it in two, and handed me half in a paint-wet wrapper.

"I hope helping me isn't keeping you from anything," he said.

"Like what?"

"Playing ball. Marbles. Cowboys and Indians."

"I don't like that stuff any more."

"How come? What about your buddies?"

My face burned. "We had a fight."

Tom took a boxing pose, pumped out left jabs and swung an uppercut right into the air. "Wham! Pow! I hope you gave them bloody noses."

"It wasn't like that." The sweet pulp of candy backed up in my throat.

But Tom didn't ask for an explanation. His face settled into seriousness. "So what do you do all day, Bobby?"

"I walk around a lot." My daily routine was to start down Elizabeth Street, turn left on Church, over to Maple, pass up and back the length of Broad, and head home on Main and Division. Our town was so small I covered the entire circuit in forty minutes, even when I had to make shopping stops. "I like to look in the store windows," I added, particularly attracted by the glitter of Praeger's Jewelry and Wallace's Clothing, where headless torsos displayed dark suits much like those that hung in my father's closet.

"What does your mom think about you walking around all day and wearing holes in your sneakers?"

"She's been in the hospital all summer."

For a second I thought Tom would reach out and touch me. But he remembered his paint-smeared fingers. "I'll bet she's going to be fine."

"Something's wrong with her blood pressure."

Tom took the piece of candy wrapper from me, wadded both halves into his pocket, and seized the paint brush again. "Well, you can help me whenever you feel like it."

Although he seemed to be working hard, it took days for Tom to finish painting the front of the building, by then his dungarees more yellow than blue. Next he had to clean out the interior in preparation for the carpenters who would shore up the floor, lay new linoleum, and partition off a rear corner.

Tom swung open the garage doors at the back of the building and light poured into the barren space, highlighting the swirls of dust raised by the breeze.

He explained that all the repair work would be done in a wooden shed at the side of the alley. "My Model A's in there now. But I don't expect we'll be needing it much. Kaisers and Frazers aren't going to break down."

"Never?"

"Not until they're, say, thirty or forty years old. I sure feel sorry for those suckers who just bought Plymouths and Chevies."

He dragged the empty boxes out to the alley, swept the floor and walls, even the ceiling, with a push broom, coughing and gagging on all the grey dust. While I watched from the doorway, my first reaction was that the store was too small, nothing like Bittner's Pontiac out on the highway, where the showroom held seven or eight cars. This place could squeeze in two at the most. My father had sworn he'd drive nothing but a Pontiac. But it hit me that if my father could be dead maybe Pontiacs would disappear too. I suddenly wanted very much to see a Kaiser and a Frazer.

While the carpenters pounded a racket inside, Tom began painting the side of the building. It was a grey humid day and he was drenched with sweat. When he stopped for his fourth Coke break, sharing every other swig with me, he asked, "Who looks after you with your mom sick?"

"My sisters, Carla and Laura."

"The twins!" Tom jumped up and slapped his forehead. "Are they your sisters?"

I nodded.

"You lucky devil!" Tom grinned down at me as if I had done something wonderful and he was about to reward me. "Hey, I want to show you something."

He led me into the repair shed and turned on a bare bulb hanging from the ceiling over a hoodless Model A. Parts lay strewn on newspaper spread over the packed dirt floor. Tom slid an accordion file from a shelf, untied it, and fumbled through to lift out a brochure. He kicked the door shut and slowly unfolded the paper to reveal greasy thumbprints and facing silhouettes of two cars in profile. "God almighty! Aren't they wonderful?"

Before I could grasp the forms, associate them with the shapes of familiar cars, he closed the brochure and returned it to the file, an anxious eye on the door the whole time. But I knew enough to realize that I had been granted a rare privilege. "They sure are swell," I told him, already cherishing the secret I shared.

When I arrived the next day, Tom barely nodded hello, peering hard at the trim he was edging with a narrow brush. But he kept sneaking glances at me. Finally, he threw the brush into the grass and kicked at the cinders of the alley.

"Good god! I sure am stupid." His hand fluttered as if he would reach out. But he just rubbed them across his tee shirt.

I looked to the spot he had been painting for some awful mistake. "What's the matter?"

"When I found out whose brother you were, I should have remembered about your father."

"That's OK." It bothered me to see him upset.

Tom retrieved his brush and picked grass blades off one by one. Then he cleared his throat. "Was your dad sick a long time?"

I shook my head. "He took me to a movie on Sunday. Then something happened Monday morning. He fell down in the bathroom when he was shaving. Mom wouldn't let me look. I had to stay in my room when the ambulance men came to carry him out on a stretcher." I had seen his face for just a second, the wide red gash on his forehead.

"Did you cry a lot?"

"No, not then."

"Later?"

"The first time I went back to school after the funeral. When Chuck Robardee said something." I sniffled back the tears that welled at the memory.

"Who's Chuck Robardee?"

"Just some kid."

"What did he say?"

"Everybody was lined up at the door for first bell and he yelled at me, 'Hey, Bobbo, I hear your old man kicked the bucket.'" The stares of the others had prickled my flesh.

"Was that the fight you told me about?"

I nodded and squeezed my blurred eyes shut.

"Well, don't you worry about him, Bobby. People like Chuck Robardee don't matter one bit."

It wasn't until Laura and Carla finally had time to sort through the laundry on my closet floor that they noticed the grease and yellow paint on my clothes. I only told them that I was helping Tom with his work, nothing more, none of our secrets.

"Tom Maxville!" They laughed in unison, the way they always did when retreating into their twinhood.

"Oh, Bobby, is he your friend?"

"He's swell to me."

"I'm sure he's very nice," Laura said, but Carla caught her eye and the two of them were sputtering again.

"What's wrong with him?" I was getting angry.

"He's such a clown," Carla said. "When we were seniors and he was a freshman, he was always following us around with a stupid grin, tripping over his big skinny feet to open doors for us."

"He thinks you're both pretty."

"I guess so," Carla said and squealed Tom's name again,

laughing by herself this time.

"I liked his brother," Laura said, her eyes suddenly grave. "Everybody liked Jim. Before he shipped overseas we made a date to go out when he came back. It was sort of a joke, but we meant it."

"Tom didn't tell me he had a brother." I felt betrayed.

"Jim was killed in the war," Carla said.

Laura nudged her. "Who knows?" she said to me. "Tom may turn out to be just like Jim in a few years."

Tom left a wall half-painted and went out to tinker with the Model A, trying to force two gears back onto the transmission shaft. It surprised me that he never cursed in frustration. When my father struggled to assemble my two-wheeler he threw a wrench across the cellar and shouted curses. Tom just grunted, sighed, and talked coaxingly to the parts as if they were pets.

"My sisters remember you," I told him.

He sat up with his squinting grin. "Really! Boy, I never thought they knew who I was. What did they say about me?"

Clown popped into my head. But I thought to say, "That you were very friendly."

"I'd sure like to find a girl like one of them someday."

"Laura would have gone out with Jim."

Tom's face went blank at the name.

"They told me about your brother."

"Oh yeah?" Tom slid back under the car and busily clanked metal.

"They said everybody liked him."

"Sure." His hammer rang against bare steel.

"Laura thinks you're going to be like Jim someday."

The pounding stopped and the silence was so great it scared me. I thought Tom would send me away right then, tell me never to come back. I stared at his face waiting for his mouth to move. But he grabbed ahold of the gears and strained to make them mesh.

After fifteen minutes in which neither of us spoke, Tom sat up, wiped more grease onto the thighs of his dungarees, and ran the fingers of both hands through his hair. The curls fell back into their normal confusion. "Maybe it'll all fit tomorrow," he said.

"My dad was great at fixing things," I blurted.

Tom sorted through a pile of bolts and springs.

"Do you think about him much?"

"Sometimes. In the middle of the night a lot." From my pillow I could look right at the closet in the hallway where my father kept his coats and suits. When I could not sleep, lying alone amid the creaks and shadows of the dark house, I would feel certain the closet door was opening, a dark figure emerging slowly, stepping toward me and then drawing back. I would shudder with the furious thumping of my heart but never screamed. I just lay there too frightened to close my eyes and wished I could run to my mother.

"How does it feel to think about him?"

"It must be awful to be dead."

"I'll bet your dad wouldn't want you to worry about that."

Finally Tom's second coat dried and the interior of the store was ready. He rolled up the layer of newspapers and razor-scraped paint splotches off the new linoleum. The partitioned cubicle was furnished with a great metal desk, a filing cabinet, telephone, typewriter, and adding machine. When West's Furniture delivered five chrome-runged chairs for customers, Tom spent half a day positioning them and a good part of another day choosing a spot on the wall to mount the Kaiser-Frazer emblem.

As he climbed down the ladder, he stepped backwards, slowly taking in the perspective of the emblem and white walls and chairs and blue linoleum. "This is terrific! This is great!" He pumped my hand, then seized me around the waist and hoisted me so high my head brushed the ceiling.

Tom's boss, Mr. McQuade, the man who would sell all the cars, started coming in most of the time now, a crewcut ex-sailor pacing around the empty store in a brown suit pinched at the shoulders and hitched at the ankles. A man unused to ties and starched collars, he was constantly poking two fingers to pull them away from his neck. Once the empty file folders were arranged and order forms stacked in a desk drawer, he had nothing to do but pace and phone invitations to the grand opening. Every afternoon at three he placed an anxious call to headquarters and was reassured that the cars were going out on trucks any day.

Tom filled his hours tinkering out in the shed and running to pick up coffee and cigarettes for his boss.

At his own initiative, he bought twenty feet of butcher's paper and printed a bright red sign to tape across the front: "COMING SOON—THE GREAT NEW"—a space for the door—"KAISERS AND FRAZERS." When it was hung, he led me across Main Street and walked up and down the block to admire its effect.

"Boy, you can't miss seeing that!" Then he worried the problem of fitting the whole town, people from miles around, into the showroom. His first thought was to pass out numbers like the bakery. Then he shrugged. "What the heck. Let them push and shove. Good gosh! All those people dying just to touch one of our cars."

His enthusiasm overwhelmed me. I cared for nothing but the grand opening, the arrival of the cars. When I spoke to my mother on the telephone, heard her voice for the first time in almost two months, I talked only of Kaisers and Frazers, begged her to buy one.

"We'll see," she said, and I realized how weary she sounded.

I rattled on endlessly to Laura and Carla, who took to running into their room and slamming the door whenever I appeared. "No more, Bobby," they pleaded, giggling together. But I made them promise to come the very first day, stay home from work if they had to.

I found Tom leaping about the alley early on a Tuesday morning, trying to do a cartwheel and sprawling on his back each time, roaring excitement. "Oh boy! Oh boy!"

"Are they coming?" I wished I could do a dance, but just stood there flatfooted and trembling.   .

"Coming? Don't be crazy. They're here! Right on the other side of that wall."

I pointed at the building. "How?"

"They brought them in the middle of the night. This is a top-secret operation. One thing, though. We have to wait till Saturday to show them. Everybody in the whole country has to wait until the same time." He was so agitated I didn't think he could hold out.

"That's OK," I told him. "It will be big news. Like hearing the war's over."

"Yeah! I never thought of that." Tom clapped his hands. "Terrific!"

"When can I see them?" I asked, frightened that he would say no, that Mr. McQuade had forbidden it, so distraught I was on the edge of breaking down into blubbering.

"You? Right now because you're my helper."

I bounced my weight from one foot to the other while he fumbled to fit a key into the padlock that secured the back doors. When it finally clicked, he pulled one door to an angle just wide enough for us to slip inside, then drew it closed at once behind him. He would not turn on a light even though the windows were still blanked white. Two large shapes shrouded in canvas filled the interior. We had to squeeze against a wall to stand between them.

Tom grabbed a corner of canvas from each car and counted slowly to ten. I swayed dizzily. He tugged and the canvas slid into a heap at his feet.

Even in the grey haze the cars dazzled, one gleaming black, the other glowing cream, their chrome brilliant. Their shapes were perfect, streamlined beyond my imagination. The absolute newness thrilled me. I inhaled wonderful odors of enamel, rubber, and fresh wax. Tentatively, unwilling to seek Tom's eyes because he might signal No, I reached out and touched the metal of one with my fingertips, lightly not to mar the shine. It felt so cool, so absolutely smooth.

When I turned to Tom, my hand still wavering in mid air, I saw tears streaming down his face. But he was smiling, his mouth in an arc of joy.

A vision of the future struck me: the streets of our town, the highway to the city, filled with rows of gleaming Kaisers, glowing Frazers, Tom at the head of them all behind the wheel of a black one with a girl prettier than Carla and Laura put together. Me right behind in the cream car, actually driving it, my mother radiant with health beside me, my awed sisters in the back. People all over pointing and saying, "There goes Bobby." And somewhere, the two of them together, my father and Jim beaming down. All of us blissful forever in a land of Kaisers, a world of Frazers.

Stories New

Tucker and Rob

From the window of the empty room Vivica had chosen for his study, Howell stared out at the garden, his view distorted by the waves and bubbles of glass panes two centuries old. Below him, Tucker and Rob were working amid the shrubbery. Rob—bare-chested and in khaki shorts—balanced atop a two-step wooden ladder, reaching with shears to trim growth from a topiary hedge shaped like a swan. Tucker, scuttling on hands and knees, gathered the cuttings into a straw basket, his long black coat spread wide on a stone path, knotted hanks of hair poking out from under the brim of his floppy black hat, a wispy mustache sagging over his lips.

Howell shuddered when he imagined himself getting up from his desk and seeing the two of them every time he looked out his window. All they did, all they seemed capable of doing, was endless gardening.

Rob lifted himself onto his toes to snip stray twigs protruding from the swan's beak. The ladder wobbled, and Howell held his breath, expecting him to topple, wishing for it, the man crashing down on Tucker, both of them too maimed to ever work again. But Tucker sprang to steady the ladder, gripping it with both hands, then sprawled flat on the path, shaking his head and laughing, his mouth wide, his head bobbing.

A breeze rattled the window in its frame, and Howell knew he would have to wedge it firm if he were going to function in that space. This part of the house needed so much maintenance—layers of chipped paint on the mullions, pigeon droppings crusted on the glass, mildew in the plaster. He doubted that anyone had tended to it in decades or that Vivica and her parents had even ventured into that wing enough to notice the disrepair. But he said nothing, not even to ask Vivica why she had selected this space so far from the heart of the house. Never in his life before her had he imagined he would have his own study.

Howell saw the garden gate swing back and Neddy, his four-year-old son, step inside, pulling his tricycle by the handlebar. Where was Vivica? She was supposed to be watching the boy. Just as he noticed Tucker on the ground, Neddy ran to him, laughing too, as if Tucker were doing something very funny, the boy and the man both laughing.

Neddy stretched out on the back of Tucker's black coat, wrapped his arms around his neck, and shouted something. Tucker lifted himself to hands and knees and began crawling around the path, hunching his shoulders, bouncing the boy up and down. Rob ignored them, continuing to trim, snipping with his shears. It sickened Howell to see his son with those two. Where was Vivica?

Howell knew by the time he hurried to the main wing of the house, down the stairs, and into the garden, Neddy would be out of sight for a good five minutes. It was better to watch. As much as he had spoken to Neddy, told him that he shouldn't be bothering the two men while they were working, the boy seemed unable to obey. When he asked Vivica to help, she told him he was being silly. Tucker and Rob were harmless beings.

Tucker reached behind and seized Neddy, rose to his feet, and began swinging him in a wide circle, until he noticed the tricycle by the gate. He set the boy down and rushed to sit on the small seat, his knees up around his shoulders, his coattails dragging as he pedaled, Neddy running behind, chasing him with happy squeals.

Howell heard Vivica's voice. Finally. She appeared in the garden, wagging a finger at Tucker as she pretended to scold him, smiling. Tucker relinquishing the tricycle, hanging his head, sputtering, "Aye, aye, missus." Vivica touched his arm, picked up the tricycle, and held Neddy's hand as she led him out of the garden, the two of them disappearing behind the house.

It stunned Howell how much he loved Neddy, the clutch in his chest whenever his son walked into a room, even just the thought of him, the image that appeared in his imagination at odd moments when he was in the car or sitting alone in the drawing room. That's because he never expected to be a father, he told himself, in fact, never expected to be married when he passed forty. Then he met Vivica at a party thrown by someone he barely spoke to in the office, surrounded by people who all their lives had known the right thing to say or do. As he stood alone by a window, realizing that he didn't belong, that he should find his coat and leave, her saw her approaching, sure she would walk past him, a thin, angular woman, one hand wrapped in a necklace of multicolored beads, her eyes wide and bright. Instead, she stopped before him and said, "Hello. You look like an interesting man." "You must mean my brother," he had answered. "Do you have a brother?" "No." She laughed and touched a finger to his wrist, transmitting warmth. Even as he sensed her great appeal, the pleasure of her company, he felt bewildered. She was so poised, so much at ease, so full of grace. Why would she have interest in a man like him? He wondered if she really had mistaken him for someone else. But before he could ask, she linked her arm through his and led him to the buffet. "Let's get a drink and chat." Howell sensed immediately this woman would not mock him.

Seated at the polished table in the formal dining room with its beamed ceiling and great chandelier, Howell poured fresh juice from their own apples for Neddy, then wine for Vivica and himself the way her father had taught him, but still nervous about spilling. Neddy wanted them to toast, reaching out to touch glasses, the boy giggling at the clink, insisting they do it again, until his mother told him that was enough.

Although the windows looked out on only a corner of the garden, Howell caught a glimpse of Rob's bare back and, immediately after, Tucker's dark coat. As much as he knew he shouldn't be saying anything, that this was not the right time or the right place, he couldn't stop himself.

"Do they have to work on Sundays?" he asked.

"It's what they choose," Vivica said.

"Seven days a week. Don't they need time off?

"But what would they do?"

"Who?" Neddy asked, his voice loud and high, the way it went whenever he thought he was being excluded.

"No one you know," his mother told him.

"The same thing over and over again, dawn till past dark. It would drive me crazy."

"Maybe not doing it would drive them crazy."

He nodded and knew he had lost the debate.

During the months after that party, Vivica came to the city every weekend, meeting Howell in her hotel room, never at his flat. When he embraced her, he always was struck by his size, how he loomed over her, her taut frame sinking into the softness of his body. Yet he felt that she was the one holding him up, that he would topple over if she stepped away. He clung so hard he feared he was hurting her, but she never cried out, never complained. Yet through all their time together he awaited an outburst, a shattering of her patience that never came.

Howell had been nervous about moving to a country village, into a great old house amid acres of apple orchards, sharing the two dozen rooms with her parents, sure he would make terrible mistakes that revealed who he really was. To his surprise, Vivica and her parents behaved as if he had always lived with them. It was a life far from any he had ever known, could barely believe was his. When his father-in-law suffered a stroke, he grieved, shaken by the absence when they had to place the man in a nursing home.

He truly liked Vivica's mother, her enthusiasm, the way she tried to cheer her bedridden husband before he died, the way—despite his apprehension—she had welcomed Howell into the family when he married Vivica. She'd only asked about his own parents once, never again after he told her "I don't see them," just nodding and saying, "It's that way sometimes." She accepted him just as he was, as Vivica often told him, "just as I do," Howell unwilling to ask who they thought they were accepting.

At times in his unease he found himself missing his small flat in the city, certainly not the living alone, but the simple ordinariness of that place—no grand ornate rooms, no cabinets filled with fine china, no polished floors or gilded frames, no wine racks in the basement, no centuries of history that had nothing to do with him. But, most of all, no Tucker and Rob in the garden.

Howell's obligation to keep the two men was sealed by the croaked whisper of his mother-in-law's deathbed instructions, the woman barely conscious from all the morphine. He'd been there at the bedside, holding one of her gaunt hands while Vivica gripped the other, weeping. "Be good to Tucker and Rob," he heard from lips that barely moved, and because Vivica was too upset to speak, he was the one to answer, "Yes, of course. We promise."

Howell couldn't have denied her wish. Now, every time he saw Tucker and Rob, he cursed that promise.

Vivica's mother had explained that Rob went off to a war and wasn't the same when he returned. He never spoke a word, and no matter how cold the weather, he wouldn't wear a shirt, just shook his head when offered one or a coat. But she never told Tucker's story to Howell beyond shaking her head and saying, "His mother was a bad lot." Vivica knew no more even though she and Tucker were the same age and she could always remember his presence in the village. He never went to the school or spent time with the other children. It wasn't that they shunned him. He always seemed happy to see them, just as he was now when he encountered another person, grinning and nodding and blurting excitement.

It took Howell some time to understand what Tucker was saying through the sounds that exploded from him, even to recognize them as words. For some reason, though Howell had never been in the military, Tucker always called him Colonel. "Good day to ye, Colonel" every time they passed on the grounds, even if it were only minutes apart.

Whenever Howell had to look at him, Tucker's eyes wouldn't hold still, darting every which way, never meeting another's glance.

To Howell's surprise, Rob and Tucker got along. At least, they were able to function as a team, Tucker seeming to know what Rob wanted him to do. Tucker called him Captain. "Aye, aye, Captain," scurrying behind Rob, handing him tools, collecting his leavings.

Rob had a home in the village, really no more than a cottage, as clean and neat as his person even though he spent little time there, puttering in the garden long past darkness. Tucker slept in one of the sheds on the grounds, behind a partition that separated his area from the yard tools and the tractor he loved to polish with old rags. Howell found himself staying inside evenings and weekends, unwilling to walk the grounds, to have to look at that shed, to run into Tucker and Ron and hear the sound of Tucker's babbling.

One evening while they lay in their bed, the lights out, a quarter moon visible above the tops of the shutters, Howell asked Vivica, "Do we really need them?"

She gave him a look of surprise. "They need us."

"Isn't there another way?"

"Where could they go? Who else would care for them?"

Howell shook his head. He didn't know.

He couldn't bring himself to tell Vivica how much their presence disturbed him. She was so natural with them, treated them as normal. He couldn't reveal how awful it was for him to be associated with defectives like Tucker and Rob.

Now the two of them passed right in front of the dining room window, Rob striding as if on a march, Tucker stooped, his coat scraping the ground. Howell turned away, so abruptly he heard his neck crack. Vivica shot him a look.

Neddy looked down at his empty plates. "May I be 'scused?"

"To do what?" Howell said.

"Ride my bike."

"All right," Vivica told him. "But stay on the paths near the house."

Together they listened to the sounds of their son's footsteps on the wooden floor of the long hallway. Vivica covered Howell's hand with hers.

Howell knew he should ask if she wanted him to open another bottle of wine. "Why not?" Vivica smiled. "It's our day to relax."

"Exactly."

"Music?"

"Fine. Let me check on Neddy first."

He stepped out to the solarium and saw Neddy in the garden, down on hands and knees beside Tucker, the two of them following Rob and picking up leaves, each one holding them up for the other to examine.

As much as Howell wanted to rush outside and seize his son, sweep him up and carry him back into the house, he knew Vivica wouldn't approve. "Neddy needs a playmate," she had told him once. "There's no reason for you to be jealous."

How could he explain to her it wasn't that? It wasn't that at all. With a last look at Neddy engrossed in his chore, he stepped back into the dining room.

Vivica had moved their glasses to the table between the leather chairs in the library and chosen the CD of a solo piano piece that to Howell sounded very modern, almost like jazz. He felt he should know the name of the musician but didn't ask her who was playing, even though he knew she wouldn't mind.

Howell set his wine glass on a coaster and closed his eyes, listening closely, liking what he heard, surprised when the percussive chords stopped and the melody turned soft and light. What seemed a sudden silence jarred him in his seat. The music was over. He looked at the clock and saw that a half-hour had passed. He had dozed and realized Vivica had the same startled look. "You too?"

"That second bottle was a mistake."

Howell stood and rubbed his eyes. "It's time for Neddy to come in."

Howell went to the garden first, but Neddy wasn't there. "Good day to ye, Colonel," Tucker said. "Where did he go?" Howell demanded. Tucker just shrugged. Howell walked the path outside the garden wall, expecting to see the boy each time he turned a corner, more and more anxious when he didn't. He took the pathway to the back of the house. As his vision adjusted to the dank shade under the huge willow, he saw the tricycle upended in a compost heap, the handlebars oddly twisted. Howell shouted his son's name and then Vivica's. He was trembling, bracing a hand against the brick of the building to keep his balance. In a clutch of fear, he shook his head to force out a vision of the boy's body in a window well, his throat slit, his head dangling at the same unnatural angle as the handlebars.

Vivica was touching his arm.

"I can't find him," Howell said.

Vivica called "Neddy, Neddy, where are you?" She paused for a moment. "He has to be on the grounds. I'll look in the orchards."

"He never goes there!" Howell's voice broke. As frightened as he was, he felt shame for his panic, the weakness he was revealing. Neddy had seen a fox prancing through orchard once and came running home in tears, crying, "I don't like those trees."

But Howell didn't stop Vivica. He forced himself to stare down into the window wells and saw nothing but wet leaves, breathed the odor of their decay. Lifting the tricycle from the compost, he set it upright and wiped off the clinging vegetation.

He could hear Vivica saying their son's name. It sounded wrong, much too composed for the state of his terror, and he screamed, "Neddy!" tearing his throat. As he walked to a corner of the house, he heard himself muttering, "Oh god, oh god."

Howell gasped when something jumped from a hedge, a jackrabbit that paused to give him a glance and then sprang across the grass. Neddy would love to have seen that, running after the creature, mimicking its hops.

When he reached the front of the house, Howell stopped and spoke aloud. "He's not here. He's not here." Ahead of him, on the other side of the semicircle of white stones surrounding the main entrance, he saw the top of Tucker's hat above the garden wall and heard him blurt a meaningless sound.

Howell started running, his shoes scattering stones, grinding at them. He pushed open the gate and went directly to Tucker. "Where's my son?"

"Good day to ye, Colonel."

Howell grabbed his shoulders, dug his fingers into the slick black oilskin. "Where the hell is my son!"

"Aye, the boy, the boy." Tucker's head bobbed up and down, his eyes darting wildly.

Rob moved up beside Tucker, staring directly at Howell. Howell had never seen the two men so close together, Rob's bare flesh, pressed against Tucker's coat.

Howell clutched the front of that coat but glared at Rob. "Tell me what you've done with my son! Talk, you goddamn freak!"

Rob seemed to press his lips together, locking in his silence. Howell drew back a fist, but Tucker reached out to close his fingers over it, the flesh filthy, the nails blackened. Instead of swinging out at Rob, Howell slapped Tucker with his other hand. Tucker dropped to the ground, burying his face between his knees, moaning, wrapping his arms around his chest and rocking back and forth.

Even though, in an instant of clarity, Howell realized neither of them had done anything to Neddy, he wanted to beat them both, give them great pain. Just as he was about to hit out, Howell heard his name, a voice shouting at him to stop. Vivica's voice.

When Howell looked up, he saw Vivica standing at the gate carrying Neddy, the boy wide-eyed in her arms. She spoke calmly now. "He fell asleep under a tree in the pachysandra. I couldn't see him in all that growth. And he didn't hear me calling."

Howell knew her words were as much for Tucker and Rob as they were for him, and he realized what she was seeing—he and Tucker and Rob posed together in the garden, the three of them joined like a triptych.

The Other Price

Doug Price had occupied the tiny place in the city on King Street for years, but now referred to the accommodation as a pied-à-terre when with friends in the country. They would laugh along with him, even though he was sure they had no idea why. It was only one very small room, up five flights of scuffed stairs, with a closet of a toilet and a claw-foot tub next to the sink. If he stood in the center of the floor and stretched out both arms, he could almost touch the pocked gray plaster walls. Originally, after he fled his parents' house at eighteen, that room was his only home. Now he used it occasionally when he came down to the city from the country. But he kept the lease because the rent was very cheap and controlled by law. He told people it suited his needs, though none of his current friends had ever seen it, and he invited no one there. Many drove up from the city to the parties he threw in the country, spending weekends crammed into the six bedrooms of the old farmhouse he had bought for a song and renovated himself. Social as he was in the country, in the city he lived a loner's life, as if he were a stranger who knew no one despite the many friends, acquaintances, and associates just a neighborhood or two away.

In the city, all he needed was his notebook computer and a modem, not even Wi-Fi. He rarely left the room, spending hours uploading code to servers halfway around the world. Usually he drew a window curtain against the thin light from the airshaft outside and didn't know whether it was night or day, warming canned food on a hotplate when he felt hungry, sprawling on a canvas cot when he began making keystroke mistakes. He didn't have to be there. His work could be done from anywhere. In the country, he had a large sun-bright office next to his bedroom, a special ergonomic chair, a super-fast Internet connection, and a view of the hills beyond his garden directly out the windows. In the country, when visiting friends didn't fill his time, he had his animals—three cats and two dogs, tropical fish, a parakeet, wild birds by the hundreds at the feeders, and a family of woodchucks that he had given names. Often he would stop his work to watch the golden finches at a thistle bag, the red-bellied woodpecker at the suet, his cats stretched out in a shaft of sunlight, the dogs curled at his feet, and tears would well in his eyes. He loved the country. He loved the creatures. Even though, when the guests were gone, he was the only person in the large house, he felt enveloped by life. Yet, now and then, in the midst of a bright day, he would feel himself swallowed by darkness and, after calling a neighbor to feed the animals, hurry to King Street, impelled by urgency.

For many of his years in the city, Doug Price had been quite poor, often hungry. Although his parents were well off, his father an executive vice president, he refused to ask them for a cent from the day he left. His only contact was sending an occasional postcard with no return address, certain it would send his father into a rage. The morning he abandoned his parents, he had gotten up very early, long before them, and loaded two dufflebags into his old Ford Falcon, stopping at the bank to close the account built from afterschool jobs and small gifts from distant relatives, not very much in total, less than a thousand. In a town just outside the city, he sold the car for several hundred more and came into the terminal by train, then sat in the waiting room with a newspaper to seek an accommodation, dialing a pay phone many times until he found the place on King Street. To save money, he had walked the forty-seven blocks with a duffle bag over each shoulder, bumping people on the sidewalk, mumbling apologies.

Of course, he wasn't poor now, not with his mastery of computer codes. He owned property, five acres, an all-terrain vehicle, rooms filled with antiques, a cellar of thick, stone walls lined with wines that he ordered by the case for his guests. On King Street, the room was still furnished with the odd pieces he had assembled during his first month there so long ago—an unraveling wicker loveseat salvaged from a curbside, a chipped yellow table and two chairs from the Salvation Army, the cot, remnants from three sets of dishes, two enamel pots, an old trunk with buckled strap hinges. The people he had collected in those early years were just as mismatched, an assortment of other strangers in the city, each one fleeing unhappiness and failure, but each with a different story and different quirks. While he was learning, gaining expertise, they wallowed in their pasts, litanies of old woes, first depressing and then boring him. At the beginning, when he had been as maudlin as they, he did things with them that he wouldn't even allow himself to think about now, things that abused his body—his soul, his parents would have said—and the bodies of others. The memories made him ashamed.

Eventually, he dropped them all and found himself amid a new circle of people like him, that is, like the Doug Price he had become, people he would arrange to meet at restaurants and galleries, people who were with him when he chose his place in the country, who helped with the renovation, who accompanied him on antique hunts, who brought gifts for his cats and dogs, ornate feeders for his birds.

It was the first day he had been in the city in more than a month, driving down on a sudden need, not checking that he had locked the door, not bothering to tell anyone where he would be, not even the neighbor who would feed his animals. He sat on the wicker loveseat, the notebook computer on his lap, half dozing while it was in the midst of a long upload, when a fist banging on the door startled him awake. He jumped up so fast he almost dropped the computer. There in the hallway stood a tall, thick man in a faded green uniform, the jacket tight and fixed with dull brass buttons. The man held a package in his face. "You D. Price?" At his nod, the man shoved a clipboard at him. "Sign here."

As the man descended the stairway, Doug called out to him. "How did you get in?"

"Front door, the way everybody does."

"Wasn't it locked?"

"Wide open."

That was odd. People in the building took great care to make sure the door locked tightly, tugging at the knob every time they left. Doug hadn't recognized the deliverer's uniform. In the country, he received FedExes almost every day, occasionally a UPS. And the company name on this package's wrapping was smeared, as if the package had been soaked with rain. Yet the past few days were dry and clear. Perhaps not in the place it was sent from.

The name and address were hand-printed—D. Price, 17 King Street. At least, it looked like a definite 17 to him. This building was 12. He held the package close to a light bulb and thought that, maybe, someone could read the 7 as a 2. The deliverer certainly. He had a careless look about him, wearing a uniform like that.

Yet, he had no idea who would be sending him material here. That hadn't happened in many years, certainly not from any of his present clients. None of them even knew about this place or its address. He hoped it wasn't anyone from his past, some person who may have recognized him on the street and wanted to be in touch again. That life was behind him.

The package had been wrapped in brown paper and strapped with rows of heavy tape. He couldn't tear it open with his hands, and had to use a kitchen knife, the sharpest he owned. When he spread the paper apart, he found a stack of religious pamphlets, a drawing of Jesus on the front, head surrounded by a ring of yellow, no doubt meant to represent gold; but this printing was cheap. And this Jesus was angry, his mouth open in a shout, his eyes narrowed in fury. His right arm was raised high above his head, fist clenched, as if about to strike a blow.

Doug heaved the pamphlets to the floor, scattering them across the bare wood. "Goddamnit!" he cursed, certain his parents had sent them, their first communication in decades. The same old crap. Repent, repent. Be saved, be saved. Prostrate yourself with fear of God. Vengeful and terrible.

When Doug looked out over the spread of pamphlets, he realized they were all different, several dozen of them, their covers each with a variation of a violent, hating Jesus. The warped belief that he had run from at eighteen. He felt himself sinking back into old emotions, knotted inside, gasping breath through his mouth.

There would be a letter or a note, most likely from his mother. She would be the one to write, never his father. He kicked a heel into the pamphlets, scattering them in search of a white sheet with her cragged handwriting. Instead, he found a laser-printed letter, more a short note, not on letterhead, without a salutation, but personal:

> *Here is the material you asked for, all but numbers 76 and 93, which are out of stock until we do a reprinting. It's a shame that I can't send the complete set because I know you will put them to good use. You always have. The city is a disgusting place, and we honor you for living there among people who are the worst of humankind. Yet they are the people who need us most. We do what we can, you most of all.*
>
> *Faithfully,*

And it was signed Charles.

Doug knew no Charles, at least no one he could remember. He searched the list of contacts entered in his computer and found only one Charles, a man he had done one project for quite a while ago, far away in another city. They had had several email exchanges, all business, nothing the slightest personal.

On a whim, he opened an Internet phone number search program, and typed in his own name and the city. The phone in this apartment was unlisted. It wouldn't turn up. But the name D. Price appeared several times, as he assumed it would in a city of millions. But, to his surprise, one had an address at 17 King Street, not 12, with a phone number nothing like his. There was someone with his name and initial only a few buildings away across the street. And he had gotten the man's package.

As much as he despised them he was glad he hadn't given into his impulse to throw the pamphlets in the trash. They belonged to someone else. He would call D. Price and tell him what had happened and that he would bring the material to his building. The phone rang five times, and Doug was about to hang up when an answering machine clicked on. "You've reached Doug Price. Please leave a message."

Doug slammed down the phone. He had expected a Donald or a David, not someone with the exact same name, and a taped voice that pronounced the first name Dewggh. He spoke it the same odd way.

What would he have said to the man? "This is Doug Price too"? Or "We have the same name"? Or just, "I've received your package by mistake"? None of it sounded right.

So Doug waited until after dark, very late, when most of the lights on King Street were out, especially those at number 17. He gathered the pamphlets, wrapped the brown paper around them, and tied the bundle with string. Then he went downstairs and crossed the street to duck into the outer doorway of 17 and place the pamphlets under the mailboxes, the man's name clearly visible. He ran back to his building and up the stairs, breathless, as if he had done something criminal.

The next morning, very early, just past 6, his phone rang. At first, he thought he was dreaming. No one called him there. The phone was for the modem. But when he sat up and rubbed his eyes, he knew it was happening. He lifted the receiver. "Yes?"

"Why did you call me last night?" someone said.

"Who is this?"

"You hung up. Didn't leave a message."

The other Doug Price. Now that the man had spoken several sentences, Doug realized that their voices were nothing alike. His own was rather high and, when he was younger, embarrassed him because it suggested weakness. The other man was abrupt and assertive. Doug didn't want to talk to him. "It was a mistake. I apologize. It won't happen again."

"Are you the one who left the package?"

"What? What are you talking about? How did you get this

number? It's unlisted."

Instead of answering, the man laughed. "I know how people behave. They call first to say, 'Your mail came to me by mistake.' But they realize they don't want to get into a conversation with a stranger. So they hang up without leaving a message. But they don't want a stranger's mail, not in their home."

"Why do you think I'm like that?" Doug asked.

"I saw you. Darting across the street with a package under your arm."

"Yes."

"Did you read them?"

"No. I didn't have to. I know what they're about."

"I can arrange to give you copies."

"No. Never! Don't call again." Doug cut off the call and immediately unplugged the phone line.

He tried to work, but it was as if he had forgotten the coding that came to him so easily. He was making mistakes, frustrated and angry at his blunders. I should leave, he thought, go back to the country. But he sat, unmoving, certain the man, the other Doug Price, was watching from a window, would see him get into his vehicle, would copy the license number and track him down. All morning he sat, his mind swarming with memories he had tried to bury for years, things he had done to strike back at his parents. He shuddered with shame, telling himself that he wasn't like that anymore.

In the early afternoon, very hungry but unable to bring himself to prepare food, he thought he would be sick. When the door shook with a loud rapping, his innards twisted in spasms. It was him. The man had come for him. But when Doug moved to the peephole, he looked out to the faded green uniform of the deliveryman. Relieved, he unlocked the door, and the man handed him a small white envelope, then turned and began the descent down the five flights. "Don't you want me to sign for it?" Doug said.

"That won't be necessary."

Inside, the door locked again, he saw that the envelope was clearly addressed to 12 in very neat handwriting but had no return address. He tore it open and slid out a folded slip of paper.

Dear Doug,

I know who you are. All about you. Everything. We should meet. We have much to share. I await your visit. I'm always at home.

Doug

Doug crumpled the note and stood with it crushed in his fist, wanting to hurl it to the floor, but froze. Eventually, he collapsed into the chair and dropped it, then reconnected the phone and pressed the number keys. The other Doug Price answered immediately, before it rang. "I don't want to know you," Doug said.

"I think it's important that we get together."

"Why? It's just a name. The accident of a name."

"I don't believe in accidents. Everything has a meaning. A purpose. Aren't you even curious?"

"I don't think so?"

"How can you know unless we meet? Come now. Just once. I promise you won't have to do it again."

There was a long silence, Doug expecting the man to say more, holding his breath, until he heard the buzzing of a dial tone. The other Doug Price had hung up.

Doug began filling the tub. It took quite a while with the building's corroded pipes, the hot spout barely trickling. He hadn't bathed in several days. Even as he stepped into the water and slid down until his body was immersed, he knew he would dress and cross over to 17, though he did not understand why. He told himself that this was the last time, that after the visit he would never come back to this room at number 12 again. He would abandon everything. This place contained nothing that he wanted. He shouldn't be there.

Shaved, dressed, out on the sidewalk, Doug realized he still had not eaten, but he didn't want to go back up the five flights. He could stop in at one of the restaurants on the block, but he wanted to get this visit over with, put it behind him and then just forget about the city, cede King Street to the other Doug Price.

The entranceway to number 17 looked very much like that to number 12. He had not paid attention when dropping off the package, but now he looked closely. The buildings could have been duplicates, perhaps designed by the same architect. But when the door buzzed open after he pressed the button for D. Price, and he stepped inside, he saw how different it was. This building was luxurious, marbled and mirrored, with two elevators, one open and waiting, all out of place for the street.

The other Doug Price also lived on the fifth floor. But the elevator stopped at a hallway with only a single door. This man occupied the entire floor. Doug saw the door was not locked, slightly ajar. He knocked lightly and then pushed it open. "It's me," he called.

"Come in, Doug," the man said. "I'm in the back."

When Doug entered, he found the apartment bathed in a dim pink light, heavy drapery over the windows. The rooms, one opening into another, were crowded with padded leather furniture, glass cases of stuffed creatures suspended from all the walls. Here in the large foyer, they were all birds—owls, hawks, shiny black crows, in the center of it all on a pedestal an eagle with its wings spread wide, as if about to pounce. The cases in the next room displayed snakes of brightly patterned skins, some coiled, some draped about bare branches, mouths wide with fangs exposed. And beyond that room, one of mammals—a fox, red squirrels, a coyote, a snarling bobcat.

Doug could barely look at them, averting his eyes, gazing down at the tiled floors, feeling sick. When he pushed into the next room it held no cases, just a large polished table under a circle of light. He gripped the edge of the table and saw a letter open flat and centered on the wood. The handwriting reminded him of his mother's, and he couldn't help reading.

Dearest Doug,

Your father and I want you to know how proud you have made us. You have fulfilled a promise far beyond our hopes and dreams for a son. We admire and applaud all that you have done and continue to do to purify an abhorrent world. You are so brave to live in that city, but we are comforted by the knowledge that you, our son, will receive an everlasting reward.

Much love,
Mother

"Where are you?" Doug called out, agitated, suddenly furious at this man. "Why are you hiding from me?"

"I'm waiting for you. I'm eager to see you—finally."

Doug stumbled when he stepped into the next room, lightheaded, his legs weak. This room was darker than the others, and it took several moments for his eyes to adjust. Glass cases again. Five of them on the floor, as if they had not yet been hung for display. When Doug looked closely at the first, he saw an orange cat very much like his. And beside it two other cats and two dogs. Stunned, he dropped to his knees and let out a cry of pain. These were his animals. His pets. Creatures he told himself he loved more than anything in the world.

He dropped to his knees and retched, doubled over, arms clutched around his middle as he rocked back and forth. But nothing came up, just a foam of spit that he wiped away with his sleeve

"What have you done?" he screamed. "What?"

"I'm waiting," a voice said.

Doug rushed toward the door to another room, pushed it open with the thrust of his shoulder, wanting to kill, to grab the other Doug Price by the throat and squeeze the life out of him.

He tripped and fell against the sharp edge of a mantle, yelping at the pain in his side. This room, a final room, was quite small, no bigger than a closet, the walls paneled with a wood so dark it was almost black. On the mantle in a hinged frame were two photographs, an elderly man and a middle-aged woman, their expressions grim, people who never smiled—his parents.

"Who are you?" Doug shouted but received no response beyond the echo of his own voice. Then he noticed the clear glass case suspended above him, much larger than those in the other rooms, and empty, large enough to hold a man.

Hide & Seek

Roger aimed his Nikon digital, quickly snapping one shot after another before the layers of purple-red sunset vanished. Paul hung a propane lantern from an aluminum pole behind the adults' table. The children were eating by themselves off at another table. Marilyn, Roger's wife, and Eleanor, Paul's wife, had served the food—sizzling ham steaks with fresh corn and snap beans bought at a vegetable stand a hundred miles back. Craig and Colette, new to the campground, immediately friendly, contributed the wine, two bottles of Bordeaux produced from their orange rucksack.

Roger zoomed in on Colette, pretending to focus, as if taking a picture. When Eleanor seemed to notice, he capped the lens and studied the sky, first closing his left eye, then his right.

Eleanor and Marilyn were sitting on a redwood bench, Paul standing behind Marilyn as he tended the grill, while Craig and Colette sprawled on the ground, his head pillowed on her stomach, her head propped against the rucksack. The adults drank the wine from plastic cups. The older children popped open soda cans, spraying each other with fizz; the younger chased fireflies.

A campfire log collapsed, sending up a shower of sparks.

"This is almost like candlelight," Eleanor said.

"Better!" Marilyn turned to Paul with a smile. He smiled back.

Roger looked through the camera again, swinging back and forth from Marilyn to Eleanor, Eleanor to Marilyn, pausing on Marilyn before he took the picture. Paul, his best friend for many years, blurred in the background.

Marilyn was a small woman, spidery thin, with a pug nose and close-cropped curls. She sat hunched, wrapped arms tight around her knees as if trying to pull herself into a tight ball. Eleanor, though only medium height, seemed tall in comparison, her auburn hair brushed back into a tight frame for a face made formal by silver-rimmed glasses. Both Roger and Paul were trim, clean-featured men who looked right in whatever clothes they wore, from business suits to their Orvis camping outfits. Any stranger could tell the couples enjoyed comfortable lives.

The men had picked the campsite from a map because it seemed so isolated, five miles deep in the woods off a single-lane dirt road. Paul towed a pop-up camper and Roger pitched a twelve-by-fifteen cabin tent. For two weeks the families had been sharing food, blankets, and fishing gear, the cooking and the cleaning up.

Craig and Colette had arrived at the campsite the previous night, long after dark, emerging into the sunrise from the cocoon of a nylon tent, waving to Roger as he gathered kindling to start a coffee fire. They said they had been traveling all summer on a motorcycle, although, like the other couples, they were in their late thirties. Craig was either growing a reddish-blond beard or was lazy about shaving. Colette, tall and full-bodied, dressed in cutoff jeans and a man's tee shirt. Her breasts hung low and widespread, nipples large and dark against the white cotton. Roger saw that Eleanor didn't approve of her, but he couldn't read Marilyn's reaction, suspecting his wife's show of friendliness.

After the meal Paul retrieved a six-pack chilling in the river and snapped open a can for each of them. Craig threw his head back and drained his in several long gulps. When he wiped his mouth with the back of his hand, Marilyn broke the silence, looking straight at Craig. "Where else have you been?"

Craig crushed his can with his fist and tossed it into the fire. "Ontario, the Michigan peninsula, the Adirondacks, Acadia."

"All on a motorcycle?" Eleanor said.

"Sure. Why not?"

"How do you shop?"

"We avoid cans and bottles," Colette said, her voice husky, "anything heavy. Except the wine. And we eat what's around us in the woods. Berries, roots. Craig's very good at knowing what's edible."

Their motorcycle had a mud-splattered license plate. Paul asked where they were from.

"We're in transit," Colette told him.

"To where?"

"Possibly Vermont. Maybe upstate New York."

"Don't you know?"

"We're not definite."

"Won't you have to decide soon?" Paul said.

Colette shrugged. "Before the first snow."

"Isn't a motorcycle bad for your kidneys?" Eleanor winced. "All that bouncing around."

"In a car," Craig said, speaking slowly as if plucking thoughts from the air, "you're all sealed in. Watching pictures flash by the windows. But on a bike you're really part of the landscape. You're attuned to everything around you."

The first impression Craig gave with his stubbled face, his torn workshirt and filthy dungarees, was that of a vagrant, the word Paul had whispered to Roger. But when he spoke, his words soft, his enunciation clear, he seemed educated.

"I'd be scared to death to be all exposed like that." Eleanor turned up her shirt collar, rolled down the sleeves.

"What's your work, Craig?" Paul asked.

Craig looked up and studied Paul closely, then stared at Roger with the same intensity. "Do you know that you two look alike?"

"Everybody says that," Eleanor offered. "Like brothers."

"But they're not." Marilyn grinned as if that pleased her.

"They're very good friends," Eleanor insisted.

"But you and Marilyn are quite different," Craig said. He framed his hands and turned from one to the other.

"How long have you all known each other?" Colette asked.

"Fifteen years," Eleanor said, proud of the number.

"Our first children were born in the same month, just twelve days apart," Marilyn added.

"Then you must all be very close," Colette said, her voice trilling on the "very."

"We're like one family." Eleanor looked to Marilyn for confirmation.

Craig smiled at them both. "It's very nice to have such dear old friends," he said.

"We share each other's memories," Paul said. Roger nodded.

"There's a comfort," Marilyn said, "in knowing someone else has the same experiences. It's like being able to verify your life through them."

"What about *you*," Eleanor asked. "Don't you feel sad about moving, parting from old friends?"

"We never stay in one place for long," Colette said.

"But when you're talking to people like us," Marilyn said, "don't you feel that you're missing something?"

Colette shrugged. "You can't have everything."

Roger felt sure she was mocking them.

Eleanor looked at her watch. "My God! We should be cleaning up." She yelled over to the children to help clear the tables. They whined that they were playing.

"Now!" Paul ordered.

"Listen to Eleanor," Roger said, glancing at Colette.

The children worked quickly, dumping paper plates, the soda and beer cans, the wine bottles into a plastic garbage bag. Then they began a spontaneous game of hide and seek under the glow of the half moon.

"Don't go far," Marilyn warned. "Stay in sight of the fire."

Shivering in the night breeze, she went into the camper for a sweater and brought one back for Eleanor. Colette said she wasn't cold, but Roger could see the goosebumps on her arms, the taut points of her nipples.

"Let's play too," Craig said.

"Play what?" Marilyn asked.

"Hide and seek of course."

"I haven't done that in twenty-five years," Paul said.

"Why not?"

Paul shrugged. "It's for kids."

"One of the advantages of being an adult," Craig said, "is that you can do anything you like."

Roger looked at Colette's broad pelvis. "I'm all for it," he said.

Eleanor began to shake her head, but Paul spoke first. "Why not? We're on vacation."

Paul argued that Craig should be it because the game had been his idea. Craig laughed and accepted. He cradled his head on the table and began to count slowly to one hundred. The others just watched until Colette asked, "Isn't anyone going to hide?" They scattered back into the trees, away from the children.

Roger watched Colette's movements and took a roundabout route to follow her down toward the launching ramp at the river where she crouched among the aluminum canoes. Paul caught Marilyn's hand and led her through a tangle of low, sweeping branches to the base of a great pine tree. Eleanor turned an anxious circle and bolted into the shadows of her camper.

Craig counted loud warning numbers that rang out through the woods: "... 98, 99, 100. Here I come. Into your secret places."

"It's nice here," Marilyn whispered to Paul. "Smell the trees."

"There's nothing like a bed of pine needles," he said.

"Do you think Craig will find us?"

"Never. We're too shrewd for him."

Roger crept up to Colette and pretended surprise when he saw her. "We've picked the same spot," he said. "We must think alike."

"I'm sure we have the same ideas about some things."

He stretched out beside her between the canoes. "We ought to keep our heads down so Craig can't see us"

"Don't worry. He won't look very hard."

"Why not?"

"Craig isn't a serious person."

"Are you?"

"Very rarely."

Even with her sweater, Eleanor was cold under the camper. She hugged her arms to her chest and lay on her side with her knees pulled up toward her middle. She felt like an idiot, annoyed that

Paul hadn't stayed close. What if one of the children should see her? Craig skipped about the clearing, chanting their names as if they were lost kittens. Once he passed so close Eleanor could have reached out and touched his shoe.

Paul held Marilyn's hand. It was the first time he had done so in all the years they had known each other, but she was not surprised. She wondered what it would feel like to slide closer and put her head on his shoulder.

"Are Roger and I really so much alike?" he asked her.

"Sometimes I mistake you from a distance."

"Up close is what matters."

"Inside," she said.

"Are we the same inside?"

It struck her that she didn't really know.

He squeezed her hand. "But we know we like each other."

"Yes, we do." She squeezed back.

Colette rolled over and looked up at the stars. Roger braced his chin in his palm to watch her chest rise and fall with each breath. Strands of her tangled hair glowed in the moonlight. When she did not speak, he became uneasy. "Do you want me to hide somewhere else?"

"Should I?"

"I was afraid I might be cramping you."

"I'll let you know."

Eleanor watched Craig light a cigarette as he moved to the edge of the trees. When he disappeared into the darkness, she felt totally alone and wanted the others with her, the children too, all pressed in the tight space under the camper, warming the night with their closeness.

"Are you glad to be away from them?" Marilyn asked Paul.

"Craig and Colette?"

She didn't answer.

"You're right," Paul said. "It's nice here."

A clatter of footsteps slapped across the bridge, childish squeals. Roger squeezed his body against the ground. When Colette started to speak, he touched a finger to her lips. She bit it with a quick snap and he jerked away.

Craig emerged from the darkness and crossed the clearing directly to the camper; he opened the door and climbed inside. Eleanor heard the creak of springs from the axle beside her as he stretched out on one of the bunks. For a moment she wanted to pound the metal bottom with her fists, but held back, afraid to make such a disturbing noise.

"We could run away," Paul told Marilyn.

"How?"

"Steal Craig and Colette's motorcycle and roar off into the night."

"How would we live?"

"I'd develop Craig's sense for what's edible."

"And the children?"

"They'd stay with Roger and Eleanor?"

"Together?"

"Would it matter?"

"Maybe Roger will run off with Eleanor first," Marilyn said.

"Highly unlikely."

"Highly."

They muffled laughter with their hands.

"What's our best argument for running off?" Marilyn asked.

"You'd finally learn how I'm different from Roger."

Tentatively, Roger returned his finger to Colette's lips. But this time she opened her mouth. He was on her in an instant, straddling her thighs with his legs, plunging his hand beneath the tee shirt.

One of the children poked his head under the trailer, startled to see Eleanor. "Go away," she hissed. "I'm hiding too."

"Why are you so quiet?" Paul asked Marilyn. "Making up your mind?"

"I'm trying to imagine what it would be like to run away with you on a motorcycle."

"How would it be?"

"Fun. For a while."

"Then what?"

"You'd miss Eleanor and I'd miss Roger."

"Are you so sure?"

"I have to believe that."

"Why?"

"If I didn't all our lives would fall apart. We'd drown in a chaos of possibilities."

Roger moved his mouth to Colette's ear, nibbling the lobe and moaning. She raked his arm with her fingernails. At the sudden stinging pain, he wondered how he would explain the scratches to the others.

Eleanor sneezed, an explosion in the still night. Then she sneezed again and decided she wasn't going to risk a bad cold just for a childish game. She pulled herself out into the open and climbed into the camper.

Craig shined a flashlight in her eyes. "So you've finally decided to come out."

"Why aren't you looking for the others?"

"I know where they are."

"Then you should go catch them."

Craig turned the light on his soft smile. "I already have."

Flower Killer

Teddy watched Jill walk about the apartment, turning on faucets, snapping on light switches, rubbing her fingertips over the pimpled wall plaster, stepping across the ragged segment of Oriental rug to open and shut closet doors. Angela had invited him to be there, ringing his doorbell in—as far as Teddy could tell—nothing but a man's frayed blue oxford shirt and announcing, "I'm subletting and this afternoon some person is coming to peek into all my crannies." That person was Jill.

"You're leaving?" Teddy had choked his panic on a mouthful of toast, once again feeling foolish in Angela's presence, even though he was almost twenty years older. Every moment with her Teddy couldn't stop being conscious of her assured grace, certain she disdained anyone who didn't measure up to her standard. And certain he didn't.

Her eyes followed Jill's anxious scrutiny, too bored to smirk. "You'd have thought she was burrowing in for life," she told Teddy later.

But Teddy knew all of Jill's frantic thoroughness was only a pretense by someone trying to hide the terror of decision-making. Teddy understood, sympathized; she was overwhelmed by everyday functioning as if it were a final exam. To Angela she must have been a creature from another species.

Angela had advertised the sublet as two and one-half rooms. Actually, when the house belonged to one family, that of a ship's captain, a hundred years before, it had been the parlor, fifteen by twenty. But now, renovated for modern times, it contained a kitchen unit built into the back wall beside the bathroom and a partitioned cubicle in one corner large enough for a bureau and single bed. Teddy's apartment was a mirror image with a common wall.

Jill stopped to admire the steel-framed French posters. "You've fixed it up nice," she said and blushed. Most of Angela's furniture was wicker, with two orange sling-back chairs on either side of a glass-topped coffee table. "I don't own a thing. Not a stick."

"Where are you living now?" Angela asked her.

"At home. With my mother."

"Aren't you happy with mother any more?"

"I'm twenty-five. It upsets her that I'm not married. If I went out on my own, maybe she could make believe I was."

Angela smiled at Jill, a brilliant smile, disarming; people like Jill were flattered to be receiving it. Whenever they were together, Teddy would keep alert to seize it in his memory even though he knew it had nothing to do with him, just a calculated reflex.

Jill seemed nice, shy enough to put him at ease with her. She had a pleasant round face and a tendency toward plumpness, with years of nervous dieting ahead before she would give in to a fifty-pound explosion. Her hair was dyed too blonde for her deep-pored skin. Angela's, loose now, shimmered rich and dark; her flesh glowed.

"I don't know what I'll do for furniture," Jill said to him. "It must be expensive to outfit even a small place."

Teddy nodded in sympathy.

"I'll sell you mine," Angela offered, waving her hand as if she held a wand.

"But what will *you* use?"

"New things for a new place."

"How much would you want?"

Angela took in the room with a sweep of her hand. "Let's say five hundred dollars."

"Is that enough for all this?"

"You'll save me the bother of moving."

Later, Jill gone, waving her check as if drying the ink, Angela told Teddy, "It didn't cost me a cent anyway. Bloomingdale's wrote off the wicker as a bad debt. The rest came from garbage picking in the better neighborhoods. You should have seen Franklin trying to stuff the mattress into his Jag."

"Welcome," Teddy said to Jill when she handed Angela another check for two month's rent.

"This is Teddy," Angela told her, forgetting he had been there when Jill first saw the apartment. "He lives behind us and is always knocking on the door with a bottle of chilled wine. You'll probably think he's fatherly."

"Why are you moving?" Jill asked her.

Teddy listened very carefully, ready to remember every nuance of her reply.

"I've been here six months. That's my limit—for places or people."

Jill giggled. "I spent my first twenty-five years in the same apartment. I'll probably spend my next twenty-five here."

"Nonsense. Places like these are only for getting your bearings."

"Do you know what made me decide to take it?"

"The posters? They stay too. Part of the furnishings."

"The posters are nice. But I like the windows best of all."

Two wide front windows took up much of the front wall.

"Look how much indirect sunlight there is," Jill said. "It's perfect for my plants."

"Plants?" Angela repeated the word with a twist of distaste.

"My African violets. They'll be the only memories I'll bring from my old life."

Teddy kept waiting for Angela's leaving, expecting her to borrow suitcases he'd never see again or—more likely—just disappear. But when, two Sundays after she signed the sublease, Jill appeared from a taxi, and Teddy helped her carry in matching plaid three-piece luggage, a garment bag, and six potted plants in a cardboard carton, Angela was still in the apartment, her belongings hanging in the closets, stored in the drawers. Angela herself sat yogi-like on the middle of the rug with a large art book spread across her thighs. She gave a startled look when Teddy pushed open the door and dropped the luggage. Then she gazed at Jill with a glimmer of recognition.

Jill froze in the doorway with shoulders sagging from the weight of the plants as if she couldn't enter without Angela's invitation.

"Is it you already?" Angela finally said.

"It's me." Jill seemed embarrassed at the admission.

"Didn't mother come?" Angela asked.

"She was crying too much." Jill made a bewildered scan of the room. "Did I mess up? Is this the wrong day?"

"I'm in a bit of a bother. My new apartment didn't ... materialize. There was a man involved. A Franklin. And, well ... I'm sure you understand."

Jill nodded even though it was clear she didn't. "I don't know what to do. I can't go back home. Not after all I went through this morning."

Teddy took the box of plants from her. Each African violet bloomed with lush flowers—blue, pink, magenta, purple. Teddy was about to tell Jill how beautiful they were, when Angela stroked three fingers down through the length of her hair and his stomach flipped.

"I have a marvelous idea," she said, her smile so dazzling Jill gaped openmouthed. "We can stay here together. For a few days. Until I make other arrangements."

"That would be great." Jill sounded relieved.

Teddy realized that he'd been about to offer Angela his apartment and find a cheap hotel.

Angela flipped the pages of her book and watched Jill unpack. "I'd help, but I'm sure you know exactly where you want everything."

Jill had to leave half her clothing in the suitcases. Then, with great care, she lifted her plants one by one from the box Teddy held and arranged them on the windowsills.

"It's perfect," she said. "They'll make new buds in no time."

"It's like living in a greenhouse," Angela told Teddy in the hallway a few evenings later. "I gag on chlorophyll, and she talks to the damn things as if they were puppies."

Teddy slipped back to his apartment for a bottle of soave and three glasses. Angela and Teddy sat and refilled their glasses while

Jill puttered about. Jill barely sipped her wine. "I get tipsy so easy."

At twilight Angela rose, picked a cashmere coat from the closet, and opened the door.

"Are you going out?" Jill asked, as disappointed as Teddy was.

"Work."

"On a Sunday night?"

"When you're a high-priced call girl you can't choose your hours." She pulled the door closed behind her.

Jill swung around and gave Teddy a look of alarm. So Teddy shook his head as fast as he could. "Angela says outrageous things."

"Where does she work?"

"Here and there," Teddy told her. "She seems to know a thousand people who do nothing but devise possibilities for her. But she refuses to stick at anything. Some days she models at Bergdorf's. Another she translates at the UN. She sells antiques, appraises jewelry, and lingers in the background of TV commercials. Tonight must be when she's supposed to take two Japanese diplomats to the opera."

"She's a fascinating person," Jill said.

"Fascinating," Teddy echoed and, as much as Teddy knew he shouldn't, spent the rest of the evening killing off the soave and detailing every nuance of Angela's fascination.

The more Teddy talked, the more he saw Jill's expression become an embarrassed recognition, and, by the time he left for his apartment with the empty bottle dangling from two fingertips, a look of pity.

Whenever Teddy tapped on their door, Jill would open it slowly while Angela stood between the windows snapping closed the skirt she had just thrown over her tights. When she and Jill were alone in the apartment, Teddy knew, Angela wore nothing but black tights and leotards that accentuated her graceful slim legs, her flat stomach, her small firm breasts. Before Jill moved in, he'd seen her without a skirt a few times, and safe in solitude let himself gasp at the memory.

Teddy could see Jill watching Angela move across the room, certain she felt her own body lumpish in comparison. She spilled, stumbled, bumped into furniture in Angela's presence.

Teddy was always tapping at their door, a bottle of wine under his arm and three stemmed glasses between his fingers, much more often than Teddy knew he should. Some evenings he'd stare at the wall that divided the apartments and warn himself not to do it. But there he'd be, out in the hallway, signaling with a dance of his fingernails on the wooden panel.

Jill would water her plants and listen to the conversation, Angela delightful in her anecdotes of the rich and famous, Teddy foolishly attempting to match wits, Jill grinning feebly.

After a month, Jill's African violets had lost their flowers and still had not budded, and Angela still had not moved, in fact stopped talking about the spectacular apartments important people were always on the verge of offering. Jill paid the rent, bought the food, and did the laundry; she even made up three months back electricity when the lights were shut off.

One evening when Angela was out working at some unspecified job, Teddy found Jill kneeling at the window feeding her violets spoonfuls of powdered nourishment in hopes of stimulating buds.

"Does she ever pay for anything?" she said.

Teddy knew he should say something just to let her know he realized how much she was being used. But he didn't want to admit it.

"If it's the money," Teddy said, "let me pay her share. But don't say a word about it."

"It's not the money as much as it is her not even wondering if she has to pay her own way. She assumes I'm around just to smooth a path for her life. That everybody is."

"If she acted any other way, she wouldn't be Angela."

Jill fixed her eyes on his. "Is it worth being abused just to have her around?"

His cheeks burned. "For me it is."

"Do you expect her ever to care anything about you?"

Teddy shook his head, his face on fire now, his forehead bubbling sweat. "The day she moves from this building, she'll forget all about me. You too."

"Then why do you bother?"

"Why don't *you* kick her out?"

Teddy couldn't remember who began crying first, the two of them suddenly embracing, weeping on each other's shoulders, squeezing harder and harder, somehow ending on the bed, Teddy sure she knew he was making love to someone else, sure she was trying to will herself to be that person.

Later, when they lay apart, only their feet touching, Jill asked if she could tell him something.

"Yes," Teddy said, half guessing what it would be about.

"When she turns out the lights at night, I lie in bed and see her roll out her sleeping bag on the rug and step out of her tights. Then I watch her outlined in the glow of the streetlight. She just stands there until I can't bear not being her and have to hide my face in the pillow."

Teddy stayed home one morning while Jill was at work to talk to Angela about her. When he entered their apartment, Angela sat mermaid-like in the sleeping bag, tossing her arms with the groans and stretches of awakening. She blinked and grimaced at the shaft of sunlight.

Teddy felt awkward not to be carrying a wine bottle, his ticket of admission. It was hard to bring himself to speak.

"What is it?" she wanted to know.

"I'd like to ask you for a favor."

"Ask me?"

"Please be nicer to Jill."

"Jill? She's such an ungainly thing."

"Your approval means a lot to her."

"What do you suggest?"

"Treat her as if she matters."

She glanced toward the violets. "Would you like me to root her in a giant urn and murmur nurturing sounds?"

"Just be kind."

"Teddy, go home."

Before he closed the door, Angela sprang from the sleeping bag, threw back her head, and spun in a dancer's twirl, loose hair floating behind her. She glided naked to the window and extended her arms to the warmth as if possessing it.

Angela began to go out early every night, return at dawn, and sleep until afternoon while Jill was away at work. As Jill told Teddy, they saw each other only for an hour or so in the evening when Jill got home and Angela was dressing.

Now and then Jill and Teddy slept together but took no real pleasure in it. "Every time she says goodbye and slams the door," Jill told him, "I shudder with loneliness."

Her plants began to wither even though she spent most of her hours in the apartment caring for them.

Teddy came by with fresh-bought pastries on a Sunday evening, surprised to find Angela home, deep in a sling chair in a silk dress and doing the crossword puzzle while Jill fed her sick violets with an eyedropper.

"The poor thing doesn't seem to be having much luck with her flowers," Angela told him.

"Not since I moved here," Jill said.

"Then why don't I bring them new life?" Angela tossed her puzzle to the floor and moved to sit cross-legged at an open window.

She held a violet up to the light in her left hand, drew back the right, and flexed her long, tapered fingers at it. "Heal!" she commanded.

The leaves were dry and brown at the tips. When Angela tried to stroke one, it crumbled. She snapped off the leaf at the stalk, paused, and then began snapping off each of the others, one by one. "I hate potted plants. I'd rather have roaches in an apartment." Jill watched numbly, too stunned to stop her. Teddy stood fascinated.

When the stalk was bare, Angela held the pot out the window, turned it upside-down, and slapped against the bottom until the dirt dropped out and burst on the sidewalk."

"Why did you do that?" Jill asked so calmly Teddy held his breath.

"I put it out of its misery," Angela said.

"Flower killer." At first, Jill almost whispered the words. Then she screamed, "Flower killer!"

"Nonsense. Look what you've done to the poor things." Angela pointed to all the pots aligned on the sill. "You're keeping them prisoner in this miserable little room."

Tearful, on the edge of blubbering, Jill rushed forward and started kicking the African violets out the window. They crashed with little mounds of dirt and quivering upended roots. By the time Teddy thought to pull her away, she had destroyed all her remaining plants.

"That was a foolish thing to do," Angela said.

A long-hooded black Jaguar appeared at the curb, and while Jill stood trembling, Angela vanished from the apartment to reappear seconds later outside the window, slipping into the passenger's seat as the car sped away with roaring acceleration.

Jill spun toward Teddy. "You get out too!" When he didn't—couldn't—move, she struck out with both hands, backing him off until Teddy retreated to the hallway and she slam-bolted the door.

Immediately, Teddy ran out onto the sidewalk and waited while Jill stood fixed in one spot by a window and watched the people who passed trample the naked plants, kick the shards of broken pots into the gutter.

When the streetlights went on and Teddy started to shiver, he watched Jill turn back into the darkening apartment and begin pulling Angela's clothing from the closets. Teddy leaped up at the window ledge, but it was just inches beyond his fingertips. He called to her: "Jill!" But she ignored him, emptying leotards, tights, and shining silk panties from the drawers, dumping everything into a heap on the floor.

Teddy ran into the house and began pounding on the door, heaving his shoulder into it. But the lock held and Teddy rushed back to the sidewalk as Jill swept Angela's perfumes and cosmetics from the bathroom shelf into a garbage bag. She removed a packet of letters from the small drawer in the night table and tossed it onto the pile. Teddy knew without reading even one that each came from a man desperate in his longing.

When all Angela's possessions were gathered on the floor, Jill scooped them up in armfuls to heave out the window. Teddy darted about trying to catch it all, but there was too much. Even as he scooped up some items from the sidewalk, Jill dropped more. While Teddy tried to fold the garments into neat stacks, Jill started dragging the wicker furniture, the coffee table, the sling-back chairs, and the scrap of rug across the room and shoved them out, scattering his stacks. Last, she threw the framed posters down as hard as she could, twisting the steel, shattering glass.

Teddy had to jump back behind a parked car. A few people stopped to watch, but most walked past as it nothing were happening, just circling off the sidewalk to avoid the mess.

Teddy salvaged what belongings he could and brought them to his apartment, then sat on the bottom of the stairway to the upper floors, sensing Jill in the darkness just a few feet away on the other side of a wall. He left the front door open to see out into the street.

Angela did not return until long after midnight, on foot, approaching from the far corner. Teddy recognized the rhythm of her movement even in the distant shadows and ran out to the sidewalk.

She stopped short half a block away when she noticed her possessions and stared up at her apartment windows. She paused with a hand in the air, as if about to make a gesture. Teddy called to her. "Angela, I saved your clothes,"

She turned and began to walk back the way she had come, refusing to look behind. When she was gone, beyond his vision, Teddy looked up and saw Jill's face pressed against the window, her body heaving with sobs. Teddy sensed her misery was as deep as his own, but knew he would never forgive her.

Seeking K

I stood at the edge of the old cemetery made dizzy by its jumble of tilted headstones, the lettering worn to shadows, vapors of strange shapes. A voice behind me said the corpses were buried ten layers deep. And that made me shiver. I sat against a wall and gasped, as if I were one of the people at the bottom, all of those caskets piled on top of me, a great smothering weight. Perhaps being dead is just like being alive, except that you're even more helpless.

But that's why I was seeking you in the first place. You thought thoughts that I was always thinking too. Unlike me, you could put your thoughts into words. Each time I read them, I kept nodding "Yes, yes, yes," at every sentence, every paragraph, every page. You could read my mind, strip bare my soul. "You know me," I wanted to tell you, speak those words the moment I found you. I'd fall to my knees, abasing myself before you, revealing the shame of my existence, begging your help.

Even before I went to the cemetery, I knew it was a foolish choice. Why should you come to a place where they stopped burying the dead hundreds of years ago? I went because I wanted to see what you had seen as a young man, as a boy, when you were still making sense of what you knew in your heart, moving it from your heart to your brain, to the place within you that held all the words you would release on paper. You saw those stones, felt the weight of those layers of broken bodies, and knew that this was the worth of a human being, to be thrown into a pit.

As I walked from the cemetery, I told myself I was finally in your city. This was the air you breathed. A paper map in my hand, I prowled the streets, knowing it would be useless to ask any of the hundreds I passed to tell me where you were. They'd pretend they didn't hear or shrug or shake their fists. Some might even reach back and slap me. I met the eyes of a woman in a fur collar and my face stung.

Of course, I wouldn't enter the places that bore your name—the restaurant, the bookstore, the building that claimed to be on the site of your birthplace, the souvenir shops in narrow alleys that sold tee shirts with the dark shape of a man alone on an empty street. Awaiting the assassins. I could barely bring myself to look at those shirts. These were the last places in the city, the last places on earth, where I would find you.

I understood what it must have been like for you to see your name spelled out on signs, printed on cheap cotton. I blinked and saw my name there in place of yours. I would flee. You would flee. What could be more terrible than to have your name exposed to the world, to have people consider you a source of diversion, to flaunt their association with your fame? If they truly absorbed your words, understood what you were revealing to them, they would tear the shirts off their backs. They would shrivel.

That must be why you put so little into print yourself, why you gave instructions to have your manuscripts thrown into a fire, reduced to ashes. Your best friend ignored your wishes, betrayed your plea. But you probably expected that he would because it's what humans do. They fail each other. They betray. They aren't to be trusted. I have never known a person I could have faith in. Except you.

When we meet, we have so much to say to each other. No, that's not right. You will speak and I will listen. Just hearing your voice will bring tears to my eyes. I will weep. I want to weep.

As I walked, I found not you, but between a synagogue and church, a statue dedicated to you, a large bronze figure, human-shaped but with a hole, an oval vacancy, instead of a head. And perched upon the shoulders of this thing, a little man with a face like yours, his little legs dangling. I stood beside the statue, barely reaching the waist of the figure, and I understood this object was revealing my insignificance. Even you, far above me, sat atop a nothingness.

It was our fathers who first gave us this feeling of being worthless. We had fathers in common. Like mine, yours was a bully and a tyrant who belittled you and made you feel like vermin, like dirt beneath his feet. Though you never mailed the letter you wrote him, I know he must have felt every word of it driven into his brain while he thrashed in sleeplessness. You told him, "What was always incomprehensible to me was your total lack of feeling for the suffering and shame you could inflict on me with your words and judgments," and I spoke that sentence into a telephone when I dialed my own father's number. But, like you, I didn't let it connect. Still, I'm sure he heard me too, heard me again and again, day and night until the moment he died. A shriveled object.

The paper map notes all the places you lived and worked and studied in the city. I found myself on a cobblestone street where your family occupied flats in buildings almost directly across from each other. In one of them your father kept his shop on the ground floor—Hermann, he was called, selling novelties and fashion accessories. What triviality. The meaningless ways people earn their livings. Now that building was a shell, sheets of metal nailed across the front, a conveyer contraption suspended to carry out the debris. Where Hermann had his shop, where you lived, now stood an emptiness of dust and naked brick. In your unsent letter, you told him how much you hated his business. Now it was a ruin. What he deserved.

Blocks away, where you endured oppression as a functionary of the Worker's Accident Insurance Company, the building had become a hotel. I don't know how any person could find pleasure sleeping in such a place, in rooms haunted by the spirits of men in stiff collars and starched cuffs suffocated by tedium. My own work was like that. Trapped in a miniscule cubicle of grey slab partitions, I saw nothing, heard only the grind of machines and garbled voices. Every few hours a person would step through the opening to gather the folders I piled on the edge of the desk and replace them with a new stack. Even though I was released every evening, I felt a prisoner, the partitions closer when I returned the next morning, my space in this world shrinking each day. I would pull my arms tight against my sides, huddle in my chair, knowing those partitions would squeeze the life out of me.

Gone was the apartment building where you wrote the story of a man transformed into an insect (about me, about us all), replaced by a luxury hotel, large black vehicles lingering in a concrete courtyard where limp flags dangled from a semicircle of poles. I imagined a guest just back from a luxury shop, arms laden with expensive packages, leaving his Mercedes to a scurrying attendant. He would ride a silent elevator to his floor, unlock the door to his room, and discover a despicable creature clinging to a wall, a rotten apple festering in the crust of its shell. My own back burns with pain; my own legs wobble as if they are wisps of straw.

Just steps from the hotel an arched bridge crossed the river. I stood on the edge of the bank, watching the rippling current, suddenly chill, folding my arms against my chest, my body trembling. Then I remembered your letter that told how often you "rowed up and then, all stretched out, floated down with the current, passing under bridges." You thought how comical you must have seemed because you were so thin, how someone said you looked like the Last Judgment, "that moment when the coffin lids have been removed but the dead still lay there motionless."

Under the bridge, lashed to a thin pole, a rowboat bobbed in the small waves. I knew what I must do. Creeping backwards down the riverbank, I clutched at rocks for balance but lost my grip and slid on my knees, ripping holes in my trousers. At the river's edge, I stepped in the water to reach the boat, an iciness spilling into my shoes. I slipped the rope over the top of the pole and pulled myself in. Two oars lay on the wooden bottom, and

I used one to push away, bracing it against a bridge piling, feeling vibrations from the vehicles overhead. A current drifted the boat to the middle of the river.

The boat leaked. At first, only a film of water coated the bottom, but soon it was up to my ankles. The sideboards were grey and splintering. I suspected the boat had been abandoned for years. Had it been meant for me, just waiting all that time?

Even after just a few strokes, an agony ate into my arms, muscles burning with each pull. I am not a strong man, not a healthy man. Every minute I had to stop and hope the current would carry me forward. Then, far ahead, I saw the shape of another boat and the figure of a man, hunched forward, pulling at his oars with a steady rhythm. It had to be you. Despite the fierce pain, the tearing in my shoulders, I rowed as hard as I could, desperate to reach you.

The castle and the church spire loomed over the city. You must have seen it every day whenever you came near the river, every moment of your rowing. Did you dream of escape? Was your goal to build up strength for the morning you would climb into your boat and row for hours, for days, down the river, miles from that castle and that spire, away from the city with its narrow, twisting streets and its graveyard of tumbled stones? You knew you would never be allowed to enter that castle. Even if you were amid the thousands of visitors who climbed the long, steep steps up to the castle grounds, clutching tickets that would allow them inside, you would have been stopped, a hand thrust into your chest. "Not you!"

I could feel the water creeping upward, saturating my trousers with wet chill, and I refused to look down. Each pull of the oars brought a terrible hurt. My own whimpering rang in my ears. The smell of the river ate deep into my lungs, sucked in with my gasping. It wasn't the taste of water, but foul, as if the layers of corpses in the cemetery, centuries of death, had seeped beneath the city into the river.

My boat passed under another bridge, and I was closing the distance between us, certain I would catch up to you just after the next bridge, the one ahead, the famous one every visitor feels compelled to cross. I could see its parapets, the heads of the endless march of tourists, the gaunt statue of a twisted man on a cross.

By the time I reached that bridge, your boat was only a few yards ahead. I called your name, trying to shout it over the splash of the river, the din of human voices, the blare of music. I called your name with a cry from the pit of my being. But you didn't turn, just sat staring straight ahead, revealing only the back of your head.

Under the bridge, I lost you in shadows, and emerged to a wall of slanted pilings that blocked the river. Ahead, a falls dropped the water to a lower level, the pilings meant to prevent danger. You had to stop, I thought. You will stop and turn, and then you will acknowledge me, know me.

But your boat slipped through the pilings, speeding toward the falls, and you rowed fiercely, even as you dropped over the edge. Then you were gone.

I let myself drift, alone on the dark surface, no longer caring where the currents took me. My boat bobbed against a piling. Eventually I would vanish too, plunge into a vast nothing. And I knew, if you had ever spoken to me, that would have been your message.

Dance with Me!

The Dixieland set ended with a thumping drumbeat, and the cornet player took the bar stool next to Hall even though several other seats were empty. A sign on the bandstand identified him as Lucky Larssen—a small man with a wispy grey goatee. Hall looked straight ahead as if studying the arrangement of cognac bottles in front of the peeling mirror, aware from the reflection that Larson was looking right at him. Uneasy, he turned to face the man.

"You weren't tapping your toes," Larssen said.

"Is that important?"

"Everybody else was." Larssen gestured toward the people behind them at the wooden tables crammed into the small semi-basement bar room. Their voices echoed off the low, beamed ceiling, mixed with bursts of laughter. "Our music makes people happy. They come here to feel good."

Hall shook his head. "I just wandered in because I was cold."

The door opened as a group of people entered, wool caps on their heads, scarves wrapped around their faces. Hall could see up the steps to the empty square outside, the night wind whipping paper scraps across the cobblestones. He shivered even though coals glowed red in the fireplace against a far wall.

"Not a night to be wandering," Larssen said.

His Danish accent was common to the people his age Hall had encountered during his two days in Copenhagen. The younger men and women spoke a neutral transatlantic English, textbook perfect. Solveig had her own way of speaking, quite musical, clearly from somewhere else, though Hall hadn't been able to guess until she told him. It was the accent that had drawn him to her, the speaker unseen among all the people standing around the refreshment table for morning coffee before the conference began. He had excused himself from the men he was chatting with to seek that voice. Even before he found her, he knew she would be lovely, though he had never imagined a face framed by a crown of pure white hair. But she wasn't old. He had seen that immediately, her skin without a wrinkle, her body lean and taut. When she met his eye and smiled, Hall said, "I'd like to know you." "Isn't that nice," she had answered. That evening at dinner he had asked about her accent. "I grew up in Norway, went to university in England, and have lived in Copenhagen for years," she told him. "Do you consider yourself Norwegian or Danish?" he wanted to know. "I consider myself an amalgamation." Hall carried the word with him from that moment on, whispered it to her again and again when they made love during the nights of the conference—"My amalgamation."

"I shouldn't be here," Hall said to Lucky Larssen.

"Where should you be?"

Hall gave him a bleak look. "I don't know any more."

"Then let's say you've found a port in a storm." The clarinetist signaled Larssen, touched a finger to his wrist. "Break over. I'll be watching your toes."

When the music started, joyful and raucous, cornet and clarinet singing to the beat of the banjo and drums, Hall felt self-conscious. Larssen's eyes kept returning to him as he threw his head back, the instrument pressed against his lips. But Hall kept his toes still, unwilling to submit. Instead he let fingers tap on the bar top, hiding them under his other hand. The bartender, a young man with a head of blond curls, noticed and gave him a smile. Hall stopped.

A ceiling light glinted off the bartender's gold earring. Hall thought he should order another beer even though he didn't want one. He pushed his glass toward the man.

"Not your style?" the bartender asked as he tilted the glass under the draft handle.

Hall shrugged.

"Not mine either. For me it's another generation. No guitars. No amps."

"They don't need amps in a place this size."

"Loud and wild for me. The louder the better. Heavy metal. Punk."

"Then working here must be dull for you," Hall said.

"Never. Something happens every night. Always a story to bring home to my girlfriend."

Hall felt something bump his shoulder, turned abruptly to see a red dress leaning against the bar. The woman had a thick braid of dark hair fixed to her head with a barrette, her eyes as dark as her hair. But they seemed to be floating in liquid, unable to focus. She held out a round, stemmed glass. "Brandy," she told the bartender.

While the bartender chose a bottle, she clicked a high heel against the floor in time with the music. Hall noticed the bartender was giving her what looked like a triple serving. "Tak," she said when he put the glass down in front of her and took a deep swig before turning back to the room. With her first step she swayed, then regained her balance.

She was a big woman, Hall saw, her weight firm and curved against the tight red dress. Shapely, she could be called, with an attractive face, but not his type. Even sober she wouldn't have appealed to him.

"Why did you give her so much?" he asked the bartender,

"Saves her return trips. I put it on her tab, and I know she's good for it. Norwegian."

So different from Solveig. "So she lives here now."

The bartender shook his head. "She shows up once a month or so to give herself a good time. That's what Norwegians do. They live in a repressed country."

"Is she having a good time?"

"Are you?" The man began washing glasses.

The music stopped again, and Hall joined in the brief applause, people at the tables quickly immersed in animated conversations, breathless laughter from one corner of the room, from behind the group standing to put on coats. Hall wondered if it was the Norwegian woman.

Lucky Larssen approached him and took the empty stool again.

"You refuse to share in the pleasures of the evening."

"Are you a social worker?"

"I play happy music. I want everybody to be happy."

"Not me. Not this time."

"But you're in wonderful Copenhagen. Why else would you be here?"

"Let's say my plans didn't work out."

"And what is her name?"

Hall's first impulse was to send him away, then realized it didn't matter. "Solveig."

"Spell it."

Hall did.

"Aha. Norwegian. Here it would be Solvej."

"Is that important?"

"You never can tell with Norwegians."

"I certainly couldn't."

"So what happened?" Larssen leaned forward and stroked his goatee.

"She has a husband."

"Many women do."

"Not in the flat when they're supposed to be on business a thousand miles away." Hall had flown for hours, climbed five flights of stairs with a bouquet of flowers, eager to embrace her, the word "amalgamation" on his lips. "And that man opens the door. She's standing behind him, smiling, saying how nice it is that I came to visit."

"So he offered you a drink, and you told him you couldn't stay. Handed her the flowers and ran."

"Something like that."

Larssen pressed a finger into his chest. "I've been there myself. The man holding flowers. Do you love her?"

"We met at a conference. I couldn't keep away from her. I'm here because I wanted to know what I felt."

"The husband will have other business trips."

"I can't just stay here until that happens. I have a job back home."

"But no wife."

"Not anymore."

Larssen grinned. "Like me. But I'm a happy man. No more wife but lots of music." He walked back to the band and wiped down his cornet with a handkerchief.

When the music started, Hall saw the Norwegian woman seize the arm of a man sitting at one of the tables. She pulled him on to the tiny dance space, joining two other couples who drew back to give her room, her red dress dominating as she swiveled and kicked off her high heels. Her partner made small movements, pumping arms, turning back to the people at his table to share their laughter. At the end of the tune, the woman tried to keep him on the space, but he shook his head, kissed her hand in an elaborate ceremony, and sat again, his back to her.

She pushed her shoes across the wood planks toward the bar and then Hall saw in the mirror her noticing him alone on his stool. She planted herself in front of him, hands on hips. "Dance with me." Her voice was hoarse, breathy in its accent. He could smell the brandy.

"I don't dance."

"With me you will."

"I can't. Not to music like this."

"You will." The words came out as a demand.

Hall turned away and faced the bar, noticing the bartender's smirk, the mirrored red hovering at his back.

"I don't even dance with my wife," he said, not remembering if he ever had.

"What wife? I don't see a wife." She closed her hands on his shoulders.

He shrugged them away. "Look. Listen to me. I said no. Even if I knew how, I'm in no mood to dance."

She locked hands on his waist and swung the stool toward her. "You *will* dance with me!"

For an instant Hall thought he would hit her but just hissed, "No!"

The woman put her hands under his arms, trying to hoist him up, grunting against his dead weight. Hall caught the bartender's eye with a pleading look, but the young man tapped his gold earring and watched. Tonight's story for his girlfriend.

The music stopped abruptly, followed by a drumroll and a silent room. Lucky Larssen stepped out into the dance space. "We dedicate our next tune to our visitor at the bar and his charming partner." He reached out in a beckoning gesture. "Please give us the pleasure of your pleasure."

People began clapping, pounding the wooden tabletops with a steady rhythm, the voices chanting, "Yes, yes, yes." The bartender joined them, his mouth at Hall's ear, his whispered "yes" like a scream. Hall contemplated fleeing, seizing his coat and vanishing into the barren night. But the way to the door was blocked, as if the others knew his intention and had moved to prevent it.

Trapped, Hall gave in, not touching the woman, not taking her hand, just following her onto the circle of wood. The drummer twirled his sticks. The room resonated with Yesses, resounding from the ceiling, louder than the music, Lucky Larssen's head thrown back, emitting blasts from his cornet.

They were the only dancers on the floor, Hall frozen, the Norwegian woman tossing her arms and legs in steps that had nothing to do with the music. Her barrette flew loose, her dark hair whipping wildly. Hall's feet began to stir, a pulsation moving up his legs and through his blood. He could feel the force of the music. With no idea what he was doing, mind empty, he let his body submit to the rhythm.

The Norwegian woman tried to spin but lost her balance, staggered, and fell forward, her red dress a heap on the floor, her hands grasping at Hall's ankles. He skipped away, his limbs shaking, his body spasmed in a jolting rhythm. The woman rolled onto her back and pointed up at him, mouth wide, her laughter lost in the shouts from the tables. The people were all banging glasses on the wood, Lucky Larssen bleating his cornet. Hall knew he looked like a fool but couldn't make himself stop.

Bird with Strings

I felt foolish even in the midst of it—arguing with Allen about Paul Whiteman. Allen said his orchestra was a jazz band. We were sitting in our four-desk cubicle in General Electric's Building 23, trainees assigned to editing ships' turbine manuals. This was during the late fifties when I was just 21, usually acquiescent in my uncertainties, trying to get a grasp on what it meant to be preparing for a career. But Allen's claim provoked me. My voice rose. "His music was white bread. That's not jazz." Allen gave me a sour look. The others—Larry and Herb—pretended they weren't listening. I didn't know why I was getting so worked up. What did it matter what Allen thought? And here I was, revealing how much I cared about jazz, suspecting people at GE, especially those above us, would consider it a form of depravity.

Gesturing through the glass partition to the next cubicle, I appealed to Josh Depree to take my side. But he was staring down on the papers on his desktop, lists of typed numbers he spent all day checking against originals. If my task as a technical editor was tedious, his was deadly. But he never complained, rarely moved from his chair, chain-smoking Camels stubbed out in an overflowing ashtray and making notations with a chewed yellow pencil.

I rapped on the glass, and Josh looked away quickly. But fuming at Allen's ignorance, I stormed around the partition to demand his support. "You're the expert. Tell him what you'd call Whiteman's music."

Josh cleared his throat, clenched his pencil in a fist, and slid down in his chair. Then he let out a series of hollow nicotine coughs and spoke in a voice like tires on gravel. "When Bix soloed, it was jazz."

"What about the orchestra?" I insisted.

"Bix was a miracle." This time Josh raised his eyes to the ceiling, a thin smile animating the deep creases of his mouth.

That was all I would get out of him. When I went back to my desk, Allen asked me, "So?" I shrugged and gave up, realizing that I had exposed Josh as much as I had myself.

Josh was an oddity in our department, Technical Publications, three decades older than the rest of us, the young tyros rotating through tasks on our path to upper management. He was going nowhere, a slight man who looked shrunken in his suits, cuffs dragging the floor, trousers bunched at the belt. His grey hair stood up straight in an overgrown flattop, deep creases lining his face. He walked with a slight gimp, dragging one foot, and his hands trembled when he held a coffee cup.

I found myself sitting with him during lunch the days I brown-bagged it while the others went to the cafeteria. For me, it was a chance to avoid another hour of career gossip—who was moving up to the carpeted sanctity of Building 6, who was being shipped off to Cincinnati. "I keep my nose clean around here," Josh told me early on, during my first month on the job. At the time I had no idea what he meant.

My fellow trainees, when their work crossed with Josh's, just dropped papers on his desk and hurried back to their side of the partition. He embarrassed them, his presence among us, like a refugee from a seedy realm they didn't want to admit existed. How had he ended up in an office with us?

I asked him, slipping the question in during one of our early lunches, after telling how I had been recruited in college by an alumnus vice president, a man in pinstripes who kept telling me I'd be set for life. I was being groomed. For what, I had only the vaguest idea. "And what brought you here?" I asked, trying to sound casual, but blushing because I was young, because I was different.

"A kid," he said. "That's what brought me here. I've got to support my kid. Christ, I'm old enough to be his grandfather." He snorted, an abrupt sound.

I scanned the desk for a photo but saw nothing but a yellow pad and wadded scraps. "He's miles from here," Josh told me. "With his mother."

Soon after, in the cafeteria with my cubicle mates, I found out that for years Josh had written a regular column for a jazz magazine. Larry revealed it in a whisper, as if exposing a disgusting habit, and the others smirked. I swallowed my impulse to defend him, to demand what right people who wasted their days in a cubicle had to feel so smug.

Our next lunch together, on a shelf beside Josh's desk, amid a stack of technical manuals, I noticed a book, *The Jazzmasters*, a collection of biographical essays on the major players. Josh hunched forward when I reached for it but didn't stop me from opening the cover. There on the contents page next to the piece on Bix Beiderbecke was Josh's name.

I had discovered jazz in the ninth grade, rushing home from school to the tiny Teletone radio in my bedroom, where I'd listen to Carl Ide's Jazz Review on WNJR from 3 to 5. He would play pieces like Billie Holiday's "Crazy He Calls Me," "Lester Leaps In," and a ton of Charlie Parker. My favorite was the album *Bird with Strings*, particularly "Repetition," the throbbing staccato strings opening for what seemed like a full minute and then Bird's horn suddenly soaring with melody. But I didn't tell anyone about it, not even my closest friends, when I was crowded into booths with them as they slid nickels into jukeboxes for Johnny Ray and the Four Aces. Happy with the pop stars of the day, they mocked what they didn't understand. So I coveted my enthusiasm, fearing ridicule.

Over the next few weeks, Josh let me draw him out, as I avoided the cafeteria more and more, going now and then only to put in an appearance. We must have made a strange pair chewing our sandwiches, me, young and closecropped in narrow three-button suits, and Josh bedraggled, looking as if he'd just survived an earthquake. I was only a listener, eager, fascinated, feeding him questions that eventually elicited long monologues. He'd run with the musicians. He'd actually heard Bix perform once, got invited to Count Basie's rehearsals, played cards with Art Tatum, tagged along with Charlie Parker to all-night sessions in Chicago. "Bird had this huge hifi speaker in his room that shook the whole goddamn apartment building. People complained, but Bird didn't give a shit."

"Did you?" I asked him.

Josh laughed, rare for him. "Hell, I was with Bird."

I wondered if any of the others, my fellow trainees, had ever heard of Bird. And yet, I was one of them, even envied by college friends for this plum position. This was real life, I kept telling myself. Grow up. Be an adult. Yet, in the evenings, when my garden apartment neighbors, all GE employees, gathered on lawn chairs, I stayed inside to listen to jazz—LPs, 45s—the volume low, my ear close to the speaker.

During one of our lunches, Josh suddenly asked me, "Who was the worst man in the world?"

"Hitler," I answered automatically.

He shook his head. "Bismark Herman Beiderbecke. The father. His son was a goddamn genius, and the man treated him like an outcast because Bix didn't go into his damn lumber business. When Bix came home after he broke down, he discovered his father had stacked all the records he sent in a closet. He never played them. He hadn't even opened the packages. I hate the sonofabitch!"

Josh's hands were shaking so much it took three matches to light his cigarette.

On a January afternoon, Larry invited everyone to a Saturday night party at his house. He was a pleasant young man, wide-hipped, sure to bloat as he grew older and more prosperous. Ever cheerful, perpetually smiling, he must have been his fraternity's social chairman. The invitations came on cards neatly lettered by his wife, the envelopes centered on our desktops when we arrived one morning. And he invited Josh. I overheard him explaining to Allen after work on the way to the parking lot. "It would have been rude to leave him out. He's part of the department."

"Maybe he won't come," Allen said.

It began snowing Friday after work, and by Saturday afternoon, we had fifteen inches. The calls went back and forth, Allen to Herb and Herb to me, then everyone to Larry. Larry checked the Public Works Department and learned that the roads probably should be plowed by evening. The party would go on.

Larry's wife, Mary, could have been his sister, the same horn-rimmed glasses, cheerful grin, and thick middle. She seemed overjoyed to see us all gathered in the small ranch house they rented at the edge of the city, putting out dips and chips and nuts on the blond wood of end tables, coffee table, hi-fi console. Allen was there when I arrived, amazed that he had no trouble with the drive, early because he had allowed an extra half hour. He was a soft man with a head of tight sandy curls, towering over his wife, Bitsy, a tiny woman with a sharp nose and muscular calves. Herb's wife, Sally, perky and athletic, was helping Mary, taking drink orders and returning with ice cubes rattling in tall glasses. Lush strings throbbed from a speaker, anonymous standards no one really heard.

I began to expect that Josh wouldn't come. Why would he want to spend an evening with the people who ignored him all day? But he showed up, late, wearing no tie and a strange plaid sport jacket several sizes too big, like a hand-me-down from a much larger man. When Sally took his drink order, he asked for a Coke and stood in one corner of the room, looking at the glass, but not drinking, instead scooping up fistfuls of nuts. I walked over to him. "What do you think of the music?"

"Sells a lot of records."

It was like a junior high school dance, the males in one group deep into talk of tire traction, but really eager for a segue into office politics, the women in another, animated by supermarket specials and fabrics, Josh with them, nodding agreement, his Coke glass still filled to the top.

Outside the snow began to fall again, but I decided to say nothing, watching the flakes swirl in the streetlight, wondering what would happen if we became snowbound. When I turned back to the room, I saw Josh drifting back into the kitchen where rye and vodka sat on the counter next to an ice bucket and quarts of cola. Ice cubes clattered in the sink. Then he reappeared with the same glass, this time filled with a clear liquid. He began telling Sally and Bitsy his method for barbecuing ribs, sipping between every sentence, setting the glass on a bookcase while he gestured with his hands, the two women feigning interest. When the glass was empty, he excused himself and went back into the kitchen.

Allen cornered me to whine about the performance rating he had received several weeks ago, an obsession with him. "How can they say I'm not creative?" Over his shoulder, I saw Josh make a sweeping gesture and knock his glass to the floor. "Oh shit!" He dropped to his knees and began mopping up the liquid with his handkerchief. "I'm really sorry. Really sorry." Sally found a roll of paper towels and stooped to help him. "Hey, it's a party," she said.

Josh retrieved the glass and headed back toward the kitchen. This time all the others stopped their conversations to stare at him. In the silence, I decided that I'd better follow. He was peering down into the empty vodka bottle, turning it upside-down and shaking.

"Keeping your nose clean?" I asked him.

"Did I ever tell you I knew Bird?" Josh said.

"Did I ever tell you I loved 'Repetition'"?

Josh grimaced. "He made that record for people like these. Strings. Shit!" He pointed toward the living room. "To them, Bird's nothing but a strungout junkie."

"They don't know any better," I said. It came out like an excuse.

"Bismark Herman Beiderbecke. What the hell are you doing here?" His voice rasped anger.

I shrugged. "What else is there for somebody like me?"

Josh grabbed my arms, shaking me so hard he lost balance and fell against the sink. "Get the fuck away, boy! Get away and don't look back!"

In a second he was out the kitchen door, coatless, tripping across the snow toward his car, leaving deep indentations in the whiteness. Snowflakes glistened in the moonlight. The night was thick with them. Josh brushed the windshield clean with swipes of a bare hand, then tugged at the door, banging it back and forth against a snow bank until the opening was wide enough for him to slide inside. The engine whined when he turned the key, so feeble I thought the battery was dead. But suddenly it roared with a cloud of black exhaust smoke. Josh shot out into the street and immediately slammed into a pile of plowed snow. He tried to back out, but his wheels just spun, faster and faster until the night stank of burning rubber.

I went into the living room and told the men we had to push him out. By the time we got coats and boots on, Josh was asleep with his head on the steering wheel. He snapped up at the sound of our voices. Larry poured sand under the back wheels, and it took us only two grunting shoves to free the car. Josh saluted and sped down the street, not turning on headlights until he reached the corner. Then he was gone.

Back inside no one said a word about Josh, Larry eventually handing me the abandoned coat from his fingertips as if it were contaminated. But I knew I'd be gone very soon myself, having no idea where I'd be going, but convinced it would be a place where people would despise Bismark Herman Beiderbecke.

Surprise

Not many minutes after Marshall arrived at Ellen's apartment the doorbell chimed. He had just draped his jacket and tie over a chair back and was unbuttoning his shirt. Ellen had slipped behind the partition into the kitchenette, and he was waiting for her to reappear and respond. When the chimes sounded again, Marshall felt a surge of anger at the interruption even though he assumed it was only a delivery. With both their schedules, they had such little time for their affair. Just arranging this meeting had taken a week of phone calls, coded messages on voice mail.

"Would you please get that," Ellen said.

"Were you expecting anybody?" he asked her.

"I'm doing something in the refrigerator," she told him.

When he opened the door, there stood Susan, his wife, and their oldest friends, Al and Cheryl. "Oh shit!" Marshall's heart turned to lead.

But instead of cursing him, Susan was smiling. So were Al and Cheryl. Al pumped his hand, Cheryl kissed his cheek, Susan embraced him.

"What's going on?" His brain reeled. This was Ellen's apartment.

"Surprise!" Al, Cheryl, and Susan shouted in unison, and Al held up a bottle of chilled Moët. The two women kissed him again, Cheryl on his ear, Susan on the lips. "Best wishes!"

"For what?" Marshall asked.

Al mock punched his shoulder. "Don't be so coy, you old son-of-a-gun."

Marshall gave them a bewildered look. "I really don't know."

"Pull the other one," Cheryl said, and Susan laughed as if she had said something really funny.

Marshall kept waiting for Ellen to appear from the kitchenette, for the screaming to start, the ranting and the sobbing. He tensed, ready to shield his face, sure someone—perhaps all of them—was going to strike out at him. But Susan and Cheryl each took a hand and led him into the living room and sat him on the sofa between them. "We want to have you all to ourselves for a while," they said.

"A while before what?" he asked.

"Before the others want you."

"Who? What others?"

"Oh no," Cheryl said. "We're not going to spoil the surprise." Al was standing at Ellen's hutch, collecting champagne glasses from behind the glass doors.

Marshall peeked at his watch. It was 12:30, and he had a 3 p.m. business appointment. Ellen had devised excuses for a long lunch, their last chance to make love for several weeks, until after her Denver trip and the launching of his new project. But now with Susan close beside him, actually touching thigh to thigh on the cushions of Ellen's sofa, he felt hollow from navel to knee.

Then Ellen stepped from the kitchen carrying a silver tray of hors d'oeuvres that she placed on the coffee table with a smile for Susan and Cheryl, even nodding across the room to Al. Marshall clenched the sides of the cushion and waited for words, for Susan to fling guacamole into Ellen's face. But Susan just nodded thanks. How do you know each other? Marshall wanted to ask her but instead folded his hands and tried to pretend that he was a stranger in that apartment himself.

"How did you get here?" He turned to Cheryl because asking her would sound more neutral.

"Al drove."

"I mean, for what?"

She squeezed his hand in both hers. "Silly man. We're here because of *you*."

"But why this place? This apartment? It's Ellen's." He spoke the name and expected thunder, as if he had violated some terrible taboo.

"The door" was all Cheryl said, though the chimes didn't sound until after she spoke.

Ellen slipped the chain and opened it wide. Marshall's entire department crowded four deep in the hallway, all the way back to the elevator—his secretary Beth, Charlie, Ted, Vivian, Lenny, everyone, even his vice president, Vince Bohm. They swarmed inside with eager greetings, giving Ellen and Susan pecks on the cheek. Beth hugged both women. She was weeping. Marshall rose as she swept toward him. She threw her arms around him, kissed him on the mouth, and burst into tears.

"What's wrong?" he asked her, genuinely concerned, convinced something terrible had happened and no one had the courage to tell him.

"You're such a wonderful man!"

She had worked for him since his promotion, and until this moment he'd never even been sure if she liked him or not—the way she always said "Marshall," as if he should have another name, as if he should be someone else. "But what have I done?" he said, trying not to sound desperate.

"What?" She wiped her tears and started laughing. The others were laughing too. "What?" they all said in unison. "Sounds like false modesty to me," Vince Bohm said, and the people from the office waited a second for his face to take on an amused expression before they laughed even louder.

Al was passing out champagne, and Cheryl helped Ellen serve, matching tea aprons tied around their waists. Beth was kissing Susan again. "You must be so pleased," Beth said. "I am, I am," Susan answered, running fingers back through her hair the way she always did in moments of perfect pleasure.

Every now and then, over the constant murmur of earnest conversations, Marshall heard the chimes and could make out more people in the doorway. The crowd had become so thick the newcomers only had an opportunity to squeeze his hand and say something like "You're terrific" before the next wave displaced them. He thought he saw several people from his high school class who had dropped out of his life twenty-five years ago. But they disappeared before he had a chance to recall their names. People spilled from the living room into Ellen's bedroom where the spread was folded back carefully, exposing a fluffed pillow and a corner of pink satin sheet.

Something had been bothering him, like an object just beyond the edge of his vision, and then he realized what it was. Everyone was very dressed, the women in cocktail gowns, the men in dark suits and even tuxedos. He was the only one in shirtsleeves. As he buttoned the collar, he looked back toward the chair where he had placed his tie and jacket. But they were gone. Someone probably had knocked them to the floor, was stepping on them at that moment.

Before he could move, two couples approached him, arms spread, grinning widely. "What a guy!" one of the men said. Marshall had a vague recollection of them. They might have been neighbors, but not from now, from someplace he had lived years before. "It's wonderful to be here," a woman said, embracing and overwhelming him with a mist of perfume. "Thanks for coming," he thought to say. "Wouldn't have missed it," the other man told him.

He felt someone tapping his back, a bit too eager, a bit too hard. He swung around about to snap annoyance when he saw his son and daughter, and in an instant was embracing them both in the sweep of his arms. "But you're in college," he finally said.

"Not today." Todd grinned widely. "I got out of two midterms when I told my profs what was happening," Crystal said.

"What is happening?" Marshall asked quickly, hoping he would finally get an answer if his question took them by surprise.

"Oh, Daddy!" Crystal waved a hand as if he were beyond belief.

"How did you get here?" Both their schools were halfway across the country.

"We flew."

"Who sent the tickets?"

"They came in the mail."

"But who invited you?" Marshall gestured at everyone gathered around them, the instant smiles when people noticed he was glancing in their direction.

"Mom called us," Todd said.

"Your mother!" Marshall gripped a chair back.

"Susan asked her to."

"Susan *did*!"

"Come on, Dad," Crystal said. "It couldn't have been that much of a surprise."

"I didn't know anything," he protested. "I still don't."

"We should go say hello to some people, shouldn't we, Sis?" Todd said, and Marshall was sure he had winked at Crystal. "Wait," he called, but they were gone.

"Marshall." His name was spoken was so softly he couldn't be sure he had actually heard it. But the voice repeated it, close to him, followed by a hand on his sleeve.

"Connie?" he said as he turned, afraid that it would be her. He looked down into the once familiar face of his first wife, his children's mother, now marked with the softening of middle age, her hair turning grey. Her eyes were smiling. The last time he had seen her, ten years ago in a lawyer's office, he had slammed the door on her rage, a stream of curses that damned him and Susan both. "I couldn't help falling in love," he had told her once before that day, knowing he was making a feeble excuse for destroying her life. He would have stayed with her if he could, but back then it would have killed him not to be with Susan.

"Why are *you* here?" he said, unable to imagine a good reason.

"It would have been awful to miss this day."

"After all that I did to you?"

"How can that matter now?"

"Do you know whose apartment this is?" For some reason he could ask that of her but not of Susan.

"Everyone does."

"And you're still here?"

"Of course."

"But why?"

Connie was about to answer when Cheryl came up to her, and the two women embraced. "Oh, my dear!" Connie said. They had been confidants once, before Marshall met Susan, when Cheryl and Al were the couple closest to Marshall and Connie just as they were now to Marshall and Susan. For a while Cheryl and Connie used to call each other, and Cheryl still sent birthday cards.

Marshall pulled Al into a corner. "You're my best friend. If you won't tell me what's going on, nobody will."

"You should have seen your face." Al seized him by the shoulders. "I wish I'd had a camera."

"Why didn't you?" Marshall asked, as if that were important.

"The one screw-up. I guess we all thought somebody else was bringing one."

"If I had pictures, I could believe all this really was happening."

"Hey, it looks like people need more drinks." Al disappeared into the kitchenette.

Before Marshall was alone for even a second, Susan came up beside him. "I think it all worked out very nicely, don't you?"

"Did you know that Connie is here?"

She nodded. "I was just talking to her."

"You were?"

"How could I not do that today?"

"And what about Ellen?"

"Ellen? She's very attractive. But then she would be, wouldn't she?"

From across the room, Ellen blew him a kiss.

"It's not what you think it is," Marshall said. "I don't really know what it is."

"That's not important now." Susan squeezed his arm.

"Betrayal? Pain?"

"No. Not any more."

"Who planned this?" Marshall asked.

"Everybody. All of us."

"Why here? Why today? What's different?"

"It's time."

"What is?"

Susan squeezed his arm.

Marshall clutched her hand and tried to meet her eyes, but he was tear-blinded. He turned his face toward the wall and could not stop sobbing, ashamed at the quivering of his body, the loud gasping noises that rose from his throat. He couldn't hear another sound, sure the others were all staring at him, sure he was ruining everything for them by making such a fool of himself. He tried to call out to them but choked on their names. When his chest stopped heaving, he realized that he no longer held Susan's hand.

When he turned toward the room and opened his eyes, everyone was gone, the apartment empty and still. Plates lay on the furniture and window ledges with remnants of food, glasses tipped beside them, dozens of empty bottles on the hutch. He saw his tie and jacket. Someone had folded them neatly and placed them on the sofa.

"Susan!" he cried, "Ellen! Connie!" His voice echoed and faded. Night had fallen outside the window, an absolute darkness.

Marshall slid the tie under his shirt collar, refusing to glance in a mirror as he adjusted the knot; then he slipped on his jacket. He stood with his hand clenched on the knob, turning it slowly, certain that when the door opened the hallway would be empty.

There's Always the Unexpected

Work had been slow for Nick. God-awful. For weeks all he'd had were what he called pissant jobs, replacing rotting sundeck wood, installing Home Depot kitchen cabinets. He'd have to hit savings soon, and there wasn't much of that. Some afternoons he just hung around the house to save gas in his truck, even though the noise of Laura's TV shows made him want to smash something. So when his cell phone rang while he was puttering in the basement, he stood up so fast he hit his head on a crossbeam, shouting a curse before he pressed Answer. "Yeah," he said, then remembered to give his business's name. It was a woman with a house that needed what she called "basic work." He didn't like her voice, the way everything she said sounded like an order, but he pretended to check his schedule and told her he could clear some time the next morning.

The moment Nick walked into that old house and shook the eager hands of the Holmans—Eleanor and Charles—he knew they were idiots for buying such a wreck. A quick glance down the hallway, at the walls, into the empty rooms on either side, told him the renovations would take months and cost a bundle. He grinned back, pumping their hands, contemplating a new truck, a fishing trip with his son, new Barbies for his two daughters, maybe a long weekend with Maggie if he could figure an excuse to give Laura. He'd stuck gold.

"It was built before the Revolutionary War," Eleanor announced, proud, Nick saw, as if she were taking credit for it. "Washington spent two winters not far away. He might have visited, stood right where we are in this living room." She tapped her shoe on a floorboard, her long legs in sharply creased tan slacks, high heels lifting her two inches above her husband.

Nick didn't like that, the woman taller, but he made a solemn face and nodded. All he knew about Washington in New Jersey was that his troops froze their balls off in Jockey Hollow while the general slept in a mansion. A museum now. He'd passed it dozens of times but never bothered to go inside. His son, Eddie, had been there years ago on a third grade trip. When Nick had asked him what it was like, the boy shrugged. "Just a lot of old shit." Laura had shaken his shoulders. "Don't say that word." But Nick couldn't help laughing. Now, remembering, he bit down on his cheeks to stop from laughing again.

"When do you want to move in?" Nick asked them.

Eleanor gave him a date.

He looked directly at Charles. "Where are you living now?"

"In town," Eleanor said. "We're selling that house."

The way she said *that* made Nick realize it wasn't up to her standards.

Charles looked soft in his sport jacket, the kind of man who wouldn't know what end of a hammer to grip. When Eleanor signaled, he led the way to the attic and pointed out the petrified roof beams cut from a variety of trees—oak, maple, chestnut—steel-hard and still covered with bark.

No insulation, Nick saw. It would take a small fortune to heat unless he stuffed fiberglass behind the walls. The bedroom ceilings were so low he could reach up and press them with the flat of his hand. Just a touch told him they were hanging loose from the crossbeams. Replacement at five thousand a pop. Nick said nothing, not yet. He'd wait until they signed a contract, his standard one with a provision for the unexpected. The basement was damp, dark marks up the stone walls. Probably got six inches of water every hard rain. French drains, that's what it would take. A week with a jackhammer. And, because the back part of the house was a 1890s addition, not historic, the Holmans wanted a new kitchen and bathrooms. The ones there now were from the thirties, the walls covered with faded fake tile linoleum. Eleanor yearned for a more authentic look. Cherry cabinets. Wide plank floors. Exposed beams. Everything else, she insisted—the original part of the house —should be preserved and restored.

"The inspector guessed about fifty thousand for the renovations," Charles told Nick, looking over to Eleanor as if waiting for her to say something. But she didn't.

Somebody paid the guy off, Nick was sure. He closed his eyes and pretended to calculate, pointing up down sideways, sucking his lower lip, drawing imaginary numbers in the air. "We want to do this right," he finally said. "Ballpark. Closer to a hundred." He knew he would end up making it at least two fifty.

"We thought it probably would come out to around that," Eleanor said, a smirk on her face as if she had just won an argument. "With the unexpected."

"Smart lady." Nick nodded. "There's always the unexpected."

Nick started slowly, just spackling the plaster of the main rooms, taping cracks in the ceilings, scraping chipped paint. The Holmans stopped by two or three times a day, side by side, arms around each other's waists, watching him work with expressions of wonder, as if he were delivering a baby. It was all he could do not to drop his tools and shout at them—"Go away! Leave me the hell alone!" But he knew with the project barely begun he could be replaced by some other guy who had a display ad in the yellow pages.

So he buddy-buddied, drank the containers of Dunkin Donuts coffee Eleanor brought, clucked sympathy at her concerns, her obsession with keeping things authentic—the Williamsburg color chips, the hand-forged tin lighting fixtures, the bubbled glass panes. Every time Nick pointed out a flaw—sagging floorboards, tilted doorframes—Charles gave that cocked head nod of his and said, "We can live with that," and Eleanor emitted her patronizing sigh —"It's historic."

When he was alone with Maggie, he cursed Eleanor— "Goddamned bitch! It's a house, not a fucking museum."

"You're getting paid," Maggie would tell him.

Nick would pull away from her and pour himself another drink. "You don't have to work for assholes."

All the easy jobs done, Nick brought in a demolition crew, a collection of guys who hung out on a street corner with barely enough English to tell a crowbar from a tape measure, and no skills beyond tearing down. He always made sure Virgilio was with him on the job those days, somebody to translate his instructions. But Virgilio couldn't be everywhere, and he'd find himself shouting directions in words he knew the others couldn't understand, his forehead veins popping with rage, he on the verge of whacking somebody with a hammer. To cool off he'd slam a bathroom door and splash water on his face.

They took down the bad ceilings first. Nick relished the Holmans' stricken look when he broke the news, shook his head in wonder at how the inspector could have missed such an obvious defect. The men loaded plaster chunks into buckets that they poured through a window into a dumpster. Grey dust hung thick in the air, coating their faces, their bare chests. Only Nick wore a mask. He figured if the others didn't have enough sense, it was their problem. When they tossed the old bathroom fixtures, white porcelain exploded against the dumpster's metal sides.

In a week the men were gone, the bathrooms gutted, the kitchen too, nothing but beams, the ceiling down, the warped 1890s flooring ripped away. As Nick straddled two-by-fours and looked down into the dark basement, out at the wall framing, he had the sensation of staring at the skeleton of a dinosaur.

Nick took to sitting in the Holmans' house after dark, hunched on the floorboards, peering out at an empty room illuminated by a harsh floodlight. Everything was wrong. Somebody had shellacked the wide pumpkin pine dark brown, like molasses. The walls sloped. The ceiling at one end of the room was six inches higher than the other. What good was his goddamned level? What was he supposed to measure against? He liked things plumb, taut right angles. Here, in this place, nothing made sense.

He told Laura he'd be working day and night. He'd been telling her that as often as he could, whenever he had a real job, for the six months since he'd hooked up with Maggie in the diner. It began with her teasing as she poured cup after cup of 6 a.m. coffee, a short-haired woman with a thick neck. "Good thing they don't give breathalyzer tests for caffeine." She said that every time. When it was slow, she sat in the booth with him, reaching down to massage a calf. "I ache already, and the day's barely begun." Nick would show her his hands, palms up, to expose cut scars and calluses, flipping them over for the swollen knuckles and blackened fingernails. "It's a tough life," he'd say. "That's why we all deserve some fun," she'd answer, and after a few times, when he caught the look in her eyes, he knew what she meant.

Around nine he'd leave the house, locking it only because of his tools, half hoping someone would break in and steal everything, down to the hand-forged nails Eleanor couldn't stop cooing about. Then he'd drive across town to Maggie's apartment, where she'd be three drinks ahead of him.

In her bed he couldn't make himself stop talking about the house, how he'd never worked on one so old, how he hardly knew where to begin, how nothing was right about it, how he couldn't picture the way it should look. That was his skill. He could envision things and make them happen, but not there, not in that fucking antique.

Nick would feel his face flushing, the blood pounding at his temples, fingers digging into the edge of the mattress. "Yeah, yeah," she'd say, reaching down to his zipper, making him hard before he even knew what was happening. Then a soft growl at his ear. "Forget that place."

He'd fling himself on top of her, thrusting, half-asleep in the darkness, imagining that he was heaving against a warped wall.

At home he barely slept. Past every midnight he sat on a

straight-back chair in his cramped kitchen, lights off, sucking on an extinguished cigar and watching clouds smother the moon. He would turn to the oven clock and curse, knowing he had to be up at five to collect whatever helper he had hired for the day ahead, stopping for breakfast at Maggie's diner, giving her a wink, inhaling the coffee steam, relieved to be out of his own house.

Finally, he would climb the stairs, one at a time, telling himself he should fix the creaking risers, trying to muffle the sounds not to disturb Eddie or his daughters, but wishing he could stomp so loud Laura would jerk awake in fright.

He would throw his clothes on the floor and slip under the covers, his wife sprawled in the darkness beside him. For the twenty years of the marriage she'd stayed thin. Maggie was overweight, her thick middle a wobbling handful when he clutched. But it didn't matter. He could barely look at Laura with her constant bitching, complaining that he spoiled Eddie and didn't pay enough attention to the girls, that their own house needed a hundred repairs, that the paint on the walls was depressing, that the washer motor was about to go. What would she do without a washer? It was his clothes, the ingrained crap from his jobs. He wondered if the fluted breathing meant she was asleep or just pretending, as disgusted with him as he was with her.

The rest of the night he would toss, kick out from under the blanket, stare into blankness, seeing Eleanor's face, hearing her pleas to be careful, not to destroy anything historic. Preserve, preserve, preserve. Agitated over putting that house back together again, he dozed into dreams where it all collapsed—walls, ceilings, cabinets— all crashing down on him. He'd writhe and cry out, Laura stirring, croaking a "Huh?"

"Nothing," he'd mutter. "It's fucking nothing."

Eddie was supposed to be helping, after school, on weekends. But Saturday morning when Nick came into the boy's bedroom and shook his shoulder, Eddie muttered, "Leave me alone," and pulled a comforter over his head. Nick's father would have gripped his ankles and dragged him out of bed, but Nick wasn't going to treat his son that way. "Be there by ten," he said, trying to be giving an order. "Not a minute later." He knew it wouldn't be till noon.

When Eddie finally arrived, he wandered around the rooms, kicked at the baseboards, checked his watch and sighed.

"Got a hot date, Dad," he told Nick after an hour.

"Lisa?"

"Yeah, Lisa." The words came out grudgingly, as if having to be with Lisa were another of life's annoyances.

But Nick found Lisa beautiful, young as she was. Tight jeans, high perky breasts, sleek dark hair, pouting lips. He couldn't bring himself to ask Eddie if they were doing it, not sure he could stand knowing.

The Holmans heard of a plumber, someone who had done good work for friends, and insisted that Nick bring him in to install the bathroom fixtures. Nick just nodded to the man and stayed as far away as he could, down on the first floor, pretending not to see him struggle a sink and toilet up the narrow stairway. At lunchtime, he ate alone sitting in a corner, refusing the man's offer to bring him coffee.

All day he could hear the man clanging metal, sawing pipes, shifting thick weight, then the rush of water in a sink, repeated flushing. Nick decided to show off his own skills, tearing away splintered baseboards, narrow wood of uneven widths, notched and gouged. He replaced them with good cedar, chose a wide s-shaped molding from the strips in his truck, satisfied that he had created a major improvement.

When the plumber came down in the late afternoon, Nick expected a reaction, ready for a nod of admiration. But the man just took in the room with a sweeping glance. "You've sure got a mess here, buddy." And he was out the door.

Nick sat for a while, then went up to the bathroom, startled by the bright white fixtures that stood firm in that wall-less space. "Well, the bitch will be happy," he said, furious at the thought of Eleanor's satisfaction when the Holmans appeared in an hour, holding hands and beaming at their man's progress.

On the morning Eddie was supposed to bring a load of lighting fixtures and hadn't shown up by noon, Nick kept poking numbers on his cell phone. The two electricians he had hired for the week drummed fingers against a window frame and gave each other exasperated looks.

"What's your problem?" Nick demanded.

"We don't like hanging around," one of the electricians, Roy, told him.

"These are hours. You're getting paid."

"We could get paid for doing something," the other one, Will, said.

"Who's in charge here?" Nick shoved the phone into his pocket before he threw it at the man.

"From the looks of things, your kid."

Roy nodded. "If it were my kid, I'd kick his ass."

"What do you know? He could have had an accident." For a second, Nick believed it.

"The only accident"—Roy spoke slowly—"was you not wearing a rubber seventeen years ago."

In an instant Nick was on him, grabbing the man by the shoulders. "You son-of-a-bitch!" Will pulled him off, a bigger man, stronger, locking Nick's arms behind his back, forcing him against a center beam. "Take it easy. We were kidding."

Nick broke away, clenching fists, shaking. "And you're fired! Get the fuck out of here. Now!"

The men picked up their tools kits and walked away without a word.

When Eleanor and Charles came by after dinner, he winced and she sputtered. "You said the lights would be hooked up today."

"I had to get rid of the electricians. Those guys don't know their asses from their earlobes."

"You hired them."

"I listened to the wrong people."

"Well, start talking to some right ones. Nothing's happening here."

"These things take time," Nick said, the words catching in his throat. "If you want it done right."

"At this point," Eleanor told him, "we'd just like it done." It sounded like an ultimatum.

Whenever Eleanor drove off, the helper of the day would thrust his pelvis, pump a hand. "Getting any of that, Nick?" "Working up to it," he would say, unwilling to admit that he couldn't stand her, that the hell of his life was going from Laura to Eleanor and back again.

He kept hearing Eleanor's demand—"We'd just like it done, We'd just like it done"—squeezing his hands, shaking them, as if he had her neck in his grip. He'd go crazy if he didn't smash something.

The wall between two front windows bulged, a bloat of plaster. Nick tore off a pink shard of striped wallpaper, ran an open palm over the pocked surface. He let the wooden mallet dangle from his other hand. It wasn't a bad bulge, not as obvious as the one on the wall along the stairway. It could be left alone. He saw Eleanor's mouth moving: Change nothing. Change nothing. Nothing. Nothing.

Nick squeezed the mallet, swung it as if the wall were her face. Once, twice, five times before he paused, his arm frozen over his head, and saw the gaps that exposed raw lathing. Too late. The wall would have to come down, he'd tell them. Worse than it looked. Ready to collapse. No choice. Had to be done.

He swung again, watching the cracks spread, first thin lines, then long and deep, with a sound like a groan, chunks clattering to the floorboards. He was destroying that wall. The sensation elated him. Sweat poured from his forehead, saturated his tee shirt. But he gained strength, emitting loud grunts as he pounded harder and harder, the pile of broken plaster covering his shoes. The wall section down to rows of lathing, he stopped, dropped the mallet and realized how much his hands hurt.

Picturing Eleanor's anguish, Charles's shocked "Hey!" he broke into a grin and turned to see his face reflected in a window, covered with white powder, ghost-like.

Nick waited for the Holmans, shifting the mallet from one hand to another, calmer than he'd been for weeks. To his surprise, Eleanor came alone that day. She cried out the moment she walked through the door. "What have you done?"

"Took care of an eyesore."

"You destroyed a wall."

"It was crap. Those people didn't know what the hell they were doing."

"That wall was older than the country. It was history."

"Fuck history!"

And he was out the door, in his truck, roaring the engine

For an hour as twilight faded to darkness, Nick sat in his truck in a park, lights out but motor idling. He'd be fired. He wouldn't bother to go back to give them the satisfaction of saying it to his face. His tools were in his truck, but he couldn't imagine using them again. Word would get out. Who'd hire him now? How would he pay the bills? "I don't give a shit," he said aloud and his breath fogged the windshield. He traced lines with a fingertip, then obliterated them with a fist.

Outside a coating of frost covered the grass, tiny crystals glittering in instants of moonlight when the clouds parted. It was almost winter, and Nick saw himself as one of Washington's men – hungry, dirty, lice in his hair, clothes like rags, shivering in a ball on a square of damp earth while an icy wind whipped through the branches of a lean-to. He closed his eyes and huddled across the seat, unable to stop shaking.

At the sound of church bells, he sat up to slam the truck in gear and edge toward the street, thinking he would head out to the highway and just drive. Instead he found himself on the route to Maggie's apartment.

He kicked off his work shoes and twisted out of his shirt as soon as she opened the door. "You're early," she said. Instead of answering, he pushed her to the bed and undid his belt, tempted to slide it from his loops and begin lashing. But at the look in her eyes, he stopped and just stood there, hovering over her, chest heaving as if he would burst into tears.

"I've had the fucking worst day of my life," he said.

"What else is new?"

Then his cell phone rang. Nick had to grope on the floor to find it in his shirt pocket. He held it out in front of him and it kept ringing.

"Answer the damn thing," Maggie told him.

He flipped it open. "Yeah?" A woman was sobbing, gulping to find her voice. His first thought was Laura and he was ready to snap the phone shut, but thought Eddie—something happened to Eddie —and began to tremble.

He heard his name—"Nick"—and immediately knew it was Eleanor.

"What the hell's wrong?"

"I went ... I used the bathroom."

"Great. Congratulations."

"I flushed. And then ... everything backed up. It wouldn't stop. It was all over the floor."

"What was?" He'd make her say it.

"Shit."

"I'll be right there." Nick slid into his shoes.

Even before he got to the house, Nick knew the problem was in the basement. A second car sat in the driveway. Charles. He'd come to be with his wife, support her in distress, the two of them wringing hands, helpless to do anything but write checks.

Both huddled in the doorway when he arrived, eyes pleading. "I'm sorry," Eleanor was saying, "so sorry to have to call you like this."

Nick grunted and carried his tool kit down the steps inside the narrow hallway door. The basement lights worked, still on the old wiring. Each breath drew in a sour dankness. He'd be wheezing for days. The foundation walls were thick jagged stone, the ceiling low, crisscrossed with pipes hanging from beams that were just rough-hewn logs. He had to stoop to avoid hitting his head, then stood up too soon and banged it on rusted metal. "Son of a bitch!"

He ignored Charles's shout from above, his "What happened?"

Nick traced the path of the drainpipes to a rear wall where they joined at a trap with a corroded iron plug. He retrieved a long Stilson wrench from his kit, clamped it to the plug and tried to pull down. It wouldn't move. The threads were frozen. He yanked again and felt a tear in his biceps. He took out a hammer and began to pound the shaft of the wrench, a loud clanging that resounded through the empty rooms. Feet moved onto the steps above him.

"Stay up there!" he shouted.

Finally, the plug budged and slowly turned. Nick could feel the bonding of decades give way with an anguished creak. He had to unclamp and clamp the wrench, twist a little at a time, until the plug came free and he could finish turning the last threads with his hand.

When he pulled the plug loose, first nothing happened. Then a dark mixture oozed out, reeking, plopping onto the concrete floor, a putrid heap. Decades of human waste, congealed from all the people who had lived in the place since there was plumbing. That's what they left behind. That was history.

He could walk up those steps, out the door, and into his truck. Abandon the Holmans to the stench of their antique. But he knew he wouldn't. He'd clean the mess. It was his job. But first he'd call them—Eleanor and Charles—down to the basement and make them know what men like him did.

Eavesdropping

When the phone rang, Jillian made frantic signals for her father to pick up the extension. "Yes," she spoke slowly, drawing out the word so that he would get on the line and hear every word the man said. "Yes, Marco, I'm here." Turning to her father, she signaled again and mouthed the words "It's him," her lips in grotesque exaggeration.

Of course it was *him*, Clark thought. Why else was Clark here, in her apartment, at 6 on a Sunday evening, the hour she said the man would call? Yet he couldn't make himself move. Despite her demand, he was ashamed to be eavesdropping on his daughter's conversation.

"You have to listen," she had pleaded. "I want you to understand why I'm so frightened." Clark had been stunned the first time she had whispered her need. Her mother, Margaret, had been in the kitchen, splashing sink water. Jillian, leaning forward, her sour breath on his face, had spoken in a harsh whisper. She didn't want her mother to know.

The urgency in her voice, the look in her eyes, weren't like his daughter at all. Yet he had known at once something was profoundly wrong. In the months since she returned from her assignment in Frankfurt, he had sensed a profound change in her. Her normal cheerfulness was only a performance, bad acting, revealed by a deep swallow whenever she laughed. He had waited for her to admit something really troubled her. If they could name it, he kept telling himself, they could fix it. But, his hand on the phone, he wasn't prepared for this moment.

Jillian glared at him and swung her arm. If he had been standing close, she would have struck him. Reluctantly, gripping with thumb and forefinger, Clark held his breath and lifted the receiver, gently, desperate to avoid making a sound, a telltale click. He flattened his other hand over the mouthpiece and felt himself redden, mortified.

"Jillian," he heard a man say, turning her name into Jill-e-ayn. "What is this?"

Clark froze, hands trembling, certain he had been discovered.

Jillian shook her head, dark hair tangling at the nape of her neck. "What is what?" She measured the words.

"The way you're acting. The way you're speaking."

"You woke me. I was dozing."

"So early? It's past midnight here."

For a second, Clark thought the man was confused, then realized he was calling from far away, another place. The tone of his voice was grave, as if the time were a matter of deadly seriousness.

Jillian had been right about the accent. Marco enunciated the English words perfectly, but the rhythms were off, the stresses flat. "He speaks many languages," Jillian had told him, "but they all sound alike, as if none of them is natural for him." "Didn't you ask him where he came from?" Clark had said. "He never answers. All he says is, My name is Marco, but don't think I'm Italian." "What does he look like?" "Dark hair, almost black, thick on his head, thick on his arms, even on his knuckles. Yet his skin is light, pale, ghostly." Jillian had shown Clark a photograph, the only one she had of the man, the two of them, taken by someone else, Marco standing beside her against the rough tan stone of a castle wall, barely taller, wearing grey trousers and a white shirt buttoned at the collar, his face dim in a line of shadow, hers blurred by the glare of the sun. The top edge of the photo was torn, as if she had started to shred it and then changed her mind.

"I can't help being tired," Jillian said. "Your calls exhaust me."

"Jillian," Marco said, "This isn't good." He spoke calmly, evenly, but Clark sensed that he was furious, his rage sending a tremor through the phone lines.

"It's awful," Jillian said.

She's going to scream, Clark thought. Instead, she fell back against a wall, her face distorted, ugly in its twisting. He had always been proud of her attractiveness, the school photos on his desk, the copies mailed to relatives. She had never given him anything to worry about. Over the years he and Margaret had spent hours telling each other how fortunate they were.

Across the room from him, Jillian slid down to the floor, her eyes imploring. He felt an impulse to enter the conversation, shout into the receiver: *Will someone please tell me what's going on?*

"I don't like the way you're acting," Marco said.

"I'm trying to live my life."

"Your life is my life, Jillian."

"It's not. It's not. It's not." She pressed her face into the wall and started to cry. All Clark could hear for what seemed like minutes was the sound of her sobbing. Then she said, the voice almost a whimper, "Please leave me alone. Stop calling."

"That will never happen. I will never stop calling."

"We're far, far apart. We live in different worlds."

"Distance is nothing. Between us there will never be distance."

I don't want to hear this. The words rang in Clark's head as if he were shouting them aloud, so insistent he missed the sound of a breaking connection, the sudden end of the conversation. Had it been Marco or Jillian? When he looked to her, his daughter sat limply, face drained, eyes empty, hands at her side.

Clark opened cabinets, eager to find her something to drink, and finally discovered a bottle of scotch behind a blue vase, like a guilty secret. He poured a glass for her, and on second thought one for himself.

He drank his quickly, in two burning gulps, before he went to her. He reached under her arms and lifted her into a chair. "Do you want this?" he asked. She nodded. He brought the glass to her lips, holding it in both hands. She sipped, swallowed, and gagged, breaking in to explosive coughing. But she took the glass from him and pressed it to her cheek.

"Now do you understand?" she said.

"He sounds like a strange man," Clark said, not understanding at all, aware how feeble he sounded.

"Strange! Is that all you can say?"

"Obsessed. Crazy with love."

"It's not love. It's nothing like love." Her eyes flashed.

"What is it then?"

"Something awful. Something terrible."

Clark hesitated, waiting for her to explain. But she said nothing more. Finally, he brought himself to ask, reddening as he spoke, "Weren't you lovers?"

"Never!"

"What then?"

"I won't tell you."

"Then how can I help?"

"I'm so ashamed. Daddy, I'm so ashamed."

She hadn't called him that in years. Clark gripped her hands. "You're my daughter. I love you. You can never make me ashamed."

Jillian shook her head and closed her eyes.

Clark sighed, realizing that he didn't want to know.

Of course, he couldn't ignore what he had heard. It was his responsibility to learn more, to make Jillian explain. He made excuses to Margaret to explain why she did not visit at their home. Their daughter's work demanded travel and overtime; it was a very busy season of the year. Instead he went to Jillian, calling first, finding her in her apartment even in the middle of the day. She had phoned in sick, she would tell him; she was calling in sick frequently, unable to face her assignments.

Clark was sure she had thrown away her mobile phone, perhaps destroyed it. That number just rang and rang when he tried it. But he didn't ask her about it.

He saw her during long lunch hours or times when he claimed to be at a meeting, aware that he was endangering his own career, sensing that it didn't matter, that his life would never be the same.

When he sat with her, their words circling her refusal to explain her anguish, the phone would ring, and she would let it go to the answering machine. His first few visits the caller was someone from her office. Jillian would respond immediately, claiming that she had been in bed unable to get to the phone. But soon the messages from Marco began: "Jillian, I know you are there. I know you are listening. You can't avoid me like this. It is impossible for you to avoid me."

Beyond tears now, she shouted back at the man who was not there, fiercely, even though he could not hear: "I won't let you win. I won't! I'll kill you first."

"Why do you say that?" Clark asked her. "You wouldn't be able to kill anyone."

"I might," she insisted. "I want to. I really want to."

"Next time let me talk to him," Clark urged.

"What could you say?

"Stop bothering my daughter. Leave her alone."

She laughed, a sound torn from her throat. "You don't know! Anything."

To Clark's surprise, one afternoon she broke a long silence and began revealing how she had met Marco. She spoke with her eyes closed, her body knotted on a chair, her voice barely above a whisper, as if speaking to an empty room. Clark did not ask her to repeat what he could not hear for fear she would stop, disclose nothing more.

Jillian's assignment in Frankfurt had only been for six months, a reward, a certain path to promotion in her company. For the first month, adjusting to the city, the language, the way of doing business, she had no time for leisure. But on a free weekend, a young German woman from the office offered to take her on a Rhine cruise. The river was wide and rapid, castles rising from the hillsides, one above each town along the way. The boatride pleased Jillian very much. In the city, the hotel, the office, she could have been anywhere. Now she was finally experiencing the sensation of knowing a place totally different, another land, another way of being.

When the boat docked at the edge of a village, the young woman, Annalise, led her though the streets to a path that climbed to a castle.

At first the path was tiered steps, then part way up turned to just steep rocks, Jillian's lungs straining, her face damp with chill sweat. Annalise called from behind: "It's more difficult than I thought. You go ahead. I'll catch up." Jillian offered to wait for her, but Annalise insisted.

Jillian was gasping by the time she reached the castle walls, gripping the cool stone and peering down at the town and the sweep of the river below. "Spectacular, isn't it?" the man said, suddenly standing beside her, pointing at the scene. That was her first sight of Marco.

He gave Jillian a lesson in history, how warrior nobles commanded the hillsides from the height of their castles, demanding tribute from those who traded along the Rhine. "It was very dangerous," he told her. "Many died brutal deaths."

Jillian expected the man to smile, relieved that life was so different now; but his face stayed fixed, and at that moment, Annalise appeared with a camera and took the photo Clark had seen.

Later Annalise told her that she had assumed Jillian knew Marco. "But how could I?" she had said. "I've just arrived." Then it struck her: "You brought me there to meet him." "That's ridiculous," Annalise had answered, but back in the office for the rest of her assignment, Jillian kept her distance.

Jillian fell into a long silence.

"Then what?" Clark asked, risking a question to make her continue.

"He started appearing outside my office building, first pretending that it was another accidental meeting, then was waiting no matter what hour I left work, as if he knew my schedule."

"What did you say to him?"

"I was polite, perhaps flattered at his attentions. I'd never known a man to be so obviously interested in me."

"Were you interested in him?"

"Curious. Why would he seek me? I'm not beautiful. Nothing special."

Clark touched her hand. "Your mother and I always thought

you were very pretty. Other people too."

"I'm ordinary!" He recoiled at the rasp that tore her voice. "I want to be ordinary!"

She turned away from him and would speak no more.

Margaret insisted that they take Jillian to dinner. "I never see my daughter." He made excuses the first few times, then knew he would have to give in. If not, his wife would become even more suspicious, and he would have to calm her anxieties too. She would pump him for information, relentless in her concern.

In the restaurant, he was relieved that Jillian smiled and kept up the small talk about her job and her apartment, nodded when Margaret offered her mother's tea set. "That would be very nice. I'll come by to pick it up." She didn't say when.

Then Margaret suddenly shifted the topic, leaned forward and cleared her throat. "Do you hear from Tim much?"

Jillian shook her head. "Not much. Not at all, really. That was so long ago."

"I always liked Tim. You two looked so lovely together."

"Tim is a very nice man." Clark could see Jillian tensing as she spoke. He reached under the tablecloth, but she pulled her hand away.

"I always hoped you would marry Tim."

"I'll never marry anyone."

Margaret's head snapped at the sting of her words.

"That's your generation," Clark said quickly. "You don't want to settle down." He could see the hurt in Margaret's eyes. They would be up all night, and he would just listen.

The next time Clark went to Jillian he asked if the man still called, hoping she would say no.

Jillian nodded. "Sometimes not for days. Then in the middle of the night, one call after another. I never answer. He leaves messages."

"What does he say?"

"The same thing. Again and again."

"Should we call the police?"

"What police? Where?"

At his desk, Clark stared at a computer screen listing Investigators—Confidential Searches, All States Detective Agency, one after another. He ran a finger across the numbers. What would he say to them? He didn't even know where the man lived, what country. They could trace calls, he supposed. But who could do anything? The man wasn't committing a crime. He wasn't making threats. Others might hear his words as lovesick pleas. Perhaps if he could convince Jillian to move back home, he could keep her safe. But from what? Awful memories? Her life was collapsing, and he didn't know how to help. He buried his face in his hands and watched his tears spread circles on the polished desktop.

The sky outside the apartment window had darkened with a mid-afternoon storm. Jillian had been abrupt when he called, not picking up until she could screen his voice on the answering machine and then eager to hang up. At the door, he felt her staring at him through the peephole for quite a while, then the loud click of locks, the slow turning of the knob.

"Are you taking vacation time?" he asked when he saw her in a wrinkled sweat suit, hair tangled, face unwashed. The telephone lay upside down on a bare floor, detached from the wall, the receiver cord dangling, the loose extension tangled beside it.

"No."

"Do you still have a job?"

"It doesn't matter."

"But *you* do."

"Maybe not."

Clark busied himself making tea while she stared out at the grey sky.

"Once over there I thought I saw Marco in a café with Annalise, sure of it," she spoke quickly. "I confronted her afterwards."

He stood in the kitchenette, hand frozen on a spoon. "And?"

197

"She said I was crazy, but I didn't believe her."

"Did he keep seeking you out?"

"More and more."

"So you finally went out with him," Clark said, wanting to believe it was nothing more than a painful romance.

"Not in the way you mean. One morning on a day like this ..." She pointed to the rain now beating on the window. "... I was walking to the bus stop in a downpour, and he pulled up beside me in his car. "It's foolish to be drenched," he said. I was so chilled and so wet. So I got in. Before I knew it, we were on the motorway. I told him to take me to my office. That I had to be at work. "I already called and said you were ill," he told me. I wanted to throw myself on him and grab the wheel, take the car away from him. But he was driving so fast, skidding into curves, spraying water. I just sat there and shook. Afraid for my life."

When she paused, rigid in her chair, Clark spoke softly to draw her out, hating the man. "Where did he take you?"

"The rain stopped and I could see the Rhine. We were driving along the river, and then he turned onto a narrow road, climbing up a hillside. By the time we got to a castle, the sun was out. This wasn't a castle like the others. It looked untended, thick weeds all around, the wood frames rotting, thick vines knotted up the stone. The place stank of sour vegetation."

"Why did he bring you there?"

"That's what I asked him."

"And what did he say?"

"Children come here."

"What children?" Clark said.

"'*Kommst du*,' he said. And I went. I followed him up a stone stairway slippery with slime. Into a room." In an instant she was sobbing, tearless gasps.

As much as he felt the need, Clark could not embrace her. He sat just inches from her. "What was in the room?"

"Something awful." Jillian turned her face into the padding of their chair.

"What?" Clark said, not sure he wanted to hear more, shaking his head. "What did you see?"

She would not answer.

Clark stayed into the evening, he and his daughter silent and unmoving. Her eyes stayed closed, squeezed shut, and he watched the darkness thicken. When he could no longer see her, he asked, "Did he keep you there? In that castle?"

She spoke so softly that at first he did not realize she had answered. "Yes."

He leaned forward. "How long?"

"I don't know."

Clark swallowed. He could feel the bile rising into his throat as he asked the question, forcing out the words. "Did he rape you?"

"No. It wasn't about that." She paused, and Clark could sense her mind working. "Maybe it was a kind of rape. He made me watch."

"What?"

She was in tears again, twisting fingers through her hair. This time he embraced her until she stopped, stroked her hair, made soothing sounds, until she stilled.

Jillian didn't answer the door. Clark implored: "It's me. It's Daddy. Come to the door." He began pounding on the wood, his hand shaking as he wrenched at the knob.

After several minutes he went down to the superintendent's apartment in the basement. The wife answered, short and plump, a toddler clinging to her leg, gazing up at him with wide eyes. When the child smiled, Clark couldn't make himself smile back. He explained that he was very worried about his daughter and gave the apartment number.

"My husband's out," the woman told him, "shopping for a new sink."

"Don't you have keys?"

"I'm not supposed to. I'm not bonded."

"Please. Something terrible could have happened." Then he blurted, "A man's been threatening her."

The woman stared at him as if finally paying attention. "I'll have to bring the baby."

"That's fine. Anything. Please hurry."

The passkeys hung on a rack over a desk beside a glowing computer monitor. The woman moved slowly, weighted down by her own bulk, slipping the key ring into a pocket, changing from slippers to shoes, lifting the child to her hip. Clark could hear her wheezing as she climbed the stairway ahead of him.

She tried several keys in Jillian's lock, one at a time, staring at the ring before she chose the next one. "Charlie knows all about these," she said. "I never ..."

Clark wanted to rip them from her hand but just clenched fists. The child giggled, opened a mouth of baby teeth.

The lock finally clicked, and the woman turned the knob. Clark rushed past her, calling Jillian's name. The living room was empty, papers spread across the coffee table, scattered on the floor. Through a doorway, he could see dishes piled in the kitchen sink, cabinet doors hanging open, unwashed pots on the stove.

The woman stood watching him. He could feel her eyes on his back, following his movements. When he stepped into the hallway to the bedroom, he heard a rasping breath, then saw Jillian in her bed, blankets pulled up to her chin. Even before he touched her burning forehead, felt her sweat-drenched hair, he shouted to the woman. "Call an ambulance!"

They wouldn't let him ride with Jillian. He drove his own car, staying close, blinkers flashing. He followed through stop signs and red lights, sensing that someone was hovering as close behind him as he was to the ambulance. But each time he looked in the mirror he saw a different car.

He had called Margaret while waiting for the EMTs, repeating, "I don't know, I don't know" to her hysterical questions. By the time Clark parked and rushed through the Emergency entrance, she was hovering over the gurney. He saw the oxygen mask on his daughter's face. Before he could tell if she were conscious, an aide wheeled her away, behind a white curtain.

A male nurse with a clipboard appeared at Clark's side, a dark man, leading Margaret and him to a cluster of metal chairs. He took down name, address, date of birth, medical insurance data, terse in his questioning. How long had their daughter been ill, he wanted to know. "Never," Margaret blurted. "She's never sick."

"I saw her two days ago," Clark told him, aware of his wife's startled reaction. "She was tired then. She's been missing work. Stress and fatigue. Never really sick."

"What's going on?" Margaret insisted when the nurse left. "Why didn't you tell me that you saw her, that she was so tired?" She pulled at the cloth of her dress, knotted it in her fingers.

"Jillian didn't want you to worry. She thought all she needed was rest." He wondered if his wife knew he was lying.

"I had a right to be told" was all she said.

The nurse returned and pointed them toward the waiting room. "You'll have to sit there," he told them. "Somebody will get you after the doctor sees her."

A television set was on, the sound low, captions appearing on the screen. Clark watched the changing colors, the moving shapes, with no idea of what he saw. Margaret spoke to him, perhaps asked questions, perhaps just talking in her agitation. He couldn't make himself pay attention. When he glanced across the room, he felt sure a man was staring at him, had been for quite a while. But the second their eyes met, the man stood up and disappeared into a corridor, so quickly Clark didn't have time to register the face. Had his eyes been dark, his hair? He couldn't be sure. For a moment, he thought of getting up to follow. But what if the doctor came?

When the doctor finally did appear, Margaret had to shake Clark's arm. He hadn't been sleeping. His mind was far away, imagining the ruin of a castle high on a hilltop, the faces of children, his daughter trapped between narrow stone walls, fists beating at green slime.

"We're not sure about the diagnosis," the doctor was saying, a young woman with a red birthmark below her ear. "She's dehydrated. Severely anemic. We're giving her fluids, preparing for a transfusion, and doing more tests. She's being moved to the fourth floor."

"When can we see her?" Clark felt Margaret gripping his wrist.

"She's going to have to be in isolation until we identify her illness. You can visit for five minutes an hour. One at a time. And you'll have to put on protective clothing. Face masks."

Margaret began to weep. Clark wrapped an arm around her shoulder and drew her to him.

On the fourth floor, they were the only people in the small waiting room, sitting on padded plastic chairs, crossing and uncrossing their legs, not speaking. Clark realized how hungry he was but said nothing, wouldn't ask Margaret if she had eaten. Hunger seemed so wrong here, now.

He let her visit first, holding her arm as she stepped into the white jump suit a nurse brought, her skirt bunched up near her waist. In the strange clothing, her face masked, her feet in paper boots, she moved oddly, each step tentative, as if learning how to walk all over again. When she looked back, Clark made himself nod at her.

He would tell her nothing. What good would that do? Their daughter was very sick now. That's all she had to know. That was bad enough.

A man appeared from around a corner of the hallway, suddenly there and immediately gone again. Was it the same man he had seen before? He couldn't be sure. Once again he hadn't gotten a good look. He couldn't even tell what the man had been wearing. It could have been a uniform, hospital staff. Perhaps not.

When it was his turn to see Jillian, he felt as awkward in the clothing as Margaret had looked, very warm, the material rubbing with an audible scratch as he stepped toward his daughter's room. The walls were white, the lights bright, oxygen canisters lined against one wall under a warning sign, pouches suspended from metal stands, needles in her arms, a tube in her nostrils, down her throat, a starched sheet pulled up to her chin. His daughter was breathing more calmly now, but it seemed shallow, her chest barely moving. Clark wanted to take her hand, but it lay under the sheet, inert against her side.

As he studied her closed eyes, the lashes soft against her flesh, he shuddered with chill, gripping the steel bed railing to keep from sinking to the floor. She would never open her eyes again.

At that moment, the door opened. When he swung around, the same man was staring in at him. "Is that Marco?" he called aloud, as if Jillian could answer. The door snapped shut, and it was over in seconds.

In the waiting room, long past midnight, Margaret sat beside him, shoulders shaking, a damp handkerchief pressed to her open mouth. Clark dug his fingers into the chair arm, fighting the force of his despair. He knew his future. Whatever happened to Jillian, he would see Marco everywhere. On street corners, on highways, in store aisles, ahead in corridors, a shape vanishing into shadows. Phones would ring in the middle of the night, shocking him from fitful sleep, an empty silence on the other end, then an odd voice saying *Jill-e-ayn's father. I will never stop calling.*

Mystery Woman

Even through the thick doors Jerry Pohl could hear pounding music and whoops from inside the student center pub. His instinct was to turn and head back to the dorm, but Cheryl had said she would be there, a casual remark he knew was an invitation. They had started talking in the hallway before their psychology course, and he really wanted to be with her. So Pohl dropped three singles on the tabletop and let a girl in a tank top stamp his wrist with a purple marker. For a moment he stared down at the illegible smear, imagining that it would never wash off, that he would have to wear it the rest of his life. Then he pulled back the door and smelled cheap beer and felt the throbbing bass from the six-foot speakers beside the bar. Stepping inside, Pohl scanned the room for Cheryl in the crowd of dancers, stoned people wild with the music, jumping up and down, shouting to be heard over the din. If Cheryl were one of them, he'd leave, tell her he couldn't make it the next time they met.

Instead of Cheryl, the first person Pohl noticed was Melody standing alone against a wall, fat and squat, pressing a transistor radio to her ear, swaying in a slow rhythm that had nothing to do with the music in the room. In the psych class she sat right in front of the instructor, constantly rattling on, first responding to the question and then—no matter what the subject—going off on some tangent about how she knew the secrets of space travel, how the faculty would soon be teaching courses about her. Initially, the instructor had been patient, letting her talk, but seeing the restlessness of the others, began to cut her off, eventually ignoring the hand she waved in his face. Pohl had watched students smirking and wondered what Cheryl thought but couldn't bring himself to ask her, not even when Melody waddled right past them clutching a jumble of books and papers. He wished he had signed up for a different section, then realized he wouldn't have known Cheryl.

If he hadn't known about Melody, from the look of her now, eyes closed behind thick, distorting glasses, moving to sounds no one else could hear, Pohl would have thought drugs, what he saw in the dorm almost every night. But the others all said it—very weird, very crazy.

To his surprise, Melody suddenly stepped into the midst of the dancers and began speaking as if delivering a lecture. Something about how in the future dancing would be psychic, how we wouldn't need our bodies, how our brain waves would soar with planetary rhythms, just the way hers already could. He could barely hear her but knew from her ramblings in class.

The dancers, male and female, closed in on her, trapping her in a tight circle, screwing fingertips into their temples, chanting her name, "Melody, Melody. Creature from outer space." Hair tangled, horn-rimmed glasses hanging off one ear, mouth open soundlessly, she swiveled frantically in search of an escape.

Pohl was ready to turn away but felt the sensation of being watched. He looked over and saw Cheryl standing in the doorway staring at him. The second their eyes met, Pohl knew he had to act. For three years he had been anonymous on campus, wanted it that way. Now he forced his way into the crowd. "That's enough. It's not funny. Leave her alone." He wrapped an arm around Melody's shoulder and pulled her from the group. The dancers let them pass, laughing, hands slapping his back.

At first he was furious to be standing beside her in that room, the others all looking, certain he had made himself a joke, a source of mockery till graduation and beyond. Then Cheryl approached, smiling, touching his arm, her hand lingering. "It's over," she told Melody. "They won't bother you again." Pohl studied Cheryl's expression, thinking how lovely she was, how sweet and soft. That's what everyone was seeing—not Melody but Cheryl and her touch. No one would ever laugh at him again.

"Let's walk Melody back to the dorm," Cheryl suggested and Pohl nodded. Outside on the pathway Melody chattered excitedly, never once referring to what had just happened. Pohl didn't pay attention. He was holding Cheryl's hand, and all he could think of was the warmth.

Soon after that night Pohl began hearing that Melody was telling stories about him, how he was the nephew of Frederick Pohl, the science fiction writer, how his uncle wanted to publish her novels. Some friends started teasing him, calling him Melody's soul mate. But he laughed it off, hugging Cheryl against him, letting them know what he really had.

"Should I tell her," Pohl asked Cheryl, "that it's a totally different family?"

"What's the harm in letting her believe?"

He nodded and she kissed him.

Melody's calls to his room began a day or two later, and they went on for years, long after graduation, following him wherever he moved.

Initially, when Pohl and Cheryl relocated halfway across the country to his first job, Melody had been hysterical when she called, always in tears, lamenting the misery of her life. How NASA never acknowledged the space ship designs she sent each week, thick packets of drawings and documentation. How people mistreated her, classmates, professors, her mean sister, her awful mother, always criticizing. "I'm abused," she would wail. "But there'll be justice. Someday they'll all be punished." She spoke of retribution, vindication, on and on, Pohl trying to interrupt, to end the conversation. "I've got to go now. Cheryl needs something." Finally, Melody still blubbering, he would just set the receiver in its cradle and walk away.

"It was her," Pohl would tell Cheryl. *Yes*, was all she would answer. He wanted to tell her how much the calls annoyed him, made him cringe every time the phone rang, but he couldn't get the words out, sure that reaction would disappoint Cheryl.

As time passed, Melody's mood changed. She stopped lamenting the way people treated her, rarely wept. Her calls became an urgent monologue, filled with great excitement about the most trivial of events—she was drawing with pastels again, someone had tacked one of an alien planet on her wall, somebody told her that her spaceship designs made more sense than NASA's.

And Melody constantly referred back to their college years, the few times they had spoken in person, what she had announced in that psych class, telling Pohl to remember her predictions from years ago—destruction of the environment, financial collapse, massacres. He agreed—"Yes, yes"—though he recalled nothing, had barely listened through all her ramblings.

Over and over Melody repeated that the space agency didn't know what it was doing. If only they had listened to her, accepted her drawings and specifications. She mocked the administrators as fools, idiots. He recalled the crude pencil sketches she had shown him in college, running after him in a corridor with her splay-footed waddle, trapping him into a corner. "See?" she would tell him, pointing to a squiggle, rattling on about vectors and trajectories. "See? I've got the answer."

Melody began calling almost every evening, sometimes twice to add something she had forgotten to tell him. One summer night, the two of them tossing in the heat, Pohl finally asked Cheryl, "What are we going to do about Melody? " She didn't answer for so long he thought she had fallen asleep. Then she said, "Don't you see how important you are to her? No one else ever did what you did for her."

"Does that mean I've got her for life? What if I had just walked away that day?"

Cheryl took his hand. "But you're not that kind of person. There's something very kind about you. You're a sensitive man."

She pressed her face against his shoulder, and Pohl remembered the moment, the look Cheryl had given him. He had done it for her, not Melody. She was the kind one, the sensitive one. It upset him that she assumed one rash act revealed who he was. And he understood Melody was the price of having Cheryl.

One lunch hour, Pohl entered a restaurant with a TV screen over the bar and learned the Challenger had exploded. He was shocked by the repeated pictures of the rocket vanishing in a great flash of light. All the time he kept thinking how Melody would call that evening, how he would have to listen to her go on and on about the disaster. He couldn't swallow his food.

When he arrived home after work, Cheryl sat rigid, staring as the TV news repeated the same footage he had seen at noon. But she had the sound off. The screen switched from the blast to shots of the astronauts in their flight suits on their way to the space capsule, waving and smiling at the camera. Cheryl had tears in her eyes, and Pohl leaned over her to massage her neck as she sniffled back her weeping, "Those poor people." Pohl wanted to hug her, wrap arms around her, but the phone rang.

"Bastards!" Melody cursed when he lifted the receiver, "NASA bastards!" Then she began speaking in a whisper. "Can you keep a secret?" Her voice pleaded.

"Of course," he told her.

"You have to promise not to say a word. Nobody else can know."

He sighed. "All right."

"I'm the Mystery Woman."

"What?"

"The Mystery Woman of the Challenger."

"Yes? " Pohl waited in bewilderment, expecting more.

"You must know." Her voice was trembling. "Everybody talks about her."

He hesitated, looking across the room to Cheryl. Had there been something on the news?

"That's me." She spoke triumphantly. Then she paused for his reaction.

"Go on," he finally said. He tried to make sense out of what she was explaining, listening much more carefully than he did to her other calls. She told about a presence in the retrieved capsule, an aura that baffled the investigators, the clear indication that someone else had been there with the other astronauts. "Me!" Melody gave one of her sputtering laughs. "Not my body. My spirit. The others wanted me with them so much. I was so close to all of them. Their families have been telepathing me. They want to know everything, how they reacted till the last second."

"How did they?" he asked, wanting this to stop.

"Like heroes. They were all heroes. As much as I tried, I couldn't save them."

All Pohl could see was the picture of that exploding space ship, imagining a pain so vivid he had to sink to the floor, covered with a chill sweat. While Melody went on he dropped the phone, kicked it across the floor. "No more! No more!" He heard himself shouting. "People were blown apart, and all she can think about is her mystery woman madness."

"She can't help it," Cheryl said.

"How long do we have to put up with this?"

"It would be cruel to stop." Cheryl had tears in her eyes. "She's part of our lives."

In bed that night, and many nights after, staring up at the ceiling, Pohl rehearsed the conversation he wanted to have with Cheryl: *It's important that I explain. What I did back then I did only to impress you, because you wanted me to. If you hadn't been there, I probably would have been like the others. When I looked at Melody, I saw a freak. People like Melody make me cringe. Since that day I've pretended to be something I'm not. Because that's who you think I am. Melody is a trap. If I admit what I really feel, I'm afraid you might hate me. I'm afraid our marriage is based on a fraud.*

But he couldn't find the courage to speak the words.

One evening after a call from Melody he finally tried, calling her aside and saying, "I have to tell you something." It was as if she knew, her head already shaking in denial, her eyes welling with tears. Although he said nothing, at that moment Pohl realized their marriage would end. Stunned, he walked out into the yard and sat in darkness gazing up at the stars.

A week after Pohl moved to an apartment, he answered the phone and heard Melody's voice. Before he could react, she blurted, "Why did you do it? "

"How did you get this number?" He demanded.

"Cheryl. I told her I would bring you to your senses." Melody let out a wail, sudden, genuine. "She loved you so much. She was perfect for you."

"Things weren't working out for us."

"You've made a terrible mistake." Now she spoke in the tone of her auguries, grave, absolute. "You'll always be sorry."

"It's better this way," he said.

"You two will always belong together."

"Never," Pohl wanted to tell her, but just hung up.

When the Columbia space shuttle disintegrated over Texas on a Saturday morning, Pohl was married to Lindsay. After sleeping late, he wandered into the kitchen for a cup of coffee and clicked the remote for the countertop TV. For a moment, he thought he was seeing old footage, then listened to the announcer and understood. Shit, he said, aloud, though he was alone in the room. His first thought was terrorism, and his second that the phone would be ringing with Melody at the other end, frantic, her voice shrill and breathless: "See! Didn't I tell you? Didn't I tell you? NASA doesn't know what it's doing. Didn't I tell you when we were in college?" And once he would have nodded, muttered, "Yes, yes," and let her go on. But now, this day, he wouldn't have to listen to her.

Pohl stared at the screen for several minutes, the trail of vapor, the stop-action shot of sudden fragmentation, the superimposed circles over the grey puffs of debris, then thought to shout upstairs to Lindsay: "Come down here. Quick!" She appeared in her robe, skin glistening, hair wrapped in a yellow towel. He pointed at the TV and she shook her head. "Not another one. It's amazing that they don't all crash."

He poured her coffee. "She'll call, you know."

Lindsay gave him a sour look. "Then we won't answer."

They hadn't been answering in months, stopping shortly after their marriage, almost a year, not since Lindsay thought to get caller ID, after shouting. "I won't have this. It's an invasion. I shudder whenever I hear the phone."

For weeks after they began ignoring her number, Melody phoned several times a day, desperate messages on the answering machine, begging, crying, "What happened? What happened?" Pohl could hear her panic but never told Lindsay of his unease. Then the calls became fewer and fewer and finally stopped.

The TV picture showed a wide swathe of field marred by a deep black mark seared into the earth. Men, tiny by comparison, paced around the edges, searching. The announcer's voice warned once again that people in the area should not touch any debris they found. It was toxic.

Pohl found himself envisioning what Cheryl must be doing at that moment, alone in the home that had been theirs, mesmerized by the television screen. She would be weeping. He imagined himself bringing his hand to her cheek, feeling the wetness of her tears as they sat together and watched scenes of disaster.

When the phone finally rang, Pohl flinched. "It's her." Lindsay's eyes fixed his with a glare of warning. On the screen he saw the flames of launch and then the grey clouds of disintegration playing over and over. Pohl stared at the telephone until the final ring, certain she would never call again. That part of his life was over.

Telling Stories

Other than Julia, Russell didn't know the people seated around the dinner table. They were her friends from the years before her divorce, and he knew he should have remembered what she had told him about them. He also knew it would be a big mistake to ask her now even if he had been able to lure her into a corner for a hurried whisper, an admission that he hadn't paid attention. They'd only been seeing each other for a few months.

"Are you aware you do most of the talking when we're together," she asked him once in the quiet after lovemaking. "And it's really not about you, just stories, and I never know whether they're true."

"I'm a writer," he had said. "I write stories."

"Well, don't write about me." She had pressed a palm to his check, and Russell couldn't decide if it had been a touch or a slap. In the dark he hadn't been able to read her face.

Here at this table he kept deliberately quiet, not silent, just offering a reinforcing comment when one of the others said something that made him think he should. The food was good and the wine even better. They were dining on a large glassed-in sun porch that Carol, the wife, kept calling an "atrium." Glowing night lamps gave a soft illumination to the deep green lawn, thick leaves of tall trees shimmering in the moonlight. Russell kept looking past the others to the garden, drawn by the colors of the vegetation and the dark shadows that seemed to be creatures rushing across the lawn. They certainly lived elegantly, Carol and Jerry. Russell wished he could recall what Julia said they did, how they made their money. He'd Google Jerry at home when he learned their last name.

The other couple, Evelyn and Alan, didn't seem to belong together, not the way Carol and Jerry matched, the two of them sandy-haired and ruddy, a bit overweight, but solid, as if they spent hours doing something physical like playing tennis. Alan sat erect on the padded chair, thin, taut, and sallow, perioodically smiling as if on a timer. When he spoke, it was extremely precise and informed. He seemed to know a lot about a lot of things. Russell understood he wasn't the kind of man you could kid about his knowledge, the way Julia teased Carol and Jerry. Often what Julia said to them was just silly, and Russell wished she had more wit.

Evelyn puzzled Russell, reminding him of a woman from his mother's generation, her grey dress out of style, her faint blonde hair pulled back in a tight bun, her glasses in a thick pink frame. She certainly wasn't fat, but beside her husband she looked thick, perhaps because when they all had been standing in the living room, Russell noted that she had wide hips and heavy thighs. He let her walk ahead of him to the sun porch and saw that she seemed to wobble in her low-heeled old ladies' shoes. She had a long face, a large jaw, and spoke with what he took to be an accent, but not foreign, not British, though she reminded him of someone from a black and white postwar film, a plucky housewife making do.

Julia reached under the table to touch Russell's hand, looking straight ahead and saying something to Jerry about a car he had owned years ago. Russell squeezed her thigh, flattened his palm against it as Jerry laughed and said, "Oh, that one. I could have made lemonade out of it."

Carol pretended to punch his arm, and Alan and Evelyn smiled, but Julia laughed out loud, her animated face making her especially pretty. Russell told himself he didn't want to do anything to spoil things between them, not here, not with people—Carol and Jerry—she liked very much, people he still was trying to decipher.

Evelyn and Julia helped Carol clean up the desert plates despite Carol's pleas for them not to bother. Russell wondered if he should volunteer too, looked for a sign from Julia, but she was focused on collecting the china. When Jerry and Alan sat fixed in their chairs, he didn't offer. Evelyn rattled cups, looking nervous as she stepped toward the kitchen, as if fearful of dropping the stack in her two hands. Russell had a thought: she's terrified of dishes. He couldn't write it down then and there but would tap it into his iPhone when no one was looking.

The idea might fit into a story. He wrote stories as much as he could, trying to get up very early for a few hours before he had to drive to his work, but managing to do that only a couple of times a week. He did write weekends, though in the months since he met Julia he had decided he'd rather be with her.

Several of his stories had been published in magazines he considered respectable, clearly not any he'd feel shame about. People, friends at work and from college, said nice things about them, and he could tell they weren't lying. In fact, some seemed impressed at his modest success, as if he were the real thing. Whatever that meant. At least he knew he wasn't deceiving himself, wasting his time. He had been writing stories in his head all his life until he finally worked up the nerve to put the words on a computer screen before printing the pages he edited with green ink. Now, more so after the publications, he was always seeking story ideas, germs of material.

He hadn't shown any of his stories to Julia, though she knew about them and even asked to read some, offhanded, not with what he took to be genuine eagerness. "Sure," he'd tell her. "I'll bring one next time," though he always managed to forget. He often thought how odd it was that they could be so intimate in bed, so unashamed, holding back nothing, and yet he so reluctant to talk about his writing. Was that the reason she said what she did about him telling stories? Had she been teasing or testing? He didn't want her judging the stories, judging him. Not yet.

When the women came back from the kitchen, Jerry brought out several cognac bottles. Russell was about to blurt, *No cigars?* But he swallowed the words, covered his mouth with a linen napkin when he coughed.

"I know what we'll do now," Carol said. "Let's tell each other about our childhoods. Some of us don't know each other well, and you can learn so much from what we did as kids."

"Great," Julia said, "I'd really like that."

Russell suspected she and Carol had planned that in the kitchen, if not before. He could see Alan contemplating, Evelyn's eyes darting. But never in Alan's direction. He thought of making up a tale, something about setting a school lab on fire and ending up in juvenile detention. Actually, he'd fantasized doing that every day in chemistry class. The fire, not detention. Of course, he wouldn't use that fabrication, not with Julia there, not with the way he was looking forward to the end of the dinner party and their time in bed, the house to themselves, her kids off visiting their father. He'd do nothing to spoil the evening. But he'd make notes about that idea, a tale about an alter ego.

He found himself eager to hear what Julia would reveal, with the thought of teasing something deeper, more intimate, out of her later in the dark, touching spots that would make her moan. But Carol volunteered to go first. "After all, it was my idea."

Jerry gave her a peck on the cheek. "And I'll fill in the details."

"Maybe I'll surprise you."

He winked at the others. "I can hardly wait."

Carol began. "When I was about to be four, I wanted nothing more than a stuffed bunny for my birthday. I asked for it at dinner one night. But my father shook his head and told me I was going to get a garbage can. He was like that—always joking around. My bothers understood. They were older and played along with him. Not me. I insisted that I didn't want a garbage can. He kept saying that he'd already bought one. I looked at my mother. She wouldn't meet my eyes. I burst into tears, wouldn't stop, even after she got up and hugged me, telling me that Daddy was only fooling. And he apologized, saying he thought I understood, saying how awful he felt."

Even though Carol was smiling, Russell suspected she was close to tears.

"Her father is a great guy," Jerry spoke quickly. "One of the kindest people I've ever met. Funny too." He reached to take Carol's hand.

Russell couldn't figure out why Carol wanted to reveal that

memory, why she had been so eager to recommend this game. Was it a message to Jerry? Did she still resent her father? Did she expect to be spoiled if she cried? He'd ponder the possibilities.

"And did you get the bunny?" Julia asked, though Russell was sure she already knew.

"Absolutely. The very next day when he got home from work. A week before my party. I got even more stuffed animals then."

"It wasn't easy to get her to make up her mind," Jerry said. "Me or that bed with all the creatures."

"You had toys in bed as an adult?" Julia's voice rose.

"Still does." Jerry winked at the others. "Only now it's me."

"My boy toy." Carol stroked his arm.

They really love each other, Russell thought and had to look away.

Julia volunteered to go next. "It's hard to come up with something Carol and Russell haven't heard before." She looked at them. "Did I tell you about my dance recital?" They shook their heads, and Russell sensed they would have even if she had.

She was supposed to have the lead role in a performance but tripped over a teammate during a gym volleyball game and wrenched her knee. Her mother wrapped the knee with icepacks for several days, keeping her home from school. Though she still had pain, she went on stage, and people—her dance teacher—told her she'd been wonderful."

"So you had a career," Russell said, assuming she'd danced for years.

Julia shook her head. "No. I quit lessons right after that as much as my parents and my teacher wanted me to go on."

"Why?" Evelyn spoke softly, as if her question were an intrusion.

"Because I knew I'd never be good enough."

"Come on," Jerry said. "You're great."

Russell nodded but wondered what else he didn't know about her, unsure why he was bothered by her quitting.

Carol picked Alan to go next. He told about winning a science project as if giving a formal report, and Russell remembered that

Julia said he did important research, though about what and for whom he had no idea. The project seemed to have been for a major competition, resulting in a prestigious scholarship. Alan made it all sound very dull.

Jerry's story was about coming off the bench in a big game to replace an injured quarterback and throwing a long, long winning pass, the ball wobbling as if tossed by a five-year-old. Russell made a mental note of that detail, then tuned out the rest of what Jerry was saying, snapping back when Carol cried out, "My hero!" and wrapped arms around him. Julia clapped.

Russell realized he should take his turn. He wondered if Julia had told Carol and Jerry about his writing, if they expected something special from him, clever and inventive. But he decided not to try, fearing he would come off as pretentious. So he talked about the hours he spent drawing comics as an eight-year-old, adventures of a superhero called Bullet Man with a bullet-shaped head and bullet-shaped car that could run down gangsters. "The main problem is that I have zip drawing talent. In fact, I'm as bad now—worse—than I was then."

Julia gave him a puzzled look as if unsure whether he was improvising on the spot. He put a hand across his heart. "Honest," he told her, relieved when she smiled.

"And you're last," Carol told Evelyn, who seemed to be shrinking into herself under the others' attention. "Batting cleanup," Jerry added.

Russell looked to Alan for his reaction, but Alan seemed to be studying his distorted reflection in a coffee spoon.

"I'm not good at this," Evelyn said, speaking so softly the others had to lean toward her. Russell was glad that Carol did not ask her to be louder and almost suggested that they let her skip. What did it matter anyway? Then he realized he was curious, especially when he saw how pale she had become, how she stared straight ahead at a blank wall.

"I wasn't a very appealing child," she began. "Overweight and ungainly. My parents had me late in life. It may have been the only time they had sex."

Russell expected her to laugh, as if she had made a joke. But she didn't, and none of the others changed expression. They seemed embarrassed, even Alan, his fingers twisted around the spoon.

Evelyn paused, and Russell thought that was it, that she had said all she would, but she swallowed and went on. "Have you ever been to a funeral home?" The others all nodded. Carol breathed out a "Yes." "All those undertakers in dark suits and solemn faces standing silently in doorways, never speaking above a whisper, trying to pretend they didn't exist. Well, that's how it was in my house. My father should have been an undertaker. But he was a small town banker, always calculating, letting others deal with people. Except on Sundays." She repeated, "Except on Sundays," and then stopped.

Russell realized he wanted her to go on. "What happened on Sundays?"

"On Sundays I poured tea. They started me at the age of five. In the afternoon after church, people would assemble, people like them, men in dark suits, women in grey dresses. I cringed every time the door chimes sounded. But I was already waiting in the kitchen, sitting on a stool in my starched dress, the pleats puffed over a crinoline petticoat, my Mary Janes gleaming. My mother had braided my hair, pulling so hard I wanted to scream. But I wouldn't. Couldn't. When everyone had arrived, my mother would speak my name. Evelyn. Just once. Never twice. And I would push out a mahogany cart with our best serving china, stopping in front of each person and asking, 'Would you like tea?' 'Please,' they all would answer, the same word in the same grim tone, and I would pour, trying not to show how terrified I was, how my hands shook."

Russell found himself clutching the bottom of his chair. When she paused the sudden silence was like a roar in his ears.

"But I never spilled," Evelyn said, almost a whisper. "In all those years I never spilled."

Russell knew he would write the story, saw in his mind print on pages in a very good magazine, but the way he would tell it the girl, the character, would smash cups in an outburst. He didn't think he would have her run out the door. That would be too much. She'd just glare at her parents and break dishes.

Evelyn spoke again, her jaw set, loud this time. "I never spilled a fucking cup."

Russell heard a gasp, unsure whether it came from Carol or Julia. He couldn't look away from Evelyn's face, grasping at every detail of her expression. "My God!" he said. "What a story."

Evelyn pushed back from the table and stood, her face red, her body trembling. Her words were barely a whisper. "It's not a story. It's my life."

The others sat in rigid silence, waiting for what would happen next. Russell knew he should say something, but before he could think of words, Evelyn bolted toward a glass door, threw it back, and ran out into the yard. Russell could see her far back in the glow of a night lamp, a dark shadow hunched and shaking. He felt sure she was weeping.

Carol and Julia stood to go to her, but Alan waved them off. "It's better for her to be alone when she's like this." He stood too, smoothed his jacket. "I think we should leave now. I'll say goodbye for Evelyn too. We'll walk around the side of the house to our car. Thank you for inviting us." He slid the glass door shut, carefully, waiting for a click.

Carol and Jerry just sat, hands folded on the table.

Julia looked at Russell. "That was awful," she told him. "Cruel."

"I'm really sorry." At that moment he meant it. "Should I go after her and apologize?"

She shook her head. "That would be worse."

"You know," Jerry said, "I was thinking the same thing. A story."

Carol nodded. "I wonder if she's ever told other people."

"Alan," Julia said. "She must have told Alan."

Russell sensed she was softening but knew not to reach for her hand. He was thinking how, in the morning, he would start the story, perhaps with an image of cups and saucers arranged on a polished cart. Or perhaps the small girl terrified to squirm in that starched dress.

Jerry reached for a cognac bottle. "Another?" The others nodded. "It's funny," he said as he poured. "Carol gave up stuffed animals, I gave up football, Julia gave up dancing, and Russell gave up drawing comics."

"And Evelyn gave up pouring tea," Carol added.

Julia smiled, and Russell knew it was all right. Soon they would go back to her house, empty of children, and they would have sex. Even now at this table he anticipated her sounds of pleasure. But he sensed that this would be the last time, that her voice would be hesitant the next time he called. And he knew he would write about her, not sure whether he would include the graphic details of their lovemaking. Those he might save for another character, some woman he created in the future.

The Author

Walter Cummins has published six previous short story collections—*Witness, Where We Live, Local Music, The End of the Circle, The Lost Ones,* and *Habitat: stories of bent realism.* More than 100 of his stories, as well as memoirs, essays, and reviews, have appeared in magazines such as *New Letters, Kansas Quarterly, Virginia Quarterly Review, Under the Sun, Arts & Letters, Confrontation, Bellevue Literary Review, Connecticut Review, The Laurel Review, Other Voices, Georgetown Review, Contrary, Sonora Review, Abiko Quarterly, Weber Studies, Midwest Quarterly, West Branch, South Carolina Review, Crosscurrents, Crescent Review, The MacGuffin,* in book collections, and on the web. With Thomas E. Kennedy, he is co-publisher of Serving House Books, an international outlet for novels, memoirs, and story, poetry, and essay collections. For more than twenty years, he was editor of *The Literary Review.* He teaches in the MFA in Creative Writing program at Fairleigh Dickinson University.

Thanks

The stories in this collection include a group first published in magazines around forty years ago and another group whose magazine publications came in the past few years. Thus, they are divided into Old and New. The many years and many magazines—the majority no longer active—mean that I have many people to thank for acceptance and support over the years. The list that follows tries to acknowledge them all, though I'm sure many others should have been included.

Here goes: Merritt Clifton, Ed Hogan, Paula G. Putney, Polly Swafford, Duff Brenna, Ricki Rycraft, the Two Bridges Writers' Group past and present, Thomas E. Kennedy, Bill and Alex Zander, Martin Donoff, Peter Selgin, Derek Alger, Renée Ashley, René Steinke, William Warner, Jack Becker, Harry and Marge Keyishian, Mary Cross, Elisabeth Murawski, Greg Herriges, Martin Green, Ted Ross, Jack Smith, Elise Salem, Steve Cameron, Christopher Klim, Vivian Shipley, Lisa del Rosso, Jayne Thomson, Susan Tekulve, Rick Mulkey, Cliff Meth, Robin Parks, Sean Toner, Ethan Joella, Stephanie Dickinson, Rob Cook, Debbie DeRosa, teaching colleagues, the host of evaluators and editors whose names I never knew, and Alison Cummins, who has borne the brunt of my story-telling habit.

WC

(Special thanks to Renée Ashley and Susan Tekulve for their wise editorial suggestions for this collection.)